MUTINY
IN THE
CARIBBEAN

SHOWELL STYLES

WILLIAM KIMBER · LONDON

First published in 1984 by
WILLIAM KIMBER & CO. LIMITED
100 Jermyn Street, London SW1Y 6EE

© Showell Styles, 1984

ISBN 0 7183 0533 7

Photoset in North Wales by
Derek Doyle & Associates, Mold, Clwyd
Printed in Great Britain by
Biddles Ltd, Guildford, Surrey

Contents

CHAPTER ONE

HMS Surprise

1

'The bone-saw, Mr Attwood.'

McMullen, the frigate's surgeon, spoke loudly to overtop the racket of noise that resonated in the narrow space between the bulkheads of *Surprise*'s orlop deck: creak and groan of timbers, stamping and shouting on deck overhead, hissing roar of waves alongside the wooden hull. Attwood, assistant surgeon, handed over the bone-saw.

'Lucky for Dobson we can give the popliteal a wide berth,' he remarked; he rubbed his chin, leaving a red stain across it. 'Stand by, Ord,' he added over his shoulder to the loblolly-boy.

Two candle-lanterns swinging from the low deckhead threw more shifting shadow than light onto the operating table where Dobson lay, a table composed of midshipmen's sea-chests pushed together and covered with an old sail. Blood from the seaman's mangled right foot glistened on the sloping canvas and dripped to the deck planking. The frigate was heeled over on the larboard tack, and the three men who bent over the improvised table balanced themselves at awkward angles. The yellow lamplight showed McMullen's angular face dark and intent, Attwood's thick lips pursed in a soundless whistle, and the wizened features of the loblolly-boy (Ord was a little superannuated seaman with white whiskers) wrinkled in pleasurable expectation.

'Take hold, Ord,' said McMullen. 'Now – '

His voice was suddenly drowned in the huge reverberant thunder of *Surprise*'s broadside, fourteen 32-pounder carronades exploding close above his head. A lesser thunder

7

followed as the gun-trucks brought up after recoil, and hard on its heels came a joyful screech and a burst of cheering.

'She's struck, sir!' piped Ord excitedly. 'They says the Spanisher's struck!'

The surgeon ignored him. 'Now, then, Mr Attwood, draw the flesh well back from my cuts, if you please.' He glanced quickly at his patient's face. 'Hold hard, Dobson.'

The wounded seaman, well dosed with spirits and with teeth clenched on the leather cud they had given him, seemed not to hear. Ord took hold of the bloody mash that had been Dobson's foot and McMullen's saw bit into bone. A second later the constricted wooden space in which they worked lurched and tilted sharply.

'God damn and blast,' said Attwood, clutching at Dobson's body to stop it from sliding off the canvas.

Surprise, turning into the wind, righted herself and the operating table came level. McMullen said, 'Steady, all' and resumed his cutting. The saw was exchanged for the knife. Ord tossed the severed foot into one of the half-tubs that stood under the bulkhead, first spitting on it for luck.

'Tenaculum, Mr Attwood. Ligatures on, and quickly. So. Swabs, Ord, and the bottle of styptic. Thus. And thus. He'll do.'

'Tidy job,' grunted Attwood. 'Bandages, Ord. Old England and Fiddler's Green for you, Dobson.'

McMullen turned away to swill his reddened arms in the cask of seawater, rolled down his shirtsleeves, shrugged on his plain blue coat and clapped his hat on his head. He could leave the rest to Attwood and Ord. He ducked under a deck-beam and started up the ladder, breathing the fresh salty air that came down from the hatch, a tonic draught after the stink of the orlop. The marine sentry on duty at the hatchway stood aside as he came up – no salute for a surgeon, a 'warrant officer of wardroom rank'. McMullen, blinking in the dazzle of late afternoon sunshine, stood for a moment to survey the scene.

The squat 32-pounders had been reloaded and run out and the gun-crews were standing-to, every man's gaze on the big schooner that lay crippled two cable-lengths away on the larboard bow. Beyond the figures of the gunners immediately in front of him, dark against the glitter of rippled water, McMullen could see *Surprise*'s longboat preparing to come alongside her late adversary, whose mainmast, shot through at half-height, trailed overside in a tangle of cordage and flapping canvas; could see, too, the white speck on the dark-blue bar of the Caribbean two miles or more distant – the second of the two Spanish privateers making good her escape.

In essence, it was a scene familiar enough to the frigate's surgeon. In October of 1796 – ten months ago – Spain had allied herself with France in the war against England, and ever since then the few ships of the British West Indies command had been busily employed in combating the swarm of Spanish privateers released to prey on British shipping in the Caribbean, with *Surprise* busiest of all; the 28-gun frigate, smallest of her class, had taken prize or destroyed seventy-nine enemy vessels since her arrival on the station. The chase, the surrender, the putting of a prize-crew on board – it had become (McMullen reflected) almost a routine.

The ensign that had just broken-out on the Spaniard's foretopmast was a white ensign, the C-in-C West Indies being vice-admiral of the white. Men were already at work clearing the wreckage of her mainmast and now the longboat put off from her side to pull back to the frigate. 'Draw charges – larboard guns secure!' came a bellow from the quarterdeck and Mr Maxwell the gunner trotted for'ard along the gangway to supervise the tricky business of withdrawing the powder-cartridges and shot. McMullen started to go aft to make his report to the captain, dodging round the busy groups of men at the guns, his keen glance scanning the brown-skinned muscular figures with something of the builder's satisfaction in his finished work.

John McMullen had been with *Surprise* since her commissioning four years ago. Then, these same lusty specimens of *homo sapiens* had been for the most part the lowest of their kind, the weedy and ill-nourished products of slums and gaols. He had seen the severe conditions of life at sea kill off more than one of the weaklings despite his utmost care; he had salved the lacerated backs of men flogged for practising the bestial brutalities they had learned on shore; he had cured some of the pox, others of the fever, and had sewn and bandaged scores of wounds of varying severity; and he had watched the conversion of a mob of pitiful wretches into a crew of confident fighting seamen. In this, he was well aware, the just but unrelaxing discipline of Captain Hamilton's rule had played a major part. But he knew that some of the credit was due to him.

'How's Jemmy Dobson, doctor?'

A large and singularly ugly seaman who was heaving on the tackle of the aftermost maindeck carronade shot the question at him in a hoarse undertone as he passed.

'Dobson has lost his right foot,' McMullen said. 'You can see him tomorrow, Bragg.'

A case to bolster his satisfaction, was Bragg. A bludgeon and a dark alley Blackfriars way with the gallows foredoomed sooner or later had been his way of life. Now the hardened criminal was the hardiest of seamen (not a wince, McMullen recalled, when he had set that badly-fractured ulna a year ago) with drunkenness his only failing – a vice which he might be said to share with the highest in the land.

The carpenter and his party were at work repairing a splintered gash in the larboard rail below the quarterdeck. Captain Hamilton's high-pitched voice spoke as McMullen mounted the ladder.

'We'll get under way, Mr Rieu, if you please.'

The surgeon, touching his hat as he stepped onto the quarterdeck, dodged round the first lieutenant and his deafening roar of orders and approached the captain.

'Surgeon's report, sir.'

'Proceed, doctor,' Hamilton said, with a quick glance under bent brows.

He was nearly a head shorter than McMullen, slim and elegant in his epauletted coat and white breeches with his cocked hat jauntily set on dark curls tied behind with a black ribbon. The two men were the same age, twenty-five, but the customarily austere set of the surgeon's bony features made him look considerably older than his captain, to whose smooth brown face two very lively brown eyes and a nose that could nearly be called snub lent an inescapably schoolboyish air.

Hamilton listened gravely to McMullen's brief report.

'The stump will heal?' he asked.

'There's a good chance of it, sir. There's the possibility of gangrene and a further amputation, of course.'

'Yes. – Well, Mr Hathaway? You have our position?'

The master, notepad in hand, touched his hat. 'Near enough, sir, though there's a deal of dead-reckoning in it. A hundred and sixty miles west-sou'-west of Cape Beata.'

Hamilton nodded. 'And the same – near enough, as you say – west-nor'-west to Morant Point. Lay me a course for Morant, sailing-master. It's a fair wind for Jamaica. Mr McMullen,' he added as the master departed, 'we'll walk, if you please.'

Under all plain sail the frigate had already left her latest prize astern and with the fresh breeze on the beam was stabbing her bowsprit at the sinking sun. Except for the carpenter's team still at work on the damaged rail her upper decks were quiet; the larboard carronades had been secured and gunports closed, and only the watch-on-deck remained at their stations by the rail. McMullen and Hamilton began their pacing up-and-down on the weather side of the quarterdeck. Captain Turpin of the marines (so named for convenience, since he was properly M. le Marquis du Tour de Pin) had dismissed his sentries and gone below and the only other occupants of the quarterdeck, Mr Rieu and Tomlin the junior midshipman, kept well over on the lee side as naval custom required. The captain and the surgeon had as much privacy as they were likely to get in a crowded fighting-ship of just over 550 tons.

The officers and crew of *Surprise* had so long been accustomed to their captain's choice of a surgeon – a warrant officer, half a civilian – as friend and confidant that it had ceased to strike them as odd. Everyone on board knew that it was only McMullen's astonishing skill in something called trepanning that had saved Edward Hamilton's life when a falling spar cracked his skull in the fight with three Spanish *guarda costas*, off Isla de Pinos eighteen months ago; and that, it seemed to them, excused any oddity. In fact, the post-captain and the surgeon, unlike as they were in temperament, had from the first discovered pleasure in each other's company and conversation as well as a mutual interest in the welfare of the common seaman. On occasions such as this, while McMullen was meticulous in maintaining the conventions of the naval hierarchy, Hamilton was accustomed to throw off all formality.

'It was the damnedest thing, John,' he was saying now, as they paced and turned. 'Dobson was over there by the rail, standing by the mizen brace. The ball – a devilish neat shot, too – smashed the rail, bounced once on the deck, and dropped on Dobson's foot next bounce, poor fellow.'

As he spoke he made vivid illustrative gestures, like an actor. McMullen smiled inwardly, remembering how he had once accused Hamilton of being an actor *manqué*. 'The captain of a King's ship needs to be an actor,' Hamilton had retorted. 'He has to play in turn the slave-driver, the jovial host, the judge, and the intrepid hero – all on the same stage and sometimes in the same day.' McMullen, himself incapable of playing a part, had come to see the truth of this.

'One casualty for the taking of four prizes is scarcely a long list, sir,' he said with intent to comfort.

'It's one too many in this game, John,' Hamilton said reprovingly. 'I'll expend my people when I have to, in a ship-to-ship battle if you like – but I don't like wasting a man in this damned hunting of small craft.'

'Small craft? Two privateer schooners – '

'One of which stayed not upon the order of her going. The other – a good plucked 'un, her captain. If he'd been navy 'stead of a privateer I'd have had him on board to dine.'

They turned together at the taffrail as the ship's bell was struck, a double clang: two bells of the last dog-watch. The widening V of the frigate's wake glinted redly across the darkening sea astern in reflection of the nascent sunset.

'I see they have the prize under way, sir,' said McMullen.

'Yes. Young Phillimore will do well enough in command.' Phillimore was the frigate's senior midshipman; two lieutenants and a master's mate had already been sent away in charge of prizes. 'I'll arrange his examination for lieutenant as soon as I can,' Hamilton added. 'Did you know he has a widowed mother and two sisters to keep?'

McMullen said he hadn't known. It was typical of Edward Hamilton, he reflected, to know the shore circumstances of all his 'people,' as he called them. They paced in silence for a few moments. Then Hamilton spoke suddenly:

'The schooner's long sixes outranged our carronades, John. We had to stand fire before we could settle her business. It was the devil's own luck that it should cost Dobson his foot.'

'I know,' McMullen said soothingly.

'Yes, but mark how the chain of fortune lengthens.' Hamilton glanced up at his vessel's inordinately tall mainmast, a mast intended for a 38-gun frigate, which he had won from Admiralty dockyard by some means known only to himself. 'But for the extra canvas on my little pet there we could never have outsailed that schooner, could never have come within range of her long sixes. But for my machinations at Portsmouth three years ago, then, James Dobson would still have two feet.'

'We've argued causality before, sir,' McMullen said firmly, 'and I tell you again that's a shallow and illogical thesis. Take it a stage further and you'll be saying the dockyard officer who took your bribe is responsible for Dobson's amputation.' He gave one of his rare chuckles. 'However, you may safely say that but for *my* little pet Dobson would very likely lose a leg rather than a foot merely.'

'Ha – the famous McMullen styptic.' Hamilton's face, red in the sunset-glow as they turned, wore a grin; his friend's 'little pet' was a medicament based on a solution of oak-galls and guaranteed to stop bleeding. 'It'll do the trick, you think?'

'I know. It did the trick for me last year, you'll remember.'

As he spoke the surgeon rubbed his left forearm, where beneath the sleeve the ridged scar of a knife-wound ran from wrist to elbow, memento of a characteristic Hamilton escapade. Acting on a rumour that information concerning the sailings of enemy privateers might be obtained at a disreputable tavern in Spanish Town, the captain had gone there in disguise one night, coercing the reluctant McMullen (who spoke fluent Spanish) into accompanying him. Possibly because Hamilton's false moustachios had fallen off into his wine, the two had been detected as spies and set upon.

McMullen's arm had intercepted a knife-thrust aimed at his friend, Hamilton had tripped their assailant and dowsed the lamp with a kick, and the two had broken out and made their escape, leaving a trail of blood which the darkness had fortunately hidden.

'I'll answer for Dobson,' McMullen went on, 'but not if he's taken into Kingston hospital. If there's a ship homeward bound, sir, Dobson should go in her.'

'He'll go –' Hamilton checked himself. 'I'd like a word with Dobson before I go to my cabin.' He raised his voice. 'Mr Rieu, you have the deck. I'll relieve you myself at eight bells.'

'Aye aye, sir.'

McMullen followed the captain down the ladder to the deck. The binnacle lamp had been lit and its yellow spark gleamed in odd contrast to the vast spread of the sunset glow overhead. Hamilton glanced aloft at the taut sails and upper spars silhouetted against the crimson sky.

'We could be in Kingston harbour before tomorrow's sunset,' he said, half to himself. '*Hermione* could be there when we arrive.'

'*Hermione*, sir?'

'Twelve-pounder frigate, thirty-two guns. I don't know her captain.'

They had reached the hatchway leading down to the orlop. Hamilton halted and looked round him. A group of deck-watch seamen, squatting below the weather rail a dozen paces away, were talking together in low tones with an occasional muted guffaw.

'No reason why you shouldn't know,' Hamilton muttered. 'You'll keep it to yourself, of course. I had it from the Admiral before we sailed that *Hermione*'s coming out to replace *Surprise* on the station – she sailed at the end of July. When next we sail from Kingston, John, it'll be for England – home.'

He started down the ladder. McMullen stood for a moment staring blankly out over the frigate's bows. The dark plain of the Caribbean stretched and merged into a sky of darkening crimson, like a sea of blood. *England – home*. He could feel no pleasure at the prospect. It meant farewell to Lucy Preston.

2

John McMullen was still thinking of Lucy Preston when *Surprise*, under reefed topsails, commenced the tricky four-mile passage through the reefs that guarded the entrance to Kingston harbour. The north-east Trade, a soldier's wind for the frigate's course, had brought the Jamaican mountains above the horizon at noon and the mid-afternoon heat smote from a brassy sky as she crept in across the shimmering water, gradually losing the cool breeze from the open sea under the lee of Gallows Point. McMullen, standing at the weather rail below the quarterdeck, watched the approaching shore, a pale-brown line below green-forested hills, and reflected that he had every reason, save one, to rejoice at the prospect of leaving Jamaica.

Surprise had been long enough on the West Indies station, her brief spells in Kingston harbour numerous enough, for him to develop a firm dislike for the place and its way of life. The island itself he could admire; the wild beauty of its craggy hills half-clad in green vegetation, its ravines and waterfalls, even the spreading plantations of sugar-cane that represented Man's interference with the natural order, had given him pleasure on jaunts ashore with Edward Hamilton or Forbes Wilson, the frigate's second lieutenant. But in the human beings who had made themselves masters of this paradisal wilderness he took no pleasure at all. The planters who had lorded it in Jamaica for a century were (it seemed to him) like the Devil's parody of an aristocracy. Waited on by legions of slaves in their tremendous mansions, answerable to no one for their treatment of the thousands of Negroes who toiled to amass their immense wealth, surrounded by black concubines and more often drunk than sober, they combined the pride of Lucifer – as Hamilton had once remarked – with the ethics of Mammon. Balls and drinking-parties were their recreations, and the presence of a military garrison and a naval squadron gave adequate excuse for an endless succession of these. McMullen's comparatively humble rank had deprived him of invitation to the more glittering functions, for which he was grateful; and he had usually managed to evade those humbler junketings designed for junior officers, his somewhat austere turn of mind making such frolics less than enjoyable. It was Captain Hamilton who had persuaded him, three months ago, to accompany him to a ball given by the officers of the 32nd at Fort Nugent, and it was there that he had met Lucy.

The ball was a lively affair attended chiefly by officers of the two Services and their ladies with a sprinkling of lesser officials from the plantations. Admiral Sir Hyde Parker graced the occasion with his podgy presence for ten minutes by way of courtesy to Colonel Spears of the 32nd but thereafter was not seen again. McMullen, an indifferent dancer and incapable of flirtatious conversation, spent the early part of the evening exchanging anecdotes of a medical nature with the regimental surgeon, but at the dinner-table he found himself seated next to a young lady introduced to him as Miss Lucy Preston, niece to the manager of the Beauchamp plantation.

Miss Preston, who was a year or two younger than himself, had no use for flirtatious conversation and proved easy to talk to, since she plied McMullen with questions about living conditions in a King's ship and the treatment of the sick, with a frank intelligence that he found remarkable. Lucy's round face was pleasant rather than pretty, her low-cut ball gown less revealing than the gowns of most of the other women, and her brown eyes reminiscent of Edward Hamilton's – all of which tended to set him at ease with her. So did the three different wines that supported the various courses of the long meal. Before it was halfway through McMullen had learned that Lucy had shocked her Jamaican friends and acquaintances by starting a small makeshift hospital for the slaves on the plantation, that she had read Defoe's *Tour thro' the Whole Island of Great Britain* and Tom Paine's *The Rights of Man*, and that it was only the tyrannies of the Directory in France that had ended her earlier sympathy with the revolutionists. And so rapidly did mutual confidence expand that before its end Lucy was possessed of most of John McMullen's life-story.

She heard how the boy, orphaned at the age of ten, was adopted by his mother's brother, a surgeon and friend of William Hunter; how he had evinced liking and aptitude for a medical career and had made such progress in it that he was one of Hunter's first students at the famous lecture-hall in Great Windmill Street; and how, left penniless after his uncle's bankruptcy and suicide, he had sat the required examinations at the Transport Board and Surgeon's Hall and taken his Royal Navy warrant as ship's surgeon.

'I must condole with you, sir,' Lucy had said, watching him covertly. 'You might have gone on to succeed Mr Hunter as surgeon to His Majesty. Instead, you have to minister to the most downtrodden of his subjects.'

Although he warmed to her sympathy McMullen had been unable to let that pass. 'I assure you I've come to be happy in that ministry, ma'am,' he had replied gravely. 'And – with your leave – there are many subjects of His Majesty a good deal more downtrodden than a British seaman.'

'But we hear of flogging and all manner of brutality in a King's ship, sir.'

'Where there is law there must be punishment for breaking it, ma'am. I've seen no worse than that.'

He had served in two ships, he told her. In his first, the *Lion* 74, there had indeed been floggings, in the main for habitual theft or sleeping on watch, but the men on the lower deck regarded these as not only just but also essential to their own comfort and safety. As for his present ship, he was fortunate in having a captain who cared as much for his crew's well-being as the surgeon himself.

'Fortunate indeed, sir.' Lucy had frowned reflectively. 'Two ships. And how many ships, at your reckoning, are there in the naval service?'

McMullen had said, not without a slight uneasiness, that he thought there must be between three and four hundred.

'So many?' Lucy had smiled suddenly. 'But let us talk of something else. I'm quite sure you won't be able to tell me what sort of pelisse the ladies were wearing in London when last you were there – but perhaps you attended a concert?'

McMullen had indeed, four years ago, been to one of the concerts given by Abel and J.C.Bach in Carlisle House, and they talked of music until the dinner and its postludes were over and Lucy's aunt, a stout lady of middle age, came to tell her the carriage was waiting.

Twelve weeks later, coming in to Kingston on this hot September afternoon, McMullen found he could recall their talk at that first meeting almost word-for-word. The stink of the harbour drifted to his nostrils and brought him back to the present. They said you could smell Kingston five miles out at sea, a legend perhaps but not far from the truth; the place was the home of filth and disease – and of Yellow Jack. One in five of the garrison soldiers, according to their regimental surgeon, could expect to die of yellow fever, that mysterious epidemic disease for which there was no cure, and 'it's the Palisades for Johnny Redcoat' was a byword among them.

The Palisades, the long rock reef that ended in Gallows Point, was in sight now a mile away on the starboard bow, with its beach of soft sand that stretched along the seaward side and was used for burying the fever victims – in very shallow graves, so that the land-crabs could complete the disposal of the bodies. In all the many times McMullen had seen the harbour entrance opening between Fort Charles and the Apostles Battery he had never failed to experience this sickening apprehension; for shore-leave there had to be, and if yellow fever was the worst danger it was only one of many that lurked ashore in Kingston. But this time – he realised suddenly – was likely to be the last. And that brought him back to Lucy Preston again.

They had met twice more since that first encounter. A performance by 'A String Trio of Talented Gentlemen' in aid of charity had chanced to coincide with *Surprise*'s next brief stay in port and he had procured a ticket, refusing to admit to himself that he hoped to see Lucy there. She was there, with her aunt. It was a shabby affair and poorly attended; the *élite* of Kingston were not much given to charity or the arts. But he won a seat next to Lucy (the aunt, Mrs Emmett by name, approving and even encouraging) and their acquaintance ripened even more swiftly than before. He learned among other things that she was an orphan like himself, her parents having lost their lives in the hurricane of '84 that had wreaked such havoc in Jamaica. Now she lived in her uncle's house on the Beauchamp plantation, five miles east of Kingston. Next time *Surprise* returned to port with her string of prizes – at the end of July, six weeks ago – he had taken his courage in both hands and paid a formal call, borrowing a horse for the purpose. It was after this visit, with the aunt's frustrating presence preventing the exchange of ideas in which he had delighted, that McMullen realised that he wanted Lucy to himself, and for a lifetime.

And now *Surprise* was to sail for England as soon as *Hermione* arrived to relieve her; the captain had told the wardroom at breakfast this morning. He knew she was long overdue for a dockyard refit and that every man on board except himself would be happy that she was homeward bound. It was a good thing for Dobson, who could continue under his care and be properly fitted with an artificial limb when they reached England – he could trust Captain Hamilton to contrive so that the man should not be taken ashore to that pestilential hospital in Kingston. To wish that *Hermione* might founder before she reached Jamaica was folly, and selfish folly at that. And yet he found himself wishing it.

The frigate, creeping slowly now across smooth water under the failing breeze, had brought Fort Charles almost abeam. There was a sudden stir on the quarterdeck, voices speaking in some excitement, but McMullen was oblivious of it, dazzled by an idea that had flashed upon him. Suppose Lucy to be his wife, and she could come with him to England in *Surprise* – Edward Hamilton would certainly afford her a passage. He blinked, shocked by his own temerity. Then he perceived it to be a mad impossibility.

Marriage and its implications had not before occurred to him in connection with Lucy Preston or anybody else. That a ship's surgeon of twenty-five with no family and no home except his ship, receiving five pounds a month from the Pay Office, should take a wife was a proposition too absurd to consider. In middle age, perhaps, there might come a final stepping-ashore and the acquisition of a small country practice and a wife, but – unless he had an independent income – a serving warrant-officer surgeon had neither the means nor the moral right (in John McMullen's opinion) to ask a woman to share his life. And Lucy –

He felt the hot blood reddening his face as he realised that he knew nothing of her feelings towards him, that his dazzling idea branded him an impertinent coxcomb. That she valued their acquaintance, short though it had been, he felt reasonably certain. There was not the least reason to think –

'Doctor!'

A voice from above his head broke into these agitated self-communings. The big brown face and sun-peeled nose of Rieu, first lieutenant, was grinning down at him from the taffrail.

'Captain's compliments and please to step up here,' said Rieu.

McMullen went up the short ladder to the quarterdeck. With second and third lieutenants absent (in harbour by now, with their prizes) and the senior midshipman away in the captured privateer, it was a depleted group of officers that awaited him: Rieu, little Hathaway the master, Turpin plump and *point-device* in his red coat, the two midshipmen Tomlin and Betts – all of them grinning delightedly at him. Hamilton, at the after rail with his telescope levelled, turned and offered him the glass. He too was smiling.

'Take a look, doctor,' he said.

Dead astern, on the blue bar of horizon far beyond the spreading furrows of *Surprise*'s wake, a speck of brilliant white caught the sun; a ship under full sail, already hull-up. McMullen steadied the glass, a recent one by Dollond with the achromatic lenses, and she sprang into instant clarity and detail, a large frigate heading for Kingston. He looked inquiringly at the captain as he returned the telescope.

'Couldn't have been more happily arranged,' said Hamilton. 'That's *Hermione*, Mr McMullen.'

McMullen's heart sank. 'You're certain of it, sir?' he asked foolishly.

'You may ask Mr Rieu here. He's served in her.'

'Not a doubt of it, doctor,' said Rieu cheerfully. 'I was second in her on the Mediterranean station in 'ninety-three, with Captain Herbert. Tonnage seven hundred and fifteen, thirty-eight guns if you count her carronades, and a broadside of sixteen twelve-pounders.'

'Nearly twice our force, in effect,' Hamilton said.

'She'll have to work damned hard to equal our record in these waters, sir, twelve-pounders or no.'

'The buzz is that the Dons are building-up a fleet of big privateers at Puerto Rico – *Surprise*'s next cruise would have been down that way.' There was more than a hint of regret in the captain's tone. '*Hermione* should be useful there.'

'Captain Herbert was in the last *Gazette*, promoted Rear-Admiral of the Blue,' said Rieu. 'There'll be a new captain in *Hermione*.'

Hard on his last word the three double clangs of the ship's bell, six bells of the afternoon watch, sounded with the fateful note of a tocsin in McMullen's ears, rousing him from dismal meditation. At the same time *Surprise* began to turn to starboard, rounding Gallows Point and opening the long east-west reach of the harbour. The white sail astern passed from view and Captain Hamilton snapped his telescope shut with an air of finality.

'Very well,' he said briskly. 'Mr Rieu, anchor parties to stations fore and aft, if you please. Captain Turpin, you may parade your men up here. Hoist our number, Mr Tomlin – and keep your eye on the flagship's yardarm. Mr Betts, my compliments to Mr Maxwell and he's to load with cartridge for vice-admiral's salute.'

The ensuing bustle recalled the surgeon to awareness of being out of place on the quarterdeck and he was moving towards the ladder when a hand dropped lightly on his shoulder and Hamilton's voice spoke in his ear.

'I fancy you leave behind more than the rest of us, John. I wish you may find compensations in England.'

McMullen frowned as he went down the ladder. He knew Edward Hamilton was aware of his acquaintance with Lucy, but he hadn't realised that his attachment to her was so obvious. Like as not the whole ship's company knew of it; in a small ship like *Surprise* one could keep nothing secret. Judging from the lively air and grinning faces of the men on deck at their various duties, the frigate's crew knew of her next destination although no word of it had been spoken outside the wardroom.

As he went for'ard on his way to examine the state of

Dobson's stump he glanced across the larboard rail to where
Kingston, its massed white buildings spreading upward and
thinning amongst the greenery of the hillside, shimmered
across pearly waters where a few small craft moved slowly
between anchored ships. It looked a paradisal place from
here; only the smell drifting across the harbour warned that
Kingston was a long remove from Paradise – farther even than
England from Jamaica.

Four thousand miles. Two months. Once that time and
distance were between them he might abandon any hope of
seeing Lucy again. Then – the alternative, the hardly-to-be-
thought-of alternative? It was all imponderables. He didn't
know how soon *Surprise* would sail, or how to set about
arranging a wedding, or whether a marriage would be possible
at all in whatever limited time was available. The frigate carried
no chaplain, or a solution might have been found there.
Hadn't he heard that a ship's captain, lacking a parson, had
authority to –

'By'r leave, doctor!'

He jumped aside to the rail to avoid the cheerful party of
seamen laying out the anchor cable, his thoughts still busy with
his problem. Those imponderables could all be ascertained
quickly, by diligent inquiry. The first thing, the one thing
needful, was Lucy's consent. McMullen brought his fist down
on the rail with a crash. He would ask her, at the earliest
opportunity.

3

Opportunity came a good deal later than McMullen could
have wished. With his resolution loaded and run up, like a
carronade, he was panting to fire his desperate shot; but
fortune was against him and a succession of shipboard
circumstances prevented him from going ashore.

No one on board *Surprise* expected any leave in the first
twenty-four hours in port; after the clewing-up and
flemishing-down and precise squaring of yards which was the
first part of the harbour 'stow,' the hands were at it again,

watch by watch, priddying the ship in every particular against
the possibility of critical visitors, among whom Vice-Admiral
Sir Hyde Parker was uppermost in everyone's mind. Captain
Hamilton, the only man to absent himself from the frigate,
went ashore to make his report at Admiralty House and (it was
rumoured) to do some preliminary bribing of storekeepers and
water-hoy skippers so that there would be no delays when
Surprise got her sailing-orders.

The surgeon and his assistant had plenty to occupy them
during this anticipated detention on board. Besides the shifting
of Dobson to more comfortable sick quarters next to
McMullen's own small cabin, they were busy taking stock of
their medical supplies and listing requirements for the long
voyage home. Coming on deck for a breath of air at sunset,
McMullen was in time to see *Hermione* rounding Gallows Point,
her topsails flushed to deep rose-colour in the lingering
radiance of the vanished sun. A beautiful vessel, he thought
her. She anchored half-a-mile astern of *Surprise* who was at her
usual berth well up towards the eastern end of the long
harbour. Before he went below again he looked across the
iridescent water to the low hill behind Fort Nugent where the
road wound over to the Beauchamp plantation and Lucy's
home, a glance half-longing, half-apprehensive. Another day
would have to pass before he travelled that road unless he
transgressed an unwritten law; which he found himself unable
to do. Since it was the captain's strict requirement that the
frigate should never be without a surgeon on board while in
port, he and Attwood had an agreement – rigidly adhered to
during *Surprise*'s time on the station – to take first leave ashore
by turns, and it chanced to be Attwood's turn this time.
McMullen could have used his seniority and gone himself but
he wasn't going to; he had been at sea long enough to know
that the breaking of agreed custom among members of a ship's
company was an unforgivable sin. The crucial moment, then,
would not come until the day after tomorrow, and he was
ashamed to find his feeling of frustration tinged with relief.
Frustration, however, was unmixed and furious when even the
day after tomorrow brought no chance of a visit to Lucy, the
sick-bay being packed with casualties.

For shore parties to return on board bruised and bleeding as the result of a brawl was the rule rather than the exception, but the fight with *Hermione*'s men had evidently been a more vicious affair than the usual tavern fracas. Fourteen men of *Surprise*'s crew had been wounded by knife-thrusts, six of them seriously, and one man (his condition not improved after being hoisted up the ship's side in a bowline) had what appeared to be a depressed fracture of the skull. McMullen and Attwood and Ord were busy stitching, swabbing and bandaging through the night and well into next morning. The Surprises were of course unanimous in maintaining that their own behaviour had been perfectly unprovocative, indeed lamblike, and that the Hermiones had outnumbered them two-to-one. Bragg, Dobson's gigantic crony, was one of the worst injured, with two terrible gashes in his chest which brought a frown to McMullen's face as he sponged away the congealing blood.

'Knifing's a dirty game, 'cept when a surgeon does it,' Attwood was saying as he bandaged the slit forearm of a man alongside Bragg. 'Englishmen use their fists.'

'Aye – Englishmen,' growled Bragg. 'If there was any English among them Hermys, sir, there warn't more'n four. Rest on 'em was Irishers and bloody foreigners. Settin' and drinkin' quiet-like we was, when they up and set on us – '

'Hold the edges of the wound together for a moment,' interrupted McMullen, threading his needle. 'You mean they attacked you without any warning?'

There was enough drink in Bragg to dull his sensitivity to pain without hindering his loquacity.

'Warning, doctor?' he repeated, without flinching as the needle penetrated for the first stitch. 'Well, now, there was what you might call a bit o' bickering twixt me and a big Hermy. Asks how many floggin's we'd had aboard *Surprise* this v'yage. Seems it's floggin' day an' night aboard *Hermione*. I tells him nary a floggin' these last two months an' he says we must be a pap-suckin' lot o' bastards. So I up an' knocks him down, same as you'd ha' done yourself sir, an' nex' minute he was at me with his knife – kickin' nasty, too. Irish he was – an' all Irishers is dirty fighters as you know, sir.'

McMullen, whose grandfather had come from County Down, concealed a smile. 'And then you all took a hand, I suppose. Mr Attwood, the roll of plaster, if you please.'

'We 'ad to 'elp Braggy, sir,' protested Attwood's patient. ' 'E'd got no knife – there weren't no knives drawn by us, swelp me if there was.'

'I'll tell the captain what you say, Gilpin. He will have to be informed of this, of course.'

McMullen gave a final pat to Bragg's plasters and went to look at the depressed fracture, incurred by a Swede named Sandell who was moaning unintelligibly, swathed in blankets and semi-conscious. Probing would have to wait until he had daylight to see by. There could be no early start tomorrow for the visit to Lucy.

In the event, it was close to noon next day when he had finished the delicate operation, lifting the bone fragment that had threatened to penetrate the regions of the brain. Sandell's condition was still serious enough, as he reported to Edward Hamilton in the privacy of the captain's cabin.

'The next twelve hours should see him out of danger, sir,' he added. 'After that I can safely leave him in Attwood's hands.'

'And borrow Doctor Muspratt's bay mare again?' said Hamilton, with a quizzical glance. 'Well, there are times when a gentleman may be forgiven for keeping a lady waiting. And by the bye – I believe you may count upon three days more.'

'Before we sail?'

'Yes. *Hermione* will almost certainly sail before we do – a quick turn-round. The Admiral wants her off Puerto Rico as soon as possible, keeping an eye on the Dons' new privateers.' Hamilton frowned suddenly. 'Tomorrow I'll take order with her captain – Pigot's his name, Hugh Pigot – concerning last night's affray. Can't have my people knifed by his ruffians. All the same, I don't much like complaining that my lads were licked by his.'

'It wasn't in fair fight!' McMullen said hotly. 'They were – '

'I know, John, I know. Two to one, and knives where it should have been fists. I'll deal with Captain Pigot, never fear.' Hamilton's brown eyes sparkled and he grinned his characteristic lop-sided grin. 'He'll be at Admiralty House tomorrow and I'm bidden there too. If I can get the Admiral on my side we may persuade Captain Pigot to deprive *Hermione*'s shore-parties of their cutlery in future.'

McMullen spent the afternoon in his sick-bay, where there were now eight patients including Dobson. All the knife-wounds seemed more likely than not to heal cleanly, and there were no signs of gangrene about Dobson's stump. Sandell was his chief anxiety, but by midnight he could sense that the crisis was past and that Attwood, following his instructions, could manage the subsequent nursing without hazard to the patient. That night he lay wakeful in his cot for a long time, forming and discarding phrases and sentences for the proposal he was to make on the morrow. He was still undecided as to what he should say when, in the early forenoon of next day, he was urging Doctor Muspratt's bay mare up the hill above Kingston.

Good fortune had provided an early start. Captain Hamilton – who could hardly have guessed the importance of his surgeon's errand – had had the gig's crew called-away to set him ashore; the surgeon of the 32nd had been ready, even eager, to loan his horse to a colleague. But if Fortune smiled the weather did not. It was September, month of intermittent heavy rains, and the downpour of the night had continued into the morning, penetrating below the turned-up collar of McMullen's tarpaulin coat as he crouched in the sternsheets of the gig. By the time he was mounted and on his way the rain had stopped, but a heavy white vapour like steam lay across the coastal hills and wooded glens. The road, a mere strip of rutted earth, was deep in mud and McMullen's best white stockings and silver-buckled shoes were caked with it. His shirt was damp against his skin, his carefully-tied stock was crumpled beyond amendment, and the cocks of his hat flapped limply as the mare, reaching the top of the hill, began to trot. He had taken off the tarpaulin coat and tied it on the crupper, but the steamy humidity all about him was making him sweat. He felt dishevelled and dispirited.

The road curled into and out of a ravine dark with dripping tropical plants and ran steeply down towards the levels of what seemed, through the mist, to be a vast green sea. A tall fence like a stockade opposed him but the gate in it was opened as he rode up by a bearded fellow with a short whip of plaited leather – a quirt, in the vernacular of the planters – hanging from his belt. He rode on between walls of sugar-cane higher than his head, meeting no one but hearing occasional distant voices and once the crack of a whiplash, until the road began to climb and the cane thinned out on the slopes of a knoll clad with low bushes. The house of the plantation manager and his wife, a substantial single-storey building of whitewashed stone, stood on the flat crest of the knoll surrounded by a fence. On his one previous visit he had admired the view to southward, which extended to the sea-coast west of Morant Point; but today there was nothing to see but the cotton-wool whiteness of the mists.

McMullen, conscious that his pulse was beating very fast – a hundred at least, he found himself thinking automatically – hitched the bay mare to the fence and went to the door. A Negro girl told him that Massa Emmett was from home but Missus was in, and Lucy's aunt, appearing at this moment to salute the visitor with a curtsey and an arch smile, said that Miss Preston was down at 'what she was pleased to call her hospital' – would Doctor McMullen come in and await Miss Preston's return? McMullen bowed his thanks and said that with Mrs Emmett's permission he would go down to the hospital; and having got away with the briefest possible exchange of courtesies he set off down a narrow path whose lower reaches were lost in the dense white vapour.

On his last, frustratingly formal, visit Lucy had pointed out this path to him and though he had longed to see what her 'hospital' was like the occasion had given no opportunity. Now, descending gingerly on the muddy slope, his mind was full of the coming encounter, though he spared a fleeting thought for Mrs Emmett. There, he suspected, was one who wouldn't be sorry to have a dependent niece taken off her hands even by a penniless ship's surgeon. With her husband the manager, a grim and silent man, McMullen had exchanged no more than half-a-dozen words but thought he was likely to be of the same mind as his wife.

Below him at the foot of the path the palm-thatched roofs of a few huts grew clearer out of the mist, and a cloaked and hooded figure beginning to climb the path towards him – Lucy!

McMullen slithered to a halt, his head a whirl of hypothecated phrases. *Pray forgive me, ma'am, if I approach a matter … The question I am about to ask will seem … I trust you will excuse my urgency …* They all seemed stilted and worse than useless. He went slowly on to meet her, noting as she came closer that her face was pale and serious.

'Good morning, ma'am – you are early abroad,' he managed to get out, doffing his hat.

His attempt at a bow on the slippery incline came within an ace of depositing him on his rump in the mud. Lucy wisely confined herself to a polite inclination of her head.

'I have a patient who needed my attention, sir,' she answered coldly. 'I am going up to the house now,' she added as McMullen, tongue-tied, still stood in her way.

'Yes – of course – naturally.' He slithered again as he stood aside. 'Will you – will you take my arm? The path is steep – '

'It's also very narrow, sir. And I manage well enough, thank you.'

She went on past him. McMullen, hurriedly seeking for something to say, followed a pace behind.

'Your patient is making a good recovery?' he asked.

Lucy made no reply for a long moment. Then she stopped, so suddenly that he almost cannoned into her, and turned to face him. Her swift movement swept aside the folds of her cloak and he saw that on the white dress beneath it there was a great bloodstain.

'My patient is a Negro, sir – a black slave.' Her voice was low and vehement. 'He has been beaten with a whip – flogged – almost to death. I've been renewing the dressings on his back.'

'Oh.' McMullen was somewhat at a loss. 'A punishment, presumably. No doubt – '

'He was half-killed because the overseer considered he was not working hard enough.'

'Indeed. The punishment seems to have been unduly severe. But if the overseer judged – '

' "The overseer judged"!' she cried in a sort of angry

triumph. 'You lay your finger on the real crime, Doctor McMullen! The overseer was judge and jury – and executioner too. The poor Negro had no one to defend him, no law to appeal to. Where is the justice in this?'

She had thrown back the hood from her dark hair and her brown eyes were blazing. McMullen could scarcely recognise in this Fury the girl who had discussed the music of Haydn with him.

'We must realise, ma'am,' he replied hesitantly, 'that a slave has no rights in common law. This Negro – '

'This Negro is a man!' she flashed at him. 'He has no rights, you say, and another man has the right – in common law, no doubt – to slash the flesh from his bones with a whip. Is that what you call justice?'

He bit his lip, a small flame of resentment alight in him. With Negro slaves, however severely flogged, he had no concern; and as to justice, he had done nothing to deserve this accusatory tone. The conversation was far off course and he tried to steer it back towards his own goal with an attempt at gallantry.

'No jury could resist Miss Preston's arguments, I'm assured,' he said, forcing a smile. 'She would charm the judge himself to her way of thinking.'

'But not you, sir!' she took him up instantly. 'For you serve in a King's ship, where such floggings are a matter of course. Your captain is merely another overseer.'

McMullen was angered despite himself. 'By your leave, ma'am, the cases are totally different. The captain – '

'They are the same, sir. One man is given power to treat other men like brute beasts – worse, indeed, than most men treat animals. And that,' added Lucy forcibly, 'is wrong – wrong – wrong!'

She turned and started up the path again. McMullen followed, seething inwardly. The chance-given opportunity, Lucy and himself alone and isolated by the mist, was fast flying from him. But for that damned Negro he might have brought it off – and now, in two or three minutes, they'd be up at the house with Aunt Emmett hampering his manoeuvres. He summoned his wits and resolution.

'Miss Preston,' he said to her cloaked back, 'this argument was none of my contriving and can be pursued, if you wish, on some other occasion. I came today to ask you a question – a question of very great moment to myself.'

The back, moving steadily on in front of him, was quite unresponsive. Something, the spirit of his Irish grandfather perhaps, prompted McMullen to throw caution and courtesy to the winds.

'Lucy!' he said sharply. 'I'm asking you to marry me.'

That halted her instantly. She swung round to stare down at him, open-mouthed and wide-eyed.

'*Surprise* sails for England in three days,' he went on quickly. 'We may never see each other again unless you'll consent – '

'You – you must be mad, sir!' she broke in, snatching away the hand he tried to clasp. 'Or else you mean to insult me. We've met but four times – '

'Doctor, ahoy!'

The hail came from close above but the hailer was invisible in the mist. McMullen, stifling a curse, hurried on with his petition.

'I know it's short notice, Lucy, and I know it's my last chance. Only say you'll be my wife and come – '

'Doctor McMullen! You down there, doctor? Wanted on board urgent – Cap'n Hamilton's orders!'

'You had better go, sir,' said Lucy, speaking between clenched teeth. 'I shall remain here awhile.'

McMullen opened his mouth and closed it. Turned away, turned back with hand half outstretched, and finally bolted up the slippery path as fast as his legs would take him, in a fury of despair. The outline of the manager's house shaped itself on the mist above and beside it the figures of a man and a horse. As he came nearer he recognised the man, small and wiry, as Antonio, captain's coxswain.

'Bit o' luck I found you so quick, doctor,' said Antonio; he was, and looked, Portuguese, but seven years on the lower deck had reformed his speech. 'Cap'n wants you immediate, sir.'

McMullen, breathless and sweating, went to unhitch the mare. 'What is it?' he snapped, over his shoulder. 'Is Dobson worse?'

'Not as I knows on, sir. Cap'n says "Find the doctor and bring him back here – tell him it's most urgent".' Antonio got into his saddle. 'I'd say he was mighty put out, was Captain Hamilton.'

McMullen mounted and swung the mare round. 'Lead on,' he said briefly.

The ride back to Kingston passed, for him, in alternations of gloomy perplexities. Was his fate with Lucy finally sealed, his last chance lost in the conjunction of her unfortunate mood and his own ineptness? She hadn't actually refused him, he recalled. Had Hamilton's summons spared him that or robbed him of possible success? And what urgency lay behind the summons? Edward Hamilton was not the man to curtail his friend's shore-leave in this manner unless the matter was important.

They cantered down the last muddy stretch of the road, past the hovels on the outskirts of Kingston and on between the warehouses to the eastern quay. There was no ship's boat waiting – no captain would trust a boat's crew alongside a Kingston quay for that long – but Antonio had secured a local wherry and they were pulled out to *Surprise* by a pair of lusty quadroons. The mist had lifted a trifle and beneath it *Hermione* was clearly visible; McMullen was too preoccupied to notice the lighters and water-hoy alongside her and the bustle of activity on board. When he came up the frigate's side the duty officer met him with hand outstretched. It was Wilson, second lieutenant, back aboard from his command of the prize.

'Captain's waiting for you in his cabin,' Wilson said as they shook hands; his thin eager face was wrinkled with concern. 'I'm damned sorry about this, John,' he added in a low voice.

McMullen didn't stay to ask what there was to be sorry about but walked quickly aft. The marine sentry stood aside and he went into Hamilton's day cabin. The captain sprang up from the table where he had been frowning over lists of stores and caught him by the arm, leading him across to the stern windows where they would be out of earshot of the sentry.

'A thousand apologies, John, for this untimely recall,' he said, looking concerned as Wilson had looked, and angry as well. 'It so happens that there's not a moment to lose.'

'We're sailing sooner than you thought, sir?'

'No. It's still three days hence. But *Hermione*'s to sail at first light tomorrow.'

Hamilton turned away, clenching his fists. He seemed to be repressing some powerful emotion.

'I had no choice!' he said suddenly, swinging round again. 'You must believe that, John – and anyway, I suppose you may not be as sorry as we are. If Miss Preston – '

'This concerns Miss Preston, then?' prompted McMullen, frowning as the captain checked himself.

'It was the damndest thing, John!' Hamilton burst out. 'A direct order from the Admiral. This Pigot – I beg his pardon, Captain Hugh Pigot of the *Hermione* – turns out to be the son of Admiral Pigot, one of the Admiralty lords with loads of interest in high places. That wouldn't influence me – you may be sure I gave him his due over this knifing affray – but you know Sir Hyde. Captain Pigot must have all he requires, Captain Pigot mustn't sail short-handed, and Captain Hamilton will damned well obey orders. No manner of use my suggesting Attwood – '

'Edward!' McMullen interrupted sharply. 'In the name of friendship, will you tell me what's happened?'

Captain Hamilton told him.

Twenty-four hours later a messenger from Kingston brought a letter to Miss Lucy Preston:

Madam,

I have little time in which to write since I have been transferred as ship's surgeon on board the frigate Hermione and sail tomorrow at dawn. I will say only that I beg you to forgive what you must have thought a most unseemly display of my true feelings for you, at our late meeting. I can plead only that I then expected to be leaving Jamaica for England, and foresaw no opportunity of putting my case before you after a more reasonable interval. I trust you will at least permit me to call and make my excuses in person, when next Hermione is in port. Until then, Madam, I venture to subscribe myself, with respect,

Your humble and obedient servant
John McMullen

CHAPTER TWO

HMS Hermione

1

McMullen woke with familiar sounds in his ears, familiar movement swaying his body on the hanging cot. There was the unceasing lamentation of a ship's timbers working in a seaway, the sibilant murmuration of water along her side, the nearer tapping and scraping of hanging clothes and other articles against the bulkhead; and the slow sideways swing of the cot, which was an oblong wooden frame with canvas stretched across it, slung fore-and-aft from two ringbolts in the deckhead. The cabin, which would have been pitch-dark but for a glimmer of light through the cracks of the doorway, was so small that the cot practically filled it, and its swinging to the ship's motion would have banged it against the sides if it had not been braced-up so close to the ringbolts that McMullen's nose was barely a foot from the deckhead planking.

He came slowly back to awareness by way of the smell. That was familiar too, to the extent that it included the tang of Stockholm tar and the all-pervasive effluvia from the bilges, but there was an overlying odour compounded of unwashed clothes and stale spirits. The present, and the immediate past, rushed into his mind and he was broad awake. The odour had been left by the late occupant of this cabin; Dogherty, ship's surgeon, had been taken ashore to the hospital in an alcoholic delirium, last of a long series and almost certain to finish him off. This was the frigate *Hermione*.

The events of the past twelve hours recurred to him in swift panorama. The hurried packing of sea-chest and instrument-case; the last-minute instructions to Attwood concerning

Dobson's stump; the gathering in the wardroom with the captain present and toasts drunk to his success and happiness in the new berth. He had been touched and surprised by their sorrow at his departure – not only Edward Hamilton, and Forbes Wilson with whom he had enjoyed many a jaunt ashore, but also Rieu the first lieutenant and 'Ham' the jovial third (whose surname was the same as the captain's) had seemed genuinely sad to lose him. As for Captain Turpin of the Marines – 'M. le ci-devant marquis' as he sometimes called himself – McMullen could have done without being embraced and kissed on both cheeks but was moved by the emotional Frenchman's tears. There were farewells from the lower-deck men, too, and his fingers still ached from the crushing handgrip administered by Seaman Bragg despite his bandaged knife-wounds. A happy ship and he had been happy in her. Would he find the same good-fellowship aboard *Hermione?*

He had come on board her at midnight. She had finished loading her stores and was strangely silent, the deck watch still and voiceless by the rail. The duty officer, a slight and somehow furtive figure in the darkness, had not been notably welcoming.

'Surgeon McMullen? Captain Pigot's abed. Report to him on deck at two bells forenoon watch. – You, there! This dunnage to the surgeon's cabin.'

He had turned away and two seamen of the watch, totally uncommunicative, had carried McMullen's belongings to the hutch below the wardroom. His last fleeting thought before sleep had swiftly claimed him was of Lucy Preston; that whatever befell him there was now the certainty of a second chance, of repairing the ill-fortune that had attended his over-impetuous proposal. That more than balanced his regret at having to leave *Surprise.*

A fist hammered on the cabin door and a deep voice called his name. 'Mr McMullen? Eight bells due and coffee's on in the wardroom.'

'Wait.' McMullen slid off his cot with the ease of long practice. 'Come in here.'

The door opened and enough light came down the companionway to reveal the grizzled hair and broad intelligent face of the big seaman who ducked under the lintel.

'Garbutt – I thought I knew that voice,' said McMullen, extending his hand. 'Petty officer in the old *Lion*.'

Garbutt returned his grip, at the same time glancing over his shoulder. 'That same, sir. But disrated to seaman now, last month.' His voice was subdued almost to a whisper.

'I'm sorry to hear it. How's the arm?'

'Good as new, sir, thanks to you.' Again he glanced apprehensively behind him. 'Dursn't stay long – duty messenger, I am.'

'Tell me this,' McMullen said quickly. 'Does this vessel carry an assistant surgeon?'

'No, sir. Solly Crump does loblolly. One sheet in the wind, he is.' Garbutt hesitated. 'You'll have your hands full, sir,' he added hurriedly, and was gone.

McMullen put on his coat, smoothed his hair, and mounted to the wardroom, guided thither by a smell of coffee that drifted along the alleyway. Four men sat at the narrow table under the low beams, waited on by a scared-looking steward. Three of them glanced up briefly as he entered and at once returned to their bread and bacon. The fourth, a skinny youth with a foppish air and a pimply face, sprang from his seat and swept an exaggerated bow.

'Why demme, it's our new medico!' he cried in shrill falsetto. 'Pray be seated, Mr – ah – McMillan, is it?'

'John McMullen, sir.'

'Indeed? Honest John, ha? – But your pardon. I have the honour to be George Fitzroy, third of this frigate. Allow me to introduce Mr Douglas, second lieutenant.' A heavily-built man with a brutal jaw scowled blackly at Fitzroy and the surgeon impartially. 'Mr Southcott, our master, and Lieutenant Boyes of the marines,' Fitzroy continued, indicating an elderly sheep-faced man and a fat officer whose red face nearly matched the colour of his uniform coat. 'Mr Reid, our – hum – duodecimo first lieutenant, is on deck at this moment. Him, and our beloved captain, you will later have the pleasure – '

'For Christ's sake stow your gab, Fitzroy!' Douglas grated savagely; he got up and went out.

At his words the eyes of both Southcott and Boyes had

flickered upward in a glance at the deckhead, above which was the quarterdeck; and McMullen was reminded for some reason of Garbutt's glances over his shoulder. Fitzroy, not at all dashed, beckoned the steward.

'Coffee, Chubb, for *Hermione*'s new surgeon – the first real coffee, Mr McMullen, we've drunk for eight weeks. And bacon, Chubb, likewise some of that fresh bread. Eat, drink and be merry, sir, while the stuff lasts. You're a glutton for blood and bones, I hope – in the way of your trade, I mean?' he added with a sidelong leer.

A sickly waft of scent came from him and McMullen had to conceal an involuntary revulsion.

'I'm not afraid of hard work, Mr Fitzroy, if that's what you mean,' he returned good-humouredly, beginning on the bacon.

'Then you'll be happy aboard *Hermione*, demme,' Fitzroy giggled. 'Your sickbay, my fearless medico, is crammed with casualties – crammed to the bulkheads, let me fall prostrate if it ain't.'

McMullen laid down his knife, frowning. 'You've been in action recently, sir? I hadn't heard of it.'

'Action?' The third lieutenant crowed with foolish laughter. 'Action indeed, dear doctor – all initiated by our beloved captain. Captain Pigot, God bless him, is unsparing in his efforts to provide action. Never a day passes but Captain Pigot, in his wisdom – '

'Mr Fitzroy!' Southcott, on his feet, interrupted in a low tremulous voice. 'I beg you – moderate your language. You go too far.'

Fitzroy grinned evilly at him and spoke more loudly. 'Why, demme, what have I said? Nothing but praises of the best captain a ship ever had, Master. You've heard me praise our beloved captain often enough before, I'm sure.'

'A bloody sight too often,' growled the marine lieutenant disgustedly. 'For God's sake do your arse-creeping where it's welcome, Fitzroy.'

'Oh, a thousand thanks, *Mister* Boyes!' shrilled Fitzroy, jumping up like a child in a pet. 'I'll be happy to acquaint Captain Pigot of your sentiments.'

'If you do,' Boyes snarled, 'he shall know of your doings in Madeira.'

The third lieutenant's only reply to this was a murderous glance as he turned to follow Southcott out of the wardroom. Boyes stood up and took his sword from a hook on the bulkhead.

'Take no notice of 'em,' he said to McMullen, buckling it onto his white belt. 'Fitzroy's a pimp and Southcott's a parasite.' He paused. 'You'll find Captain Pigot keeps a strict discipline aboard this ship – in my opinion we'd be a bloody shambles if he didn't.'

He departed abruptly. Left alone, McMullen finished his bacon and coffee. Both were excellent, as was to be expected when *Hermione* had just replenished her food store; but he couldn't enjoy them. It was already apparent that in exchanging *Surprise* for *Hermione* he had not made the best of bargains. Had the egregious Fitzroy spoken the truth about the sickbay full of casualties? He had better find out, and without delay.

The fresh cool breeze on deck was a welcome tonic after the oppressive atmospheres of cabin and wardroom. He stood for a moment at the rail below the quarterdeck to savour it. *Hermione* was under all sail to the royals, close-hauled on the larboard tack with the steady northerly Trade speeding her across a dark-blue sea towards the imminent sunrise. McMullen was just in time to see the flash of white gold as the sun's rim climbed over the horizon to become, in a matter of seconds, a full and dazzling disc that set the blue furrows a-glitter and turned the frigate's towers of canvas to shining ivory pyramids. Below them the deck was busy. For'ard of the mizen-mast rows of kneeling men clad in canvas drawers, their brown backs (many of them scarred, he noticed) and their posture giving them the look of Muslims at prayer, were holystoning the planking under the stern eyes of two petty officers, while on either gangway other parties dragged the 'bear' to and fro – a great stone sewn in a canvas cover. Beyond them, on the foredeck, small gangs of men were at the shot-nettings of the guns, blackleading the 12-pounder balls. McMullen had heard of this practice among ship-proud captains; it had never been done in *Surprise*, for Edward Hamilton – as proud of his ship as any man – disdained show. A quick glance round showed him that everything in sight was ordered to perfection, paintwork glistening and unscratched, the falls of the halyards coiled-down to a nicety, brasswork winking whitely in the rays of the new-risen sun. His own ship (he still thought of her as that) had been taut and trig enough but not to such ostentatious effect. Another difference was the silence. Apart from the ceaseless scraping of the holystones and the sounds of the wind in sails and rigging there was a curious silence; no mutter of gossip or jest, no smothered chuckle, no human sound from the forty or fifty men at work.

A few paces away was the quartermaster at the big wheel. Mr Southcott, standing near him, caught McMullen's glance and looked quickly away. McMullen had been about to ask where the sickbay was to be found, but he left the question unasked and decided to find out for himself since no one seemed to be anxious to show him. His years as ship's surgeon, the most independent officer in any King's ship, had not decreased his natural independence.

He remembered as he began to walk for'ard along the tilted deck that at two bells he was to report to the captain on the quarterdeck, and turned to look aft; it could not be far off two bells now. There were four men on the quarterdeck, Lieutenant Boyes at the taffrail talking with a tall midshipman and Fitzroy pacing the lee side in company with a little spindle-shanked man whom (remembering the expression used by the derisive Fitzroy) he could identify as the first lieutenant, Mr Reid. Of the captain there was as yet no sign. He went on, edging past the holystoners, not one of whom looked up as he passed, and accosted the man who was supervising the blackleading of the shot. This was a squat, ape-like person wearing a dark-blue smock and white trousers and holding a short thick rattan cane in a fist like a chunk of oak.

'Good morning, boatswain,' said McMullen briskly. 'I'm seeking the sickbay. Where is it?'

The boatswain turned his big head slowly and favoured him with a scowl. 'And who may *you* be?' he demanded.

'McMullen, ship's surgeon. I asked where the sickbay – '

'You slab-fingered bugger!'

The boatswain, whirling round, had launched a vicious blow of his cane – blindly, as it seemed to McMullen – at his closely-grouped charges. An olive-skinned seaman yelped with pain as the rattan bit into his bare shoulder and all but dropped his can of blacklead, which was caught in the nick of time by his neighbour. The boatswain ripped out a string of oaths and simultaneously came the sound of two bells being sounded on the after-deck.

'One spot on my paintwork and by God it'll be the cat – 'stead of *this*!'

A second blow of the cane, delivered with uncontrolled force, glanced off the man's warding arm and thudded into his neck between jaw and shoulder. His knees crumpled under him and he collapsed on the deck.

'Bucket of water, Snape – and no dallying or you'll get the same.' The boatswain turned as McMullen tapped him on the shoulder. 'Well, mister?'

McMullen's eyes were blazing but he had his voice under control. 'This, mister – I don't know your name.'

'Pascoe.'

'Well then, Mr Pascoe, I'll have you know that was a foul and dangerous blow. Presumably you've no knowledge of anatomy – '

'What the hell is it to do with you?'

'Listen to me!' rasped the surgeon. 'But for the obstruction you could have broken the man's neck. As it was, the jugular vein – '

'Stow your bloody mumbo-jumbo, Mr Whoever-you-are,' Pascoe interrupted with a sneer. 'When I start teaching you your duty you can teach me mine.'

He was in the right of it, McMullen knew. How an executive officer performed his duties was no business of a ship's surgeon; moreover, Pascoe was a warrant officer like himself and in no way his subordinate. But his blood was up and he couldn't let the matter rest there.

'I hope I know my duty, Mr Pascoe,' he returned sternly. 'I'm required by my warrant to maintain this ship's company in a fit state to work the ship and fight an enemy. If you're going to break their necks you're working against me.'

'When I've finished with 'em you can have 'em,' said Pascoe brutally.

There was a hot reply on McMullen's lips but it remained unspoken. A pasty-faced midshipman with a look of premature age and a furtive manner (last night's duty officer, probably) had arrived breathless at his side.

'Mr McMullen – on the quarterdeck – instantly,' he panted.

Swallowing his anger, McMullen followed him aft. The deck was steeply tilted to starboard now, for with the climbing sun had come a sudden increase in the wind and *Hermione*'s lee rail was leaning above racing whitecaps. They passed the holystoning party hurrying for'ard, their task completed; a sullen-looking crowd, black skins and yellow among them, with not a word spoken or a sidelong glance, herded along by the petty officers. It was small wonder, McMullen thought, that men so cowed and constrained turned into fighting demons when they were let loose ashore. He went up to the quarterdeck, touching his hat as he topped the ladder, and found himself confronting the captain of the *Hermione*.

Hugh Pigot was a man scarcely older than McMullen and as tall as him, but full-fleshed where the surgeon was lean, his handsome face showing unmistakable dewlaps below the round white chin. He stood with his hands behind his back, well-shaped legs in snowy breeches and stockings astraddle, his slightly protuberant eyes staring at McMullen as he approached. But his stare shifted away without recognition of the surgeon's presence and he turned to speak to the first lieutenant. McMullen's first glance had noted two perhaps trivial but slightly odd things: while most of those on board were tanned by wind and sun, Captain Pigot's face was as pink-and-white as a milkmaid's; and despite his immaculate blue coat with its glittering gold braid and epaulettes a central button of the white waistcoat beneath it was affixed to the wrong buttonhole.

'Mr Reid, I will have the topgallants off her.' The captain's voice was deep and resonant. 'And see that the men look sharp about it.'

'Aye aye, sir.' Mr Reid almost fell over himself in his haste to get to the taffrail. 'Hands to make sail! Off t'garns'ls and look sharp!'

His thin strident voice matched his skinny figure. Captain Pigot took three strides and shouldered him aside. His voice rose easily above the shouts of the boatswain's mates and the muffled trampling of feet as the men rushed to the shrouds.

'And a flogging for the last man down!'

He turned on his heel and came to stand facing the surgeon. His full red lips were wet as if he had just passed his tongue over them and his eyes, of a pale grey colour, were glittering with excitement. The glitter faded, leaving a hard grey stare, but the lips were smiling as he spoke.

'Mr McMullen? I believe you were to report to me at two bells.'

'I'm sorry if I was a little late, sir.'

' "A little late",' the captain repeated musingly. 'Aboard my ship, Mr McMullen, that is *too* late. You will learn, Mr McMullen – and for your own sake you will learn quickly – that all here is done according to my will.' His voice began to rise. 'For those who deviate in the slightest there is punishment, Mr McMullen, punishment! The laggard, the insolent, the clumsy and the careless, none shall escape the lash!' It was a hysterical stridency now. 'They shall suffer and bleed, Mr McMullen, and for those who claim immunity such as you there are other punishments to be devised, never fear! I tell you none shall escape me – none – none shall – '

His voice suddenly trailed away and stopped. A trickle of saliva had run down his chin from the corner of his mouth and he wiped it away with a lace handkerchief, at the same time darting a suspicious glance round him. Two lieutenants, the marine officer and two midshipmen were on the quarterdeck and all were studiously gazing aloft. Pigot shut his eyes, shook his head twice, and then looked at McMullen as if he was seeing him for the first time.

'Ah, yes,' he said in a normal tone. 'I have work for you in our sickbay, Mr McMullen. I want those idlers back to their duty without delay. You will hand your report to Mr Reid at noon.'

'Aye aye, sir. I was about to – '

'You have not yet visited the sickbay?'

'No, sir. I was on my way there when – ' McMullen, hesitating, found he had to brace himself – 'when I was forced to intervene with the boatswain.'

As concisely as he could, McMullen described the blow he had seen given and its possible consequences. Pigot's eye was on the topmen who were now racing down to the deck with their job completed. There was a faint smile on his lips and it was difficult to tell whether he was listening or not. When McMullen had finished he made no comment but spoke instead to the first lieutenant.

'Well, Mr Reid?'

'Carver was last down, sir,' said Reid, rubbing his hands together nervously.

'He shall have six at the capstan. You will not pipe all hands, Mr Reid – my presence will be sufficient.'

'Aye aye, sir,' said the first lieutenant with an ingratiating smile. 'Of course, sir.'

Pigot turned and McMullen saw that his lips gleamed wetly and the strange glitter was back in his eyes.

'Mr Casey, you will take Mr McMullen to the sickbay. Do not delay your return or it will be the worse for you.'

'Aye aye, sir.'

The lanky midshipman stepped hastily forward. He was an overgrown youth of sixteen or seventeen, presumably junior to the elderly-seeming young man who had interrupted the skirmish with the boatswain. McMullen was following Casey down the ladder when the captain's resonant voice boomed from behind them.

'Mr Pascoe! Those men are idling. Use your cane, and spare not.'

The slight was so open and gratuitous that McMullen found himself shaking with repressed anger. To steady himself he tried to open a conversation with Casey.

'This wind's fair enough for Puerto Rico, Mr Casey. That's where we're bound to, I hear.'

The midshipman nodded and quickened his pace. With her upper sails gone the frigate was listing less heavily and they could move for'ard at a good speed. McMullen tried again, voicing a thought that had occurred to him earlier.

'The last man down from the shrouds is surely likely to have been the first up on the yard. Don't you think it's scarcely fair to penalise him?'

There was naked terror in the sidelong glance that Casey darted at him.

'Don't, sir – please don't!' he said in a shaky whisper; and that was all.

They reached the forehatch and the midshipman halted irresolute, looking quickly over his shoulder towards the quarterdeck.

'Do you wish me to conduct you,' he began.

'Tell me where it is and get back with you,' McMullen told him impatiently.

'Starboard side of the fo'c'sle. Turn left at the bottom of the companion and right at the end of the alleyway.'

Casey scuttled away aft. McMullen went down two steps of the companion-ladder and stopped dead. Above the high-pitched shrilling of the wind in the rigging rose the shriek of a man in agony, repeated again and again. Carver, the last man down. And if it hadn't been Carver another of the topmen – the smartest men in the ship and the most daring – would have suffered under the cat. Before the war with Spain McMullen had spent eight months at the Salamanca lectures of Herero Pidal, pioneer researcher into mental disorders. He was already beginning to wonder about Captain Pigot.

Before he had reached the foot of the ladder he was met by the stink. At the turn of the alleyway it was so thick and offensive that despite his habituation to the inevitable odour below-decks he had to brace himself before going on. The stench of bilges long overdue for cleaning was almost swamped by a horrible fetor compounded of excrement, vomit, and stale blood. He pushed aside a filthy canvas screen and was in the sickbay, with a hoarse murmuring of groans and oaths in his ears. A single smoky lamp lit a space considerably larger than *Surprise*'s orlop but not large enough for the ten or twelve men who lay sprawled on the dirty canvas spread on the planking; most of them lay face-downwards, some with bloodstained cloths or swabs across their backs and others without dressings so that the oozing dark-purple flesh, like liver that had been hacked with a knife, was exposed. From the shadows at the far end a voice croaked '*water – water – water*' and stopped. A little man with a head too big for his body got up from a corner and took a panikin towards the sound, stepping over the recumbent bodies.

McMullen, teeth hard clenched, took it all in at a glance. Here was the result of 'action initiated by our beloved captain,' as Fitzroy had put it – of that and of the shortcomings of Mr Dogherty.

'Solly Crump!' he said loudly above the chorus of groaning. 'Give that man his drink and then come here.'

He took off his coat and looked round him in the dim light for somewhere to put it, eventually finding a hook well above the foul mess on the planking. A cupboard on the bulkhead had its door swinging half-open, ends of cloth protruded from a large chest at one end of the cabin. The loblolly-boy stumbled towards him. He was well past middle-age, with a shock of greying hair and a big nose; his mouth hung open in a gap-toothed grin but there was a spark of intelligence in the bleary eyes.

'I'm the new surgeon, Solly,' said McMullen. 'You're on duty alone here?'

'Yeth, thir.' Solly chuckled gleefully. 'Mr Dogherty, he's gone to – '

'I know about Mr Dogherty. You're going to help me, Solly. We've a deal of work to do. Dressings in this chest? Right. Take down that lantern and stand here, by me. Now, then.'

McMullen rolled up his sleeves.

2

The frigate *Hermione* had commissioned at Plymouth in May. Her complement was 220 men and she had sailed fifteen short of complement having had trouble in finding enough seamen to man her. A nucleus of crew transferred from a ship that was paying-off consisted mainly of Irishmen. The rest included a large number of pressed landsmen and a quota of convicted criminals sent from Exeter Assizes. Three men had died on the voyage out from England.

These and a few other items of information McMullen gleaned from the eleven men in his sickbay during his first day on board *Hermione*. Three were foreigners – two Danes and a Neapolitan – and the floggings eight of the eleven had received had been administered at sunset yesterday at the gangway, for misdemeanours during the loading of stores. He learned this much with difficulty and often by inference, for none of the men was willing to talk and no word as to the nature of their transgressions or complaint about their punishment passed their lips; this surgeon might be a deal handier with his salves and kindlier of tongue than his predecessor but he was a wardroom officer none the less, on the side of the hierarchy 'aft'. But such men, illiterate and brutish, had little skill in hiding their feelings and it was not difficult to perceive the hatred and resentment that smouldered in them.

A naval surgeon, however deeply committed to the service of suffering humanity, owed primary allegiance to the King and the King's Navy. The Admiralty had shown unusual forethought (so McMullen had often thought) in allotting the surgeon wardroom rank, so that he associated with men dedicated to their ship and their Service above all other things. McMullen's six years in the Navy had given him an insight into the problem confronting a captain and his officers called upon to take a newly-manned ship to sea; the appalling prospect of having to fight an enemy or weather a gale with a crew of untrained and unwilling landsmen. He had seen Edward Hamilton and his first lieutenant deal with this situation – a cruel situation that made a cruel remedy inevitable – and could sympathise with Captain Pigot's predicament at Portsmouth. But where Hamilton's methods had brought order and a happy ship Pigot's seemed to have brought about a ship of slaves, governed by terror. He could imagine the hell this frigate had been for the past four months with a captain like Hugh Pigot; a hell more crippling to the spirit in some cases than in others but lighting in every man the flame of hatred.

Carver, flogged for being last man down, came down to the sickbay while McMullen was attending to the second of his patients. He was escorted according to custom by two of his messmates, one of whom carried his shirt, but he disdained any help from them. He was a big man and the blood oozing from his lacerated back was clogged by matted black hair.

'A swill o' water'll do, doctor,' he said hardily. 'Six wi' the cat's naught to me.'

'You 'owled, Bill,' remarked one of his supporters.

' 'Course I 'owled. A couple of "Ohs" and then "Oh my God" – they think it ain't 'urtin' you, else, and lays on 'arder. What's that you're swabbin' me with, doctor?'

'Styptic,' said McMullen, 'to stop the bleeding. I'll strap a dressing on and you'd better take a make-and-mend for the rest of the – '

'Not me!' Carver interrupted boastfully. 'All right for Nobby there – 'ow many did you get last dog-watch, Nobby?'

'A dozen,' muttered the man McMullen had been attending to.

'Aye, and a cursed shame it – ' Carver bit the sentence off short, with a covert glance at McMullen. ' 'And me that shirt, matey. I'm goin' on deck an' fit for duty. I'll show 'em, see?'

He swaggered out with his admiring messmates. McMullen went on with his work, frowning. Carver's was not one of the broken spirits; but then, the man was of the type that is not so very far above the beasts. What happened when men like Carver reached the breaking-point, as eventually they must do.

With salve and fresh dressings on their torn backs seven of the eight flogging cases could rejoin their messes and undertake light duties, he decided. The eighth, a severe case some of whose four dozen lashes had cut through to the spinal bone, would have to remain under his care. The remaining three 'casualties' had not suffered under the cat. Two were twitching and babbling in the throes of fever and the other, a young Irishman with a shock of red hair and a vacant expression, had had the toes of his right foot crushed beneath a recoiling gun-truck. McMullen did what he could for the fever cases, relieved to find that neither was suffering from gaol-fever or Yellow Jack, and examined the crushed foot. The injury had been incurred a fortnight ago, the Irishman told him; his name was Mahoney. And Surgeon Dogherty, thought

McMullen, must have been sober when he treated it for the
injury was making a fast recovery. The firm bandaging he
applied should – as he told Mahoney – find him fit for light
duties in two days' time.

Bare feet drummed reverberantly on the planking overhead.
A smart *thwack*! followed instantly by a cry of pain; a distant
yelling of orders; and the frigate's hull swung and tilted as she
went about on the starboard tack. As had often happened
before, McMullen experienced a fleeting mental start at this
reminder that he and his immediate preoccupations were in
fact sailing across the Caribbean. Puerto Rico, he remembered,
was a good 800 miles east of Kingston and using the almost
unvarying north-east Trades *Hermione* would make long
reaches on the larboard tack and short ones on the starboard
in order to arrive off the island. Four or five days. Today was
September 17th – but the prospect of even five days in *Hermione*
so lowered his spirits that he stopped himself from looking
ahead. A drift of fresh air wafted down the alleyway by the
frigate's change of course made him suddenly aware that the
fetid air down here was almost asphyxiating him, and with a
word to Solly Crump he climbed up to the deck.

The sun was high and over the starboard quarter now.
Along the decks the hands were trimming and belaying the
sheets, close-hauling on the new course, without any of the
yo-ho-ing and jocular muttering he had been accustomed to in
Surprise. Looking aft beyond the long row of 12-pounders he
could see the captain and Douglas the second lieutenant on the
quarterdeck, leaning on the taffrail and watching a group of
hands who were hauling on the mizen sheets. As he looked,
Pigot shot out his hand, pointing to the group. Instantly
Douglas went down the ladder at a bound, seized an
undersized seaman by the collar, and knocked him down with
a vicious blow in the face. The man rolled over feebly and got
to his hands and knees. Douglas kicked him down again before
mounting leisurely to the quarterdeck. Captain Pigot's hearty
laugh, as deep and resonant as his speech, came clearly to
McMullen's ears.

He turned abruptly and went down the companion-ladder,
smothering as best he could the sudden blaze of anger. What

use was it to be angry? He could do nothing about things like that – nobody could. He could do something about this terrible stink, though; his duty required him to make application to the captain for cleaning of bilges and fumigation of lower-deck, and if ever there was excuse for such an application it was here and now. Mere prudence, however, he reflected as he went along the alleyway, dictated an interval before he applied. He was a new broom, he had made a bad start, and Pigot's malice (or, perhaps, partial dementia) could impel him to refuse if he was approached thus early in his service aboard the frigate. But he could make a start himself – and Solly would help him. Half-witted Solly Crump might be, but he was willing; besides being the only helpful and friendly creature McMullen had so far encountered in *Hermione*.

'Some of you more comfortable, lads, I hope?' he said as he entered the sickbay.

Grunts and groans answered him – a sullen lot, he thought. But one voice piped up, to hearten him: 'Aye, sir – and thankee.'

'Good. My report goes to the first lieutenant at eight bells,' McMullen went on briskly, 'and I hope he'll have some of you moved to healthier quarters. Meanwhile – buckets, Solly, and mops, and water. A great deal of water. We'll shift some of this filth off the deck.'

Five minutes before noon McMullen was in his hutch of a cabin, scowling at the brief report he had written and feeling, like Job, that his flesh was clothed with worms and clods of dust. There was more cleaning-out yet to do in the sickbay but he had left it unfinished in order to be punctual with his report; and the hurried wash in cold water hadn't rid him of the stink. He could legitimately have demanded a working-party to swab-out the sickbay, he reflected irritably. Why hadn't he done so? Partly because he hadn't been twenty-four hours in this ship yet and it was clear enough that he would have to tread warily, but partly also – he admitted it reluctantly – because he was already infected by the fear-ridden atmosphere on board. He was afraid of Pigot. No. He amended that. Not of Hugh Pigot the man, but of a captain's almost unlimited authority wielded by a man unbalanced and childishly vindictive. He flung introspection angrily aside and went out into the sunshine and breeze of the deck.

To the eye all was peace and order. Steadily *Hermione* held her course, the watch-on-deck squatting in an orderly row under the weather rail, the helmsman (it was Garbutt, he noticed, once of the *Lion*) erect and motionless except for the movement of hands and forearms as he balanced the frigate's movement with slight turns of the wheel. On the quarterdeck they were standing ready for the noon sights, two lieutenants, two midshipmen and Southcott the master all with sextants in their hands. The captain was absent – Hamilton, McMullen remembered, had never failed to be on the quarterdeck at noon. Five sextants all rose together to their owners' eyes and the sextant arms were moved to bring the sun's limb to the horizon.

'Noon, sir,' said Southcott to Reid.

'Make it twelve, Mr Southcott,' said Reid.

Four double clangs rang out on the ship's bell and with no sound but the muffled thudding of bare feet the watch-below came up to relieve their fellows. The effect of order and precision was to some extent spoiled by the boatswain, who had come on deck with the new watch. Pascoe, pointing to the capstan, barked a harsh order and two hands ran with cloths to scrub at the capstan's base, removing some lingering stain. It was where Carver had been flogged. McMullen, banishing a frown, went up to the quarterdeck and touched his hat to the first lieutenant.

'Surgeon's report, sir,' he said, proffering it.

Reid had prominent teeth and sallow pouchy cheeks, and the glare he directed at McMullen gave him the look of a rabbit trying to appear ferocious. He snatched the paper without a word and scowled at it.

'May I draw your attention, sir, to two matters?' McMullen said with careful deference. 'Mahoney, the man with the crushed foot, will be fit for light duties only in two days' time. And the man who received four dozen, Hammond, must remain in sickbay for somewhat longer.'

'He won't like that,' Reid muttered.

'Hammond will have to lump it, I fear. The nature of his

injuries – '

'I said Captain Pigot won't like it!' shrilled the first lieutenant angrily. 'God damn it, sir, are you a numbskull? Captain Pigot don't spare malingerers, Mr McMullen!'

McMullen would have liked to ask if men were flogged for not immediately recovering after a savage flogging; but he kept the thought to himself.

'Yes, sir,' he said, wooden-faced. 'And as to the fever cases, I'd like to shift them to healthier quarters. It would speed their recovery.'

'Put the rogues where you like, for Christ's sake!' Reid interrupted, turning away. 'Keep your stinking cripples off my upper decks – that's all I ask.'

Mr Reid's decks were spotless under McMullen's eye as he went down the ladder. Above his head the snowy canvas rose in curves of perfect beauty against the blue. A lovely ship, he thought, and they'd made a whore of her; all paint and prettiness on the outside and rottenness underneath. 'Who can bring a clean thing out of an unclean?' That was Job again. Well, he could at least take up the old prophet's challenge and see what he could do with the sickbay.

3

For a frigate bound from Jamaica to Puerto Rico the next few days were fortunate enough. A slight northerly shift of the Trade enabled her to bear up and hold her easterly course on a strong and steady wind. Before nightfall of the second day the lookout's hail from the masthead announced Cape Beata on Hispaniola on the larboard beam, and morning found her halfway to her destination.

The eastern Caribbean, 30,000 square miles of sea rimmed on north and east by a chain of islands large and small many of which were in possession of England's enemies – French, Dutch, and Spanish – and on the south by the long indented coast of Spanish America, was an area of busy trade despite the war. Yet *Hermione* on her course across the northern waters of this vast lagoon spoke only one vessel, a merchantman

westward bound out of Castries on St Lucia. Half-a-dozen
times, indeed, a distant sail was reported from the masthead,
usually to northward, but none of the ships sighted came any
nearer than that to the frigate's course and Captain Pigot never
deviated from it; his orders, it could be presumed, required
him to reach his cruising-ground off Puerto Rico at the earliest
possible date.

These days did nothing to reduce McMullen's intense dislike
of his new berth and much to increase his growing uneasiness.
He tried to forget both in devoting himself to his sickbay and
his patients. With no watchkeeping duties and no one of the
ship's hierarchy apparently interested in his doings he saw no
impropriety in avoiding the society of the wardroom except at
mealtimes, which were gloomy occasions and mostly silent
unless Fitzroy happened to be present to parade his shrill
inanities. He made one attempt to establish friendly relations
with the marine lieutenant, the only wardroom officer with a
trace of normal sociability; but as Boyes could talk of nothing
but his own experiences in brothels at home and abroad he
didn't pursue his efforts.

Captain Pigot, it appeared, occasionally invited one of his
lieutenants to dine in the captain's cabin, Fitzroy being
especially favoured. He kept no watches and came on the
quarterdeck when he felt inclined, his appearance (McMullen
noted) always coinciding with an increase in the petty
brutalities of the deck officers and the activity of Pascoe's
'starter'. He ordered two seamen to be flogged on the second
day, ten lashes each for alleged slackness reported by the
second lieutenant; and on the third day there was a twenty-lash
flogging of a man supposed to have 'made an ugly face at the
boatswain', a punishment which brought into the sickbay a
youngster of 17 bleeding and half-insensible. These were all
summary punishments, the victim being made to strip and
bend himself across the capstan. And Captain Pigot left his
quarterdeck in order to observe the punishment at close
quarters.

It was this continual flogging at the capstan that shocked
McMullen as much as anything. In *Surprise* he had witnessed
three floggings, two for repeated theft and one for a sexual

offence against one of the ship's boys; and each had been the occasion of a ceremonial as solemn as any court of justice ashore. Captain Hamilton's usual method of punishment, involving the 'booked' offenders of a month or more, was to have a sea-cock opened and set the men pumping clean water through the bilges, but for graver crimes he insisted on making it clear to all on board that the flogging he had ordered was an administration of justice. There had been the piping aft of all hands, marines paraded, junior officers ranked at the break of the poop, captain and lieutenants in their best uniforms on the quarterdeck; the witnesses called to attest, the Article of War that had been infringed read, the culprit asked if he had anything to say in extentuation. And then the flogging at the gratings previously rigged, with all the accepted ritual of the nine-tailed cat being produced from its red baize bag and the preliminary drawing of the knotted tails through the fingers of the boatswain's mate appointed to execute punishment. Brutal spectacle it might be but the assembled seamen, sticklers for correct ritual in all things from the serving of a rum ration to burial at sea, returned satisfied to the mess-decks. Garbutt had once told McMullen that in the *Lion* 74 the punishment devised for a detected thief by his own messmates was a good deal more painful than twelve lashes with the cat.

McMullen was beginning to suspect that the floggings in *Hermione* were first and foremost for the satisfaction of her captain's depraved appetites. The floating community of the ship was like a Tyranny of the dark ages, with Pigot as the tyrant, Douglas the purveyor of victims, Reid an attendant sycophant, and Fitzroy a favoured jester, while the boatswain represented the chief torturer. And its underlings, slaves in all but name, must be aware that it was not in their bond to be slaves.

In his goings to and fro along the decks and in his sickbay McMullen made covert observation. Under the eye of officers and petty officers the hands worked stony-faced and sheep-like, taking oaths and blows in sullen silence. Fear of instant retribution had achieved thus much. But when they chanced to be unwatched for a moment there were scowls and murmurings, glances of pure hatred directed aft, horny fists clenched until the knuckles whitened. Below, on the mess-decks, there was none of the noisy chaffing and blasphemous argument he was accustomed to in *Surprise*. The inboard bulkhead of the sickbay divided it from the starboard mess-deck and when the starboard watch was off duty he could hear their voices, though not their words for they talked in low tones. Often the mutterings would swell in a subdued roar like the growl of an angry sea, to subside at a sharp word of warning from someone among them. If McMullen thought these signs ominous, he saw no reason to report them to the first lieutenant; his sympathies were with *Hermione*'s crew.

At night in his cot he thought of Lucy Preston. Once, he remembered, she had hinted that service in two ships of war was not sufficient basis for his arguments in favour of naval disciplinary methods. There was reason in that, he saw now. 'One man is given power to treat other men like brute beasts,' she had said, 'and that is wrong – wrong – wrong!' He would not grant that; such power in a captain's hands was essential to the safety of his ship, whether in a gale or in a fight. But in the wrong hands – the hands of a man like Pigot – it could be a great and growing evil, and when *Hermione* returned to Kingston and he could visit Lucy again he would concede that much.

To their last brief and abortive meeting he gave much thought as he lay on the swaying cot in the darkness, picturing Lucy's face and hearing her voice responding to his ill-advised proposal. He was able without much difficulty to persuade himself that she wouldn't refuse to see him, that he would be afforded an opportunity of recapturing the lost ground. After all, she hadn't said 'No'. And he recalled his fleeting impression that in spite of her words about being insulted she hadn't been entirely displeased. When would he see her again? A month or six weeks, perhaps – the frigate's cruise would hardly be longer. It was a pleasant eventuality on which to rest his thoughts while he drifted into sleep.

On the 20th, a Sunday, *Hermione* ran into darker weather, a clouded sky and a fitful wind. Her royals were hoisted shortly after dawn and taken in half-an-hour later, only to be let fall once again to catch the failing breeze that set in at two bells of the forenoon watch. The activities of the topmen aloft for the third time were watched by the captain. McMullen, returning aft from visiting his fever cases (their hammocks were now slung in a nook above the orlop) noted with relief that for once Pigot ordered no flogging for the last man down; perhaps, he thought bitterly, abstinence from physical cruelty was the man's one concession to the Sabbath. In this, however, he was proved wrong.

At six bells the beat of the marines' drum and the pipes of the boatswain's mates summoned all hands aft. McMullen took his place with the junior officers below the quarterdeck ladder, Boyes and his dozen marines were drawn up behind Pigot and the three lieutenants on the quarterdeck, and the captain stepped forward to the head of the ladder with a book in his hand. *Hermione*, like *Surprise*, carried no chaplain and McMullen, remembering Edward Hamilton's practice, expected a reading from the Book of Common Prayer; but Captain Pigot's reading was the Articles of War. He read them well, in a deep sonorous voice that gave weight to every word, speaking into a silence unusual on the frigate's upper deck because the wind had fallen away. She was moving slowly over a dark and sullen sea beneath an overcast sky streaked with sooty cloud, and the only noises were an occasional flapping of half-filled sails and hiss of water along her sides.

McMullen listened with half an ear, for he was aware of a tension in the atmosphere that had nothing to do with the ominous weather. It was as if an invisible cloud hung above the silent crowd massed in their Sunday rig on the after-deck, a cloud charged with a restrained passion of hatred. The impression was so strong that he glanced aside at the men nearest him, the two midshipmen and Pascoe and Mr Searle the gunner; but their expressions told him nothing. Perhaps it was merely a reflection of his own inner feelings. His attention returned to the captain, who was beginning to read the Nineteenth Article.

So far as McMullen could tell he laid no special emphasis on the words, but the slight movement among the silent crew, the shifting of feet or changing of posture inevitable when two hundred men were assembled, ceased utterly as he pronounced them. '*If any person in or belonging to the fleet shall make or endeavour to make any mutinous assembly upon any offence whatsoever, every person offending therein, and being convicted by the sentence of the court-martial, shall suffer death.*' And no alternative, the surgeon reflected; no *or such other punishment*, as other of the Articles had appended. The penalty was final and absolute for merely endeavouring to make a mutinous assembly.

Captain Pigot, having read on to the end and added no comment, descended to the deck with his three lieutenants and made a surprisingly rapid inspection of his crew. It occurred to McMullen that lack of a button or hair in need of cutting could hardly be made the occasion for a flogging of any magnitude; and this possibly uncharitable thought was not dispelled by the captain's expression as he passed on his way back to the quarterdeck. Pigot's handsome heavy-jowled face wore a look of brooding dissatisfaction and his voice rang harshly as he turned at the taffrail.

'Mr Reid, you may dismiss the hands.'

At the first lieutenant's yell silence and stillness ended. The men crowded hurriedly along the gangways, Pascoe and his mates sprang away to herd them for'ard. Pigot, leaning from the taffrail, watched like a hawk. One man, limping, lagged behind the crowd surging along the larboard gangway – it was Mahoney, the man with the crushed foot, McMullen saw – and suddenly stumbled and fell. Pascoe dashed at him with a shouted curse and his rattan uplifted. In the same instant a big seaman just in front of Mahoney turned and bent to help the fallen man to his feet, so that Pascoe's blow fell on his shoulder. He started up, one arm raised to ward off a second blow.

'*Still!*'

The captain's tremendous roar arrested all movement on the upper deck. McMullen, who had not moved from his place below the quarterdeck, turned to look up at him. Pigot's face had flushed dark red, but not with anger. He was grinning in evident delight, his pale eyes wide and glistening. He reminded McMullen, absurdly, of a picture in a childhood book of Little Jack Horner anticipating his pie. He pointed with a shaking hand.

'That man, Mr Reid – that man,' he said in a kind of triumph. 'His name?'

Reid, invisible behind him, said something.

'Garbutt,' Pigot repeated with relish. 'Garbutt raised his hand against a superior officer. You saw it. One hundred lashes for Garbutt, Mr Reid – here and now, before the ship's company. Have the gratings rigged.'

Reid screeched orders that were echoed by Pascoe's bawlings and the men surged back again to their packed ranks on the after deck. Hounded and cuffed by the boatswain, four hands raised two of the wooden gratings that covered the hatchways, reared one of them against the bulkhead below the quarterdeck, and laid the other flat at its foot. Garbutt was led forward, his wrists fast in the grip of the boatswain's mates.

'Strip and seize him up!' Pigot vociferated; he was making little up-and-down bobs, like an excited boy.

Garbutt's shirt was pulled off and he stood with face and chest pressed against the upright grating, arms upstretched while the boatswain's mates lashed his wrists to the upper corners with spunyarn.

'Do your duty!'

The captain's voice was like a cock crowing. McMullen had to repress an urgent desire to be sick. He found himself unable to look at Garbutt, crucified there on the grating while the bigger of the two boatswain's mates cleared the nine knotted tails with a flick. His averted gaze passed beyond the men massed at the larboard rail to the dark sea that moved restlessly under the clouded sky. Above the black bar of the horizon a slit of pallor widened momently across the north, and the big mizen course overhead flapped and filled again.

The swish and thud of the first lash brought no sound from Garbutt. Again. Again. Ten – eleven – twelve – and now short inhuman cries broke from him. McMullen closed his eyes. A hundred lashes. The man would lose consciousness long before the last was given. It was a meagre comfort. Thirty-four. Thirty-five. Garbutt had ceased to cry out. The gap of pale sky was spreading rapidly, pushing back a level rim of dark cloud and shedding a ghastly light that showed Garbutt's upper body a black and glistening mass. Rain streaked suddenly down, a dense barrier of silver rods, in a few seconds soaking the clothing of men and officers. The lash rose and fell, rose and fell. Fifty-one, fifty-two, and abruptly *Hermione* lurched and shuddered as if she too had come under the blows of the cat. Successive gusts banged erratically at her canvas, jibs and foresails flapped and cracked like pistol-shots. The man at the wheel, who had remained intent on ship and course throughout, spun his spokes in a hurry and glanced anxiously over his shoulder.

'Lay on, damn you!' Pigot yelled furiously at the boatswain's mate.

The squall struck her a moment later, first taking her aback and then laying her over. From the canted quarterdeck urgent voices sounded, and glancing up McMullen saw Pigot snatch off his hat and hurl it on to the deck. Reid's piercing shout cut through the rising whistle of the wind.

'Larboard sheets – jump to it! Jib and fore sheets! Larboard helm, hard over!'

The after deck emptied of seamen except for the parties hauling on the mizen sheets and clearing-away the apparatus of punishment. Garbutt, dangling limply, was cut down and dragged for'ard with trailing heels, leaving a runlet of blood to mingle with the rainwater that swilled across the deck. And as McMullen dodged past the men hauling on the mainsheet the frigate, her sails filling on the larboard tack, raced away south-eastward.

Down in the lamplit sick-bay ten minutes later McMullen straightened himself and tossed a double handful of reddened swabs into the bucket held by Solly Crump. For a moment he stood contemplating the bloated livid cushion of flesh, raw and bleeding, that had been Garbutt's large sunbrowned back. The big seaman, sprawled face-downwards across the makeshift table, had groaned once or twice but had given no further sign of consciousness. The only other patient, Hammond, was in a cot at the end of the sick-bay and seemed to be asleep. McMullen withdrew his frowning gaze from the oozing mess. His lips were tightly compressed and when he spoke to his vacantly-grinning assistant it was jerkily, through clenched teeth.

'Styptic bottle, Solly. And a clean cloth.'

Inwardly he was seething with a rage the more furious because he knew it was utterly useless. It was the rank injustice of the punishment that infuriated him rather than the savagery of the flogging; that and the knowledge that there was nothing he could do about it, no appeal against the will of a man whose word was absolute law – a man, moreover, who was constitutionally unfit to have command. Of that he was now convinced. For he had caught sight of Pigot's face at the moment when he had dashed his hat to the deck, and it was the face of a man possessed by devils.

'To all intents a maniac – a raving lunatic!' Involuntarily he spoke the words aloud, giving vent to his thoughts and his anger together. The instant look of terror in Solly's bleary eyes brought a prick of compunction and some abatement of his anger.

'Not you, Solly Crump,' he said with a smile. 'You've more sense than some of us. Pull that box of dressings over here.'

Garbutt's tortured flesh had twitched as the oak-gall styptic was applied and he had given a groan. Now, without stirring, he spoke in a low voice.

'Is it – bad, sir?'

'Bad enough.' McMullen was laying the dressings across the network of cuts. 'You'll feel it for many a day.'

'Give me a tight strapping, sir, if you please. I don't want to be off duty no longer 'n I has to.'

He was silent for a moment or two while the surgeon went on with his work. Then he spoke again.

'I did naught to deserve this, sir,' he muttered.

McMullen's anger boiled up and over. 'By God you didn't!' he said fiercely. 'I saw it all – your arm went up to fend off Pascoe's cane. Captain Pigot – ' He checked himself abruptly, aware of the enormity he had been about to commit. 'I'm going to pass this bandage under your belly. Raise yourself a little if you can.'

A voice spoke unexpectedly from the shadows. McMullen had forgotten Hammond was there.

'If it 'adn't been you, 'Arry,' said Hammond, ' 'twould 'ave been some other pore bugger.'

'You'll please to keep your mouth shut, Hammond,' McMullen said sharply.

'It's true what he says, sir.' Garbutt's words were spoken into a fold of the sailcloth on which he was lying, and came with muffled intensity. 'He has to have a flogging. It's like drink to him. We've seen it long enough, longer'n you have, sir, and it's same as brandy was to Mr Dogherty. You saw it. He'd have let the ship go sooner'n stop my hundred lashes.'

McMullen could find nothing to say though he knew he had to stop this talk. This was so precisely his own impression.

'I heard something you said just now, sir,' Garbutt went on quickly. 'D'you think he's wrong in the head, sir – mad?'

'I think you'll regret it if you say another word,' McMullen said strongly. 'Both of you will forget what's been said and so shall I. Solly, I order you to keep quiet about this. You understand?'

'Aye aye, thir,' beamed Solly.

'Very well. Garbutt, lie as you are without stirring. I shall be back shortly and we'll rig a cot for you. See that he has some water, Solly.'

He pulled on his coat, soaking wet from the rain-squall, and climbed to the deck. The wind met him as he emerged from the hatchway, striking wet and cold on his cheek, and a gout of spray lopped over the weather rail to spatter his face; but he scarcely noticed them in the confusion of his thoughts. He had listened to words spoken against the captain, questioning Pigot's authority, and his plain duty was to report them. He knew that nothing could persuade him to do so. The conflict between the respect for authority his years in the Navy had given him and his growing conviction that Pigot was mentally unhinged tormented him.

A wave shattered itself against the weather bow and McMullen dodged behind the base of the foremast to escape the flying sheet of seawater. The wind was rising, the weather worsening, and he was enough of a seaman to perceive that the frigate was over-canvassed. As the thought struck him, ousting other anxieties from his mind, a roar from the quarterdeck summoned the hands to take in sail. It was the hurricane season, though *Hermione* was not in the normal path taken by the hurricanes. McMullen found himself wishing for a natural cataclysm that should end the increasing tension he felt around him; and tossed his fancy impatiently aside. Only some gigantic wave sweeping the quarterdeck clear of Pigot and his officers could do that.

CHAPTER THREE

A Choice of Loyalties

1

The northerly gale that swept *Hermione* far to the southward of her course endured for thirty-six hours. According to Southcott, the master, it was the offshoot of a hurricane passing westward from the Leeward Islands to blow itself out in the Gulf of Mexico, and the frigate was lucky to miss it. The storm was fierce enough, for all that, and for a day and most of a night *Hermione* rode it out under reefed topsails and jib, drifting all the time farther from her objective. She was a well-found ship, but the big seas that hammered her hull started the planking and the pumps were manned continuously. Water found its way into McMullen's little cabin and oozed into the sickbay where he spent most of his time.

Perhaps because he had enough to occupy him in nursing his ship Captain Pigot ordered no floggings during the period of the storm, but other injuries kept the surgeon busy. These were the sort of injuries he had become accustomed to in *Surprise* in rough weather, the cuts and broken heads and the occasional cracked rib inevitable when men were flung about by the violent motions of their ship. He noted, as he had often noted before, that most of them were incurred in the first watch. There were always men who would save their noon rum ration and add it to the issue made at the end of the first dog-watch, thus obtaining half-a-pint of liquor to gulp at a draught. Primed with this, it was easy to forget not only the hardships of a seaman's life but also the lowness of deckhead beams and the slipperiness of ladders. It was a marvel McMullen had never ceased to wonder at that these same

61

half-drunken men could swarm aloft and run out on a swaying yard to take in a reef without missing handhold or foothold – or, if they did, without failing to stop themselves from falling. He had indeed heard of men falling from aloft but he had never seen it happen. Edward Hamilton had once gravely assured him that it was simply a matter of faith; every seaman, he asserted, firmly believed in the sweet little cherub of Dibdin's song –

> *That sits up aloft*
> *To keep watch for the life of poor Jack.*

McMullen inclined to the more scientific theory that the human organism faced with explicit peril generated some lymph or ichor which counteracted the effect of alcohol.

The minor casualties of the gale (there was a broken nose among them) he had to treat in the handicapping conditions of an ill-lit box shaken in the hand of a giant. Any serious operation would have been impossible with *Hermione* bucking and rearing like a maddened horse, but nothing of the kind came his way and his half-dozen patients were all back on full duty within the hour. Only Garbutt and Hammond remained as full-time patients, and Hammond's back was sufficiently healed for him to return to the mess-decks with a light bandaging in another twenty-four hours. Between them McMullen and Solly had rigged a hanging cot for Garbutt on which he could lie face-downwards without being rolled over by the frigate's tossing; relieving-tackles of spunyarn prevented it from crashing against the bulkheads when it swung but even so he had to be secured with rope to prevent him from being thrown off. Garbutt himself appeared impatient with these precautions.

'I could stand, sir,' he protested more than once. 'Aye, and walk the deck. Scarce half-a-hundred I was given, the lads say, and what's that?'

'That's fifty flesh-wounds, Garbutt,' McMullen told him severely. 'Move before they're healed and they'll open again.'

The man's impatience to be up and about seemed odd to McMullen. In this ship of all ships there was no likelihood of a lower-deck rating wanting to resume his duty prematurely out of loyalty to his officers. It was as though Garbutt's enforced idleness was delaying some cherished project he had been engaged on. McMullen grew uneasy; and his uneasiness was not lessened by the number of visitors that came to the sick-bay.

That the men should be allowed to visit their sick messmates was naval custom, and in twos and threes hands from the watch-below, or from the deck watch coming off duty, would sidle down the alleyway and ask to have a bit of a yarn with Harry Garbutt; and McMullen would of course allow it. On the first two occasions he seized the chance to make the comfortless journey aft along the spray-swept deck to his cabin, escaping for five minutes from the sick-bay stench that could not now be rectified until calmer weather. Both times, on his return, he had the impression of a low-voiced excited conversation interrupted by his entrance, an impression strengthened by transparent attempts on the part of the visitors to appear at ease. Moreover, though some of the men who came in were messmates of Garbutt's others were not in his watch. One of these, a hatchet-faced seaman with long grey hair, by name Meyer and one of the oldest hands on board, joined the sick-bay condolence party whenever it was his watch-below. Shrink from the conclusion he might, but the sum of what he had seen and heard made it inescapable. They were plotting – mutiny.

For the first time he had let the word frankly into his mind, with all its sinister implications. That night as he lay sleepless on his wildly-swinging cot he heard it yelled by the gale and thundered in ceaseless repetition by the angry seas. Beneath these mighty voices an inner voice nagged on and on of duty and loyalty to the Service and the safety of the ship's officers, and this voice he tried again and again to answer. To whom would he report his suspicions? To Reid, Douglas, Fitzroy? From none of them could he expect any attempt to reason with the hands. The report would be passed at once to the captain and he would act instantly. Garbutt, Meyer, Hammond – he, McMullen, would have to name them – would be put in irons until they could be hanged with due formality at Kingston.

Many others would no doubt be flogged; Pigot might well decide to flog his way through the whole crew, twenty a day. And for this the final responsibility would rest on the word of John McMullen. What was worse still, the men would die and suffer for nothing, for the cause of the disease would remain.

Who would agree with his diagnosis of Hugh Pigot's condition if ever he tried to state it openly? Medical research into the diseases of the mind was in its infancy, and the theories of Herero Pidal, if they had yet reached London from Salamanca, would have been studied only by a very few of the more progressive physicians. He could visualise the page of his notebook written seven years ago.

Con qué motivo ... For what reason does the subject perform these cruelties? It is that the diseased mind has substituted them for the more normal lusts of the flesh, and as with drink and sexual desire indulgence develops increased craving for satisfaction. Curative treatment is still to seek. For the present, close confinement under observation ...

How to confine Captain Pigot? There was no possibility of it. And yet it was the foulest injustice that men should suffer pain and death because of another man's infirmity.

McMullen perceived that he had two consciences. The unresolved conflict between them, he told himself, was based on nothing more than a suspicion, and until that suspicion was confirmed he need take no irrevocable action. But he would have to confront Garbutt, who seemed likely to be a prime mover in whatever was going forward, early tomorrow. That such a confrontation would obviously place him in a perilous position was something to offset what he felt to be his dereliction of duty. This decision taken, he was able to try and get some sleep. And *Hermione*, decreasing the violence of her tossing as wind and sea moderated, assisted him.

At dawn of the next day, September 22nd, the frigate was swooping over dark rollers unflecked with white, under a sky whose high overcast of cloud showed through narrow rifts the paling stars. The wind had veered right round to the south-east, and well before sunrise she was running under courses, topsails, and topgallants with a stiff and rising breeze over her starboard quarter. McMullen, slipping into the wardroom for coffee and bread, found tempers there more equable than usual.

'Bid you good morning, Honest John,' crowed Fitzroy as he came in. 'You're in time to observe our second lieutenant looking pleasant for the first time in recorded history. It's a fair wind, d'ye see.'

'A fair wind if Southcott's done his sums right,' Douglas growled. 'The devil may take him if he hasn't.'

'I suppose we've been blown far off our course,' McMullen said for the sake of being sociable. 'What is our present position?'

'God only knows, my dear medico.' Fitzroy gave a giggle. 'But demme if He hasn't imparted his knowledge to His prophet, our master here.'

Southcott looked annoyed. 'As I've told you, Mr Fitzroy, I have only dead-reckoning to go by. I put the ship's position, as an approximation, at three hundred miles sou'-sou'-west of Puerto Rico island.'

'And as another approximation,' Fitzroy echoed mockingly, 'we're two hundred miles north of the coast of Spanish America. Why, demme!' he added with the air of one making a great discovery, 'had the gale endured for two days more our honest Sawbones might have gone ashore to collect Peruvian bark – a sovereign remedy for sore backs, I'm assured.'

McMullen contrived to look amused by this sally and then, finishing his coffee, left the wardroom and went for'ard to the sickbay. He found Hammond sitting on his mattress while Solly, kneeling behind him, trimmed his hair with a large sheath-knife. Garbutt lay prone on his cot.

'Your knife, Hammond?' McMullen said sharply.

'Yes, sir. Just 'avin' a bit of a – '

'You know the rule – no knives, tobacco, or rum in a ship's sick-bay?'

'Yes, sir,' said Hammond sullenly.

'Well, you'd lose your knife, Hammond, but that I think you'll rejoin your mess today – light duties only, mind. Let's have a look at your back.'

He examined the healing cuts, applied plaster where it was needed, and dismissed Hammond to his mess. Solly he despatched to the galley to get his breakfast and bring Garbutt's breakfast back with him when he returned. Then he drew a deep breath and turned, to find that Garbutt had slid down from his cot and was trying to pull his shirt on over his bandages.

'What's this?' he demanded, frowning.

'What you might call an experiment, sir, by'r leave.' Garbutt set his teeth and tugged the shirt fully on. 'Ha. Easy as silk on a woman. I'm wishful to report fit for duty, sir.'

'For duty, Garbutt?' McMullen decided to rush his fence. 'Or for this other matter you've been planning?'

'Other matter, sir?' Garbutt repeated, staring hard at him.

McMullen turned away and began picking up the soiled dressings he had removed from Hammond's back.

'Yes,' he said over his shoulder. 'Mutiny, Garbutt.'

There was a dead silence behind him. He put the dressings in a spitkid and faced the seaman. Garbutt's eyes were narrowed to slits and his weatherbeaten face was grim.

'You're either a fool or a brave man,' he muttered. 'You've just told me there's only yourself between some of us and Execution Dock. I could have broken your neck a second ago.'

'I know that. Why didn't you?'

'Because I know you, sir. We were shipmates in the old *Lion* before this and you're not the sort to blab without a warning. What's more, you're on our side – '

'Nothing of the sort!' McMullen interrupted angrily. 'I'm telling you now, Garbutt, you're heading for destruction – a lee shore and an onshore gale. The hands have a grievance, I've seen that. But even if a mutiny should succeed – and you've long odds against you – you'll never see England again, or any British port in these seas. You and your mates will have two choices, and two only. One's to wander the face of the earth till the end of your days, like outlaws. The other's Execution Dock, as you call it.'

'Either one of 'em's better'n what we've got now,' Garbutt said fiercely; he shot out a hand and gripped the surgeon's arm. 'Listen to me, Mr McMullen. You say the hands have a grievance and you've seen it. How long have you been in this ship? Five days. We've been in her five months, and every day the same as what you've seen. We can't stand no more, sir, and that's God's truth. And Captain Pigot's mad, ain't he?'

'Take your hand from my arm,' said McMullen quietly.

Garbutt released his grip instantly. 'Beg pardon, sir. But mad's what he is. I heard you say as much.'

'In my opinion,' McMullen said slowly, 'Captain Pigot is suffering from a form of mental sickness.'

'That's it, sir. And when a captain's too sick to command his ship proper the surgeon tells the first lieutenant so and he takes over. If you was to tell Mr Reid firm-like that the captain's mad – '

'Don't be a fool, man. Would Mr Reid, or any of the other officers for that matter, take notice of my opinion?'

'No, sir,' Garbutt said with a sort of gloomy satisfaction. 'And that's what me and Meyer reckoned. There ain't but the one hope for us, and that's to take the ship ourselves. So the plan we've made – '

'I don't want to hear it!' McMullen cried out suddenly, turning away. 'I'll not be a party to mutiny!'

Even as he said the words he knew that they were futile. Garbutt's deep voice echoed his thought.

'You've gone too far for that, sir. Either you're with us or you'll go to the captain and send us all to hell.'

The man's evident confidence that he would not go to the captain was not the less exasperating for McMullen's awareness that he was right.

'You'd best hear me out,' Garbutt went on in tones low but emphatic. 'There'll be no bloodshed. They're a rough lot on board here, sir, rougher 'n most – foreigners, half of 'em. But me and Meyer, we've got 'em well in hand. The armoury first and the redcoats under hatches. Then – '

'Wait.' McMullen gulped down conflicting emotions. 'When is this – this thing to be?'

'Soon as she's inside a hundred mile from the nearest land. All officers bar the master into the cutter with a week's food and water, and shoved off. We'll need Mr Southcott to navigate us – '

He broke off short as footsteps sounded descending the ladder. Solly Crump, carrying a covered bowl, sidled in past the canvas curtain. McMullen took the bowl from him with hands that trembled uncontrollably and tried to speak with his usual briskness.

'Burgoo, and not made with mildewed oatmeal this time. Get that inside you, Garbutt. I'll consider your application to return to duty, and the other matter – ' he hesitated, but only for a second – 'stays in my head until I've considered that too.'

He went out abruptly and up the ladder to the deck. The wind had freshened, he noted absently, and *Hermione* was plunging through the dark rollers and sending clouds of spray flying over her bows. He started along the gangway towards his cabin and halted halfway along it to grip the rail and stare unseeing at the furrowed sea. There was nothing to consider, after all. It was inconceivable that he should betray Garbutt now. He remembered the *Bounty* mutiny of eight years ago, a mutiny with far less excuse than *Hermione*'s crew had; and how Captain Bligh, put with 17 others into an open boat inadequately provisioned, had come safely out of it after a voyage of nearly 4,000 miles. Pigot's lot would be far better. And though it would mean a lifetime of exile for the mutineers he could see no hope for them save mutiny.

As he turned to go aft he saw that Captain Pigot was on the quarterdeck. Pigot said something to the first lieutenant, who sprang to the taffrail shouting orders.

'Hands to reef tops'ls! Aloft with you, there!'

The captain's deep voice followed instantly. 'Look lively, you scum! Boatswain, start those laggards. And by God there'll be fifty lashes for the last man down!'

McMullen was near enough now to see the savage grin on Pigot's heavy-jowled face and the mad glitter in his eyes as he stared up at the men climbing frantically to the mizen topsail yard. Out along the footropes moved the tiny figures high above the deck, shouldering each other in their haste. The long fold of canvas was gathered in, the knots tied; the line of men balanced and shuffled hastily back along the yard to launch themselves down the tenuous ladder of the shrouds. The two men who had been outermost on the weather end of the yardarm were still edging towards the mast when the foremost of their mates were halfway down to the deck. One or other of those two, McMullen told himself, would be Pigot's victim.

Precisely how it happened he was unable to see. The two spidery figures high overhead detached themselves from the yard at the same time, as if they had simultaneously resolved to take that perilous short cut – the leap through empty air from the yard to the shrouds. Perhaps they collided as they jumped. He couldn't tell. Both men hurtled down a fathom clear of their objective and fell with a frightful double thud onto the after deck a few paces from him.

2

McMullen sprang forward and knelt beside the fallen men. They lay close together, one flat on his back with arms and legs outspread and the other in a crumpled heap that moved and collapsed as he bent to examine it. One look was sufficient; the man had pitched on his head and the smashed cranium was an oozing mass of glistening red and grey. His hands moved on the body of the second man. Neck broken and probably the lower spine as well. He looked up at the taffrail, where the captain still stood unmoving.

'Both dead,' he said.

Pigot nodded curtly. He was no longer grinning, but his scowl was one of annoyance – or perhaps, McMullen thought, frustration. He glared at the hands who had crowded aft to stare in a kind of awe at their dead shipmates, and waggled an imperious finger at the bodies on the deck below him.

'Heave those lubbers overboard!' he ordered.

It was not so much the callousness of the order as its blatant insanity that made McMullen gasp. A canvas shroud and the reading of the Burial Service was required when a seaman died on board, and every man of *Hermione*'s crew of two hundred knew it. A low growl like the sound of distant thunder rose from the little crowd of hands but no one moved.

'Heave 'em overboard, d'ye hear!' Pigot thundered. 'Mr Pascoe! Use your starter.'

Before the boatswain could use his cane half-a-dozen men ran forward to the bodies. They lifted them awkwardly, hurried them to the lee rail, and pitched them over the side. The captain kept his gaze on the close-packed throng of seamen.

'The first man to speak or move,' he said slowly, 'gets five hundred lashes. I'll flog the life out of him, by God I will!' His voice began to rise, harsh and hysterical as McMullen had heard it once before. 'I'll have my orders obeyed on the instant, d'ye hear? I'll flog every man on board if I have to – aye, every God-damned bastard! I'll flog – I'll – flog – '

The harsh voice ceased abruptly. Pigot gulped, passed his handkerchief across his lips and spoke to the first lieutenant in his ordinary voice.

'Send those men about their duties, Mr Reid,' he said, 'and have the deck swabbed and scoured. I will have this vessel immaculate.'

He turned to descend the quarterdeck ladder as Reid began screeching the orders. McMullen, who had retreated to the rail, watched him as he came down the steps. There was a small secret smile on the full lips and the pale eyes, wide and staring, passed over the surgeon apparently without seeing him. He went into his cabin below the quarterdeck. Four of the hands with mops and a bucket trotted up and began to slosh and scrub at the stained deck where the broken bodies had lain; and McMullen's stomach, which he had always regarded as proof against emotional disturbance, heaved unpleasantly. He went below and past the door of his cabin into the little quarter-gallery over the stern which was used as an officers' privy, where he could vomit without being observed. Afterwards he sat for a long time on the sea-chest below his hanging cot, with his head in his hands.

He was past anger now. As well be angry with a fever case in delirium as with Hugh Pigot. The man was wholly evil, or demented, or possessed by a devil – it made no difference what the thing was called, there was no cure for it. On land his place would be in the Infirmary of St Mary of Bethlehem in Bishopsgate, 'put away' where his dementia could do no harm to his fellow-men; at sea, lacking a Bedlam, the plain remedy was to put him away in a boat. And with him, of course, the officers who pandered to his perverted lust. But – was it 'of course'? Should he not at least try to confer with them apart, one by one, and lay his diagnosis before them? He reviewed them in his mind: Reid, Douglas, Fitzroy. If he broached the matter to any of them he would find himself in irons. Southcott he might persuade, he thought, but the master struck him as ineffectual and most unlikely to influence the others.

At this point his gloomy reflections were interrupted by a cautious double-knock on his cabin door and a gruff voice, lowered almost to a whisper, inquired if he was within. His reply brought Mr Searle the gunner sidling in through the door, which he closed very carefully behind him.

'I'd like a wee word with you, Mr McMullen,' said Searle in the same hoarse whisper. 'With your leave, that's to say.'

He was a small man, sharp-featured and narrow-eyed, with a close thatch of grey curls that made him look more like a lawyer than a warrant officer in the Navy. McMullen had seen little of Mr Searle and exchanged no word with him so far, for he messed in the gunroom and the guns had not been exercised since the frigate left Kingston.

'Yes, of course, Mr Searle,' said McMullen warily, getting up; he had reached a state in which he felt that wherever he trod it was upon thin ice. 'There's only the chest to sit on,' he added. 'Pray take it.'

'Thankee.' Searle squatted on the sea-chest and took a small box from the pocket of his blue coat. 'Ye'll take a pinch? No? Then mayhap ye'll allow me.'

He helped himself liberally to snuff. The dim light of the cabin lantern struck a glint from his little eyes as he fixed them on the surgeon.

'I'm thinking there's a gey unchancey smell about, Mr McMullen,' he said solemnly, and sneezed.

'Indeed?' McMullen tried to speak lightly. 'Then I trust you'll not blame me. The late occupant of this cabin – '

'About this vessel, is my meaning,' the gunner amplified, frowning. 'I might call it a minacious smell, if ye appreciate the word.'

'I think I do. But in what respect, Mr Searle?'

Mr Searle took time to answer, brushing snuff from his chest. 'I'll not conceal from ye,' he said at last, weighing his words, 'that very recent events, and I'll say nae more than that, have given us in the gunroom cause for disquietude. Nay – ' he raised a corrective finger – 'have conseederably enlarged the disquietude already felt.'

'You're referring to Captain Pigot's unceremonious disposal of two dead men. That indeed has given rise to a good deal of discontent.'

Mr Searle, McMullen noticed, was not immune from the apprehensive over-the-shoulder glance that affected the rest of the ship's company.

'Nae word of that, Mr McMullen, nae word of that,' he said, lowering his voice still further. 'But true it is that if all the rum on board had been jettisoned it would have had nae worse effect on the men than the circumstance ye mention.'

'You may well be right,' said McMullen, carefully non-committal.

'And this being so,' Searle continued ponderously, 'we – the gunroom officers, that's to say – have debated the possibility that the hands may take some sort of – um – injudeecious action.'

They're planning to mutiny. I can name the ringleaders. The words that passed through McMullen's mind remained unspoken. What could Searle do but report them to the captain?

'And you think that's likely?' he said.

The gunner wagged his head, frowning. 'The gude knows. There's a gey strict discipline aboard this vessel, as ye've seen. Mayhap it'll hold, mayhap it'll break. And mayhap – 'tis what we had in mind – ye'll be the man can tell us which airt the wind's blowing.'

Plainly well satisfied with this pronouncement, he took snuff again. McMullen could see what was coming and took refuge in prevarication.

'I, Mr Searle? I joined this ship only five days ago. How should I know what's in the minds of her crew?'

Searle sneezed heartily. 'Aye,' he said when he had recovered. 'But ye're the surgeon and ye've had men to tend in your sickbay. Men that have suffered flogging by the captain's order – by the captain's just command, that's to say. Ye'll have heard their mutterings and grumblings. And it could well be that ye gathered some inkling of the general feeling consarning these same just punishments.'

This, McMullen realised, was the crucial moment. The Rubicon lay before him and his next words could take him across it. With only the slightest hesitation he made the irrevocable decision.

'I see, I see,' he said, feigning an amused enlightenment. 'But I assure you, Mr Searle, you've little cause for alarm – so far as I can judge, that is. The men I've attended to have complained of their pain, naturally, but of nothing else that I've heard.'

'Is that so, now?'

Searle's needle-sharp stare seemed to bore into him. McMullen felt he must produce some elaboration of his lie.

'To be honest with you, Mr Searle,' he said confidentially, 'I'm not accustomed to the kind of discipline you maintain here. A week ago I'd have said it was too strictly imposed. But if its object is to break rebellious spirits, as I suppose, it has certainly succeeded. In my opinion there's not a man on board with the spirit to take the sort of – um – injudicious action you have in mind.'

He couldn't resist the malicious echo of Searle's euphemism but the gunner appeared not to notice it. Nor, it seemed, was he fully satisfied.

'There's this chiel Garbutt,' he said without shifting his penetrating stare. 'The captain disrated him from petty officer for neglecting his duty. I hear you and Garbutt were in the *Lion* seventy-four together, Mr McMullen.'

'So we were.' Was there danger here? 'I recall treating the man for a broken arm – a dull fellow I thought him then, lacking in initiative. But I'm surprised to hear he neglected his duty.'

'He neglected the duty of using his cane on laggards,' Searle said drily.

'Oh. And on that account – yes, I see. You think he'd be in sympathy with men planning a – '

'An injudicious action,' the gunner said quickly. 'I'll no'

deny I thought it likely. Garbutt was disrated syne and he was flogged twa days ago. I'm thinking the man would be sore disgruntled.'

McMullen shook his head. 'He's under my care now and his back's in a bad way. I'd say he thinks of nothing beyond that, Mr Searle. I may be wrong, of course,' he added politely.

'I'd prefer ye to be right,' Searle said somewhat grimly, getting up. 'Aweel, I'll awa' back and tell the gunroom your opeenion. Ye'll have jaloused I'm a wee deputation sent to get it. Mr Price – the carpenter, ye ken – thinks as you do, so *he'll* be satisfied, at the least.'

When the cabin door had closed behind him McMullen sat down heavily on the chest and mopped his brow with a swab he found in his pocket. He was inclined to like Mr Searle, and the way he had treated him brought a pang of remorse. But this passed almost at once, succeeded by a feeling of relief now that the burden of decision no longer weighed him down. He had lied to defend the intending mutineers, he had made himself one with them. There could be no changing sides now.

Searle's visit, however, had left him slightly uneasy. In the gunner's manner he thought to have distinguished suspicion of himself, and he remembered unguarded actions and expressions that might well have aroused it; his interference with Pascoe on the first day, for instance, and the betraying emotions an observer might have seen on his face during Garbutt's flogging. He would have to be more careful in the future. And for how long? Two hundred and fifty miles to Puerto Rico by Southcott's estimate, which meant that *Hermione* would be within a hundred miles of land by this time tomorrow. But the hands wouldn't rise against their officers in daytime. It would be tomorrow night, then –

He got up, suddenly aware that he needed urgently to talk with Garbutt. There were half-a-dozen questions that had to be asked.

On deck the second officer was blasphemously directing the hoisting of additional canvas. The steady favouring wind had died away, leaving the frigate moving slowly across a long swell beneath a sky of grey monotone. The mazarine of the Caribbean was transmuted to lead, and *Hermione* might have

been off the Kentish Banks instead of several hundred miles
south of the Tropic of Cancer, but for the oppressive warmth
that closed in upon her as she lost way. McMullen made his
way for'ard and down to the sickbay. Only Solly was there,
asleep and snoring on the mattress. Garbutt, it seemed, had
forestalled his permission to rejoin his mess.

He hesitated for a moment, thinking of those urgent
unresolved questions. But it wouldn't do to enter the
messdecks looking for Garbutt; there was the chance of a petty
officer observing him and report of his visit coming to ears
cocked for suspicious happenings – Mr Searle's, perhaps. He
woke Solly and set him to tidying the sickbay while he himself
went to the orlop to inspect Ayers and Zadowa, the fever cases.
Ayers was through the worst of it and sleeping peacefully, but
Zadowa showed signs of relapsing and was groaning and
muttering in mild delirium.

McMullen spent the rest of the day in tending the delirious
man and directing Solly in a further cleansing of the sickbay.
He made the needs of Zadowa his excuse for not taking his
meals in the wardroom, contenting himself instead with bread
and cold beef and coffee obtained from Chubb the wardroom
steward; the sense of betrayal was inescapable and he could not
bring himself to eat with men for whose imminent downfall he
was in a way responsible.

At two bells of the first watch *Hermione* was moving very
slowly through a warm darkness, with the slightest of swells
lifting her and barely enough breeze to give her steerage-way.
McMullen gave some final attentions to his fever patients, left
Solly in charge with orders to call him if there was any notable
change in Zadowa's condition, and groped his way aft past the
massive rumps of the guns and the huddled dark forms of the
watch-on-deck. There had been no floggings this day, he
reflected; perhaps Captain Pigot deemed two violent deaths a
sufficient satisfaction of his appetites. Slits and slivers of light
gleamed from Pigot's cabin and there was a light in the
wardroom, but otherwise the only light on deck was from the
binnacle lamp, which threw an upward glow that showed
dimly the features of the man at the wheel blankly hollowed
like a skull.

McMullen's cabin had a stout lock and he had locked it when he left, after blowing out the lantern. Letting himself in, he found the tinder-box and lit the lantern. His eye caught a slip of brown stuff on the planking a few feet from the door, and he bent and picked it up. It was a piece of thin leather, and on it markings had been made with charcoal. A single word: *Tonight.*

3

In a ship at sea there is never silence. And yet the frigate *Hermione*, creeping across the black waters on that night of September 22nd, seemed to move with an uncanny muteness. Her hull scarcely lifted on the gentle swell, and the myriad sounds that usually accompanied her progress were hushed to a sleepy murmur that a listening ear assimilated and forgot. She was like a ship of the dead, thought McMullen.

He was lying fully dressed on his cot in the darkness, not with any thought of sleep – sleep was out of the question – but because he could no longer endure the restless standing and sitting, listening for some significant noise, which had occupied him for three hours. The recumbent position did something to ease his physical self but it could not ease the turmoil of his thoughts. He lay on a bed of unrest, at one moment with every muscle tense and ears strained to the uttermost, at another vainly seeking the answer to one or other of several questions vitally important to himself.

It was strange, when he came to think of it, that in his concern with the rights and wrongs of mutiny and their relation to the special case of Hugh Pigot he had omitted to ask what was to become of himself. Was he to be 'put away' with Pigot and his officers in the cutter, to share with them the chances of an open boat and a possible landfall – Puerto Rico and imprisonment, or one of the British Leeward Islands and eventual return to Jamaica? (Lucy Preston seemed very far away at this moment.) Or, having thrown in his lot with the mutineers, would he be kept on board? In the first alternative he could expect no mercy from the men in the cutter, since it was impossible that his part in the mutiny could be kept secret once the hands had taken over; and in the other his case would be no better, for he could never return to Jamaica except in irons and Lucy must be lost to him for ever. He saw now that he was by his own choice walking a road that led only to black disaster for himself.

He saw, too, that he had one last chance, a chance that diminished with every second of time. Even now he could raise the alarm, with some tale of a plot overheard, and appear as the saviour of Pigot and his ship. He dismissed the thought as soon as it occurred to him, ashamed that it had entered his mind. That it should have done so he attributed to the fact that it was the one course that could bring him to Lucy again; but he knew that he could never look her in the face with such a burden of treachery upon him.

A sudden clang brought him slithering off the cot to stand rigid and alert. The ship's bell – that was all. Eight bells: *the iron tongue of midnight* and the beginning of the middle watch. Footsteps and curt voices marked the changing of the watch-on-deck; a cabin door banged shut; silence again but for a dull rhythmic thudding that would be the relieving officer pacing the quarterdeck overhead. McMullen loosened his stock, for it was hot in the cabin and he was sweating. For some time he stood leaning against the bulkhead at his old game of straining his ears, and then bethought him that there was nothing to stop him from taking the air on deck or visiting his sickbay if he wished to. He went out to the after deck.

Invisible above the unbroken drift of low cloud the moon, nearing her last quarter, diffused a glimmering light. His eyes, long accustomed to the pitch darkness of the cabin, took in the familiar details of a quiet and orderly deck: the black perspective of the rail, with the indeterminate masses of the hands grouped motionless along it; the faintly etched lines of the shrouds soaring up to the great dark curves of the sails; the pillar-like bases of main and mizen masts and beyond them the shapes of *Hermione*'s three boats stowed on the spar deck aft of the foremast. He moved a few paces along the rail to look up at the quarterdeck. A small figure came and went, its silhouette bobbing up at the taffrail against the dusky sky and vanishing as it paced away aft: Reid was officer of the watch, then, and the other two dimly discernible up there would probably be one of the midshipmen and Southcott the master. Below the narrow overhang of the quarterdeck the helmsman was invisible behind the glow of the binnacle lamp, but he could make out the white crossbelts of the marine sentry on duty outside the captain's cabin. There were still narrow strips of light outlining Pigot's door, he noted. The occasional rustle of upper sails in the light and fitful breeze, the susurration of the frigate's lazy progress, merged in an undercurrent of sound into which Reid's scarcely-audible footsteps wove an ordered pattern. Nothing, thought McMullen, could seem more peaceful.

A vagrant waft of air stirred the hair at the back of his neck, reminding him with absurd irrelevance that it was long since he had had it trimmed, and of a sudden he had a mental picture of Solly Crump in the sickbay trimming Hammond's greasy locks with a sheath-knife. Hammond's knife; a knife such as every seaman carried, but it must have been razor-sharp. McMullen gave an involuntary shudder. Warm though the night air was it was chilling his body, which was damp with sweat. He retreated to the sheltered corner where the rail met the rise of the quarterdeck, and settled himself there to wait.

Tonight. It must of course have been Garbutt, who had previously told him that tomorrow night was the time fixed for action, who had contrived that warning for him. What had caused the putting-forward of the mutineers' plan? A reasonable guess was that Pigot's conduct after the two seamen had fallen to their deaths had so enraged the crew that the ringleaders could hold them back no longer. And that raised in his mind the question of how much control could be exercised by Garbutt and Meyer, and whoever else shared the leadership, over two hundred infuriated seamen. He reflected uneasily that he knew nothing, or next to nothing, about the plans or organisation of a revolt he had committed himself to support – and in which he had been allotted no part. The reflection irked him, for beneath the man of medicine with his academic upbringing there lurked the man of action. To wait, and when the moment came to have no rôle but that of bystander, aggravated his present acute impatience. But there was nothing he could do about it. He braced himself against the rail, motionless in his corner, and resumed his tense listening for the first sign of disturbance.

When it came the thing was different from his vague anticipations.

A seaman, a big man, came trotting aft to the break of the quarterdeck where the bell hung. After a moment the double clang sounded, two bells of the middle watch. But the seaman did not return for'ard. Peering below the ladder close beside him McMullen discerned dim shapes engaged in a brief struggle. There came a bubbling groan and the metallic noise of a musket falling to the deck. Before he had time to realise that a man had been stabbed to death a few paces from him another sound made him swing round to face the deck, a sound like thunder continuous and close at hand. Some heavy object clanked into the scuppers near him and trundled away. Roundshot from the nettings were being rolled across the deck.

'What the devil's afoot, there?'

That was Reid's screech, from the head of the ladder. There was no reply and the thunder of the rolling shot grew louder.

'By God, some of you shall pay for this!' Reid clattered down the ladder and out across the deck. 'Pass the word for the boatswain! Where – '

He checked on the word and turned about to run. Simultaneously McMullen saw the surging wave.

Or that was what it looked like in the first instant of perception – a great wave that had somehow flooded over the bows and was rushing aft along both gangways. But it was a wave of men. He saw it reach and overwhelm the first lieutenant before he had gained the foot of the ladder. Saw the dull gleam of steel and heard a scream like that of a stuck pig, horribly cut short. Then the outer wing of the mob was upon him and he was seized by the throat.

'Who's this?'

The man's spittle was hot on his face.

'McMullen – surgeon,' he choked. 'Loose me, damn you!'

'He's with us,' said another voice, and he was freed.

From below decks amidships came a sudden clamour of yells and screams – the marines' quarters. It ended the strange silence with which the crowd of men had made their onset. An uproar of hoarse cheers, bellowed commands, and oaths in several languages rose in savage crescendo. McMullen, dazed for an instant, recovered his senses. They were murdering – it was to be a slaughter of officers!

A yelling throng was pouring up to the quarterdeck but the main body was surging against the cabins below. A door was wrenched open, releasing a flood of light. He hurled himself through the gap below the ladder, thrusting and hammering his way between striving bodies towards the open door. A face appeared suddenly close to his – Southcott, with blood streaming from a slash across the cheek. Then Southcott had gone and he was in the doorway, striking and shouldering with blind urgency, shouting at the top of his voice: 'Stand back! Stand back!'

His words were drowned in the deafening pandemonium of yells and curses but he struggled on, smiting and kicking. A waft of scent came to his nostrils, he caught a glimpse of coloured tapestries and cushions. Pigot's cabin. It was packed with shouting, struggling men. McMullen slammed his fist into the neck of a man who blocked his way, the man turned on him a bearded face distorted with fury, and he felt the impact of the knife that slashed across his upper arm. If there was pain he was oblivious of it, for it was then that he saw the captain.

Hugh Pigot's upper body rose above the close-packed men that pressed upon him, as if it was being squeezed upward by the pressure that forced him against the stern window of the cabin. The shirt that was his only garment had been white but was now crimson, and the crimson glistened wetly in the yellow lamplight. His eyes were wide and staring, the lower part of his face had been smashed to a shapeless red pulp, and from the gash that had been his mouth came an inarticulate babbling. Hands grasping knives swung and threatened above the heads of the yelling men nearest Pigot. A knife stabbed into his belly and blood spurted. A voice screeched above the uproar: 'Into the drink with him!' Others took it up: 'The drink! The drink!'

A stool crashed at the stern window, smashing the panes and opening a jagged gap into the darkness of sky and sea.

McMullen saw Captain Pigot, still babbling, thrust bodily out through the gap, naked hairy legs kicking feebly as he vanished. In a wild unreasoning access of fury he flung himself forward striking vainly at Pigot's murderers. Then the whole scene of glaring eyes and bloody hands and shattered window fled into oblivion as a heavy fist smote down on his head from behind.

CHAPTER FOUR

Escape

1

Someone was crooning a little song, repetitive and interminable:

> *Se si spezz' oi-li, oi-la*
> *Se si spezza, buona sera,*
> *Non si puo raccomodar.*

It blended with McMullen's returning consciousness, a sad sequence of notes, sometimes hummed and sometimes sung softly in a man's voice, over and over again. The sound came from near at hand, only a few feet away. As McMullen realised this he realised also that he was in pain; not severe pain but coming from more than one source. He had a splitting headache, his left arm below the shoulder burned and throbbed, and a slight movement of his aching head brought an agonising twinge at the base of his neck. He was lying on some flat surface that swayed under him and a familiar odour confirmed that this was the cot in his cabin. He opened his eyes and received further confirmation from the sight of the lantern swinging from its usual hook on the deckhead. For a moment, and as if Time had slipped back a few cogs, he was newly come on board *Hermione* after last night's farewells in his old ship, leaving in Attwood's care the two fever cases Zadowa and Ayers – and here, with the effect of a whirling wheel, his mind regained the true present. Ayers and Zadowa were his patients in *Hermione*. There had been mutiny, bloodshed. The remembrance of Pigot's half-naked body, blood-boltered and feebly writhing, being forced out through the stern window flashed vividly across his thoughts. He tried to raise himself on the cot and fell back with a groan of pain.

The humming ceased and a brown face, thin and pockmarked, rose into view. McMullen, turning his head with an effort, recognised the man as a Neapolitan seaman named Ruffo.

'*Come!*' said Ruffo with a flash of white teeth. 'The *signor* is all alive-oh. I tell zem now.'

He turned away. McMullen, recollection of recent events crowding upon him, found his voice.

'Stay! Tell me what's happened. Where are the other officers?'

'*Avvetate, signor,*' Ruffo said soothingly. 'I bring Garbutt.'

He picked up a musket from beside the seachest where he had been sitting and went out, locking the door behind him. McMullen lay staring up at the deckhead, trying to order his confused thoughts. He was a prisoner, it seemed. And, as was evident when he tried to move, in an enfeebled state. His left arm above the elbow was swathed in bandaging crudely applied; the knife-slash in Pigot's cabin had done some damage, then, though cautious flexing of the muscles reassured him that this was no more than a flesh wound. His weakness was probably due to considerable loss of blood, he thought. He remembered now the sledgehammer blow on his head administered from behind, which no doubt accounted for his other pains. With that blow had ended his futile attempt to save Pigot. What had happened since?

The frigate, he could tell, was making good speed through a moderate sea, with a beam wind. Above the usual ship noises he could hear occasional hoarse yells on deck, and once a roar of laughter. The mutiny, of course, had been successful and now *Hermione* was in the hands of her long-suffering crew – and bound, no doubt, for some coast or island out of reach of the penalty they had incurred. Mutiny and murder. That meant hanging for every man on board, if and when he was caught. For John McMullen, too. He'd been a fool to accept Garbutt's assurance that there would be no bloodshed. But for that, he told himself, he would never have stood aside from what was certainly his duty. Anger against Garbutt rose in him and seemed to infuse his weakened body with more strength, so that he was essaying to sit up on the cot when the key grated in the lock and Garbutt entered the cabin carrying a steaming bowl. Ruffo, musket in hand, followed him in.

'Happy to see you're none so bad, sir,' Garbutt said gruffly. 'You've been out and under long enough. – You can take a spell on deck,' he added to Ruffo.

'*Oibo, amico caro*,' the man objected. 'Me, I am responseeble to the Committee for this *signor*.'

'Well, and ain't I one of the Committee?' growled Garbutt. 'Cut your stick and do as I say.'

Ruffo shrugged his shoulders carelessly and departed.

'So you've a Committee – on the Jacobin model, I presume,' McMullen said bitterly. 'Where's your guillotine, may I ask?'

'There's a soup of beef and taters here,' Garbutt said stolidly, 'and you'd best get it down.' He put the bowl down on the deck. 'Settin' on the seachest, I reckon.'

McMullen found himself picked up like a baby and lifted to the deck, where, as his legs refused to support him, he was forced to sit down on the chest.

'You murdered Captain Pigot,' he said, a trifle breathlessly. 'What of the other officers?'

Garbutt handed him the bowl and a spoon. 'If you can use your left hand to steady it you can manage. You've been layin' there without grub best part of four watches.'

'You gave me your word there was to be no bloodshed, Garbutt, and I saw Captain Pigot – '

'Eat that soup, sir,' the seaman interrupted sharply. 'I'll tell you, as best I can, while you're at it.'

The contents of the bowl smelt delicious. McMullen discovered that he was ravenously hungry, and without his willing it his hand dipped the spoon. Garbutt squatted on his haunches beside the seachest and passed a horny hand over the grey bristles on his unshaven chin. The yellow lantern-light showed his weatherbeaten face deeply lined, his mouth grimly set. The bandaging that covered back and shoulders beneath his shirt gave him the look of a hunchback.

'I should ha' known,' he said heavily. 'Carver, he'd said

more'n once as he'd do Mr Reid's business for him if he got
the chance, and Carver headed the rush. It wasn't only the
captain they went for, Mr McMullen. Mr Douglas, Mr Fitzroy,
Mr Boyes, Midshipman Hollins, and the bo'sun – all of 'em
down with Davy Jones now. Not to mention seven of Mr
Boyes's Jollies as showed fight. The rest came in with us.'

McMullen, rigid and staring with his spoon halfway to his
lips, let out a gasp of horror.

'By Christ!' he whispered hoarsely. 'You slaughtered them
all – you spared none?'

'The lads came to their senses, like,' Garbutt went on in the
same dull tone. 'The gunner, the master, and Mr Casey, they
was lashed up unhurt. Same with the carpenter and Billy
Moncrieff, the cook. Them five, sir, we put off in the cutter this
forenoon with food an' water for a week. The wind's backed
northerly so they'll make St Vincent or St Lucia, I reckon.
Three days' sailin', with a fair wind and no hurricanes, from
where we – '

'Twelve men were murdered. Their blood is on your head.'

'And none of it on yourn, Mr McMullen?' said Garbutt
harshly. 'Think on that, and eat your soup.'

His words hit McMullen like a blow. He had forgotten the
part he had played; keeping silence when a word would have
saved the lives of those twelve men. Automatically he went on
eating, balancing the bowl against the lift and tilt of the
frigate's progress. For the moment he could find no reply to
the seaman's hinted accusation. Garbutt, who had rested his
head on his hands for a few seconds like a man utterly weary,
went on with his tale.

'Nor was twelve dead the sum of it. Meyer pistolled two
seamen, dead as mutton, both of 'em. 'Twas when we had
trouble over the drink – Pigot's wine an' suchlike. Me and
Meyer, we reckoned to pitch it overboard and hold to the
reg'lar rum issue. Let a sailor loose among the liquor and the
ship's as good as lost. Some o' the hands objected. Two had to
be shot before they'd see reason – Carver was one. After that
we set up a Committee, elected by vote all right an' proper.
Nine of us, d'ye see, so there can't be no equal sides when we
vote. But – ' He hesitated, then broke out with a desperate

sincerity. 'Before God, sir, it was never any plan of mine to kill the officers. You'll believe that?'

McMullen set down the empty bowl on the deck. He had sorely needed that good hot food, and now that it was inside him he could feel his strength returning and his mind adjusting to its normal clarity. Already he had perceived that twelve deaths by violence must be balanced against the alternative of a hundred or more deaths by hanging which would have resulted from his speaking that unspoken word.

'I'll believe that, Garbutt,' he said with something of his old briskness, 'and there let us leave the matter. The thing is done. Every man in this ship, including her surgeon, has a hangman's noose waiting for him.' He moved his head and winced as pain stabbed at the base of his skull. 'And the surgeon is a prisoner, it appears.'

'Not by my will, sir. 'Twas the Committee decided to set a guard in the cabin till you came to yourself.'

'Because of what happened in the captain's cabin?'

'Aye. You hit Lynch, leadin' seaman – 'twas he who gave you that.' Garbutt nodded at McMullen's bandaged arm. 'And Lynch was 'lected to the Committee, d'ye see. But you was fair hammering wherever you could land a fist, sir, an' yelling at 'em to let Pigot alone. I saw you.'

'You were there – in Pigot's cabin? Why in God's name didn't you help me?'

Garbutt took a second or two to answer. 'I reckon I helped you, sir, in a way,' he said slowly, 'though I was too late to help the captain. This goddamned back o' mine was like a sea-anchor slowin' me up, so I was at the back o' the crowd at the rush. Soon as I saw Carver stab Reid I ran for the cabin. Right astern of you I was, when you started to use your fists and shout. Every man of 'em was fightin' mad an' they didn't like it – 'twasn't only Lynch's knife that was lifted agin you. So, d'ye see – ' he paused and rubbed his chin – 'I reckoned you'd be safer put to sleep an' layin' on the deck.'

'You? It was you that hit me?'

'Me it was, sir. With this.' Garbutt held up a clenched fist massive as a knot of oak. 'An' if the time you was out is anything to go by I hit harder than what I meant to, which I'm sorry for it. Afterwards Solly Crump an' me got you in here – bleedin' like a stuck pig, you was – an' Solly got them bandages on you.'

'I see,' McMullen said with a wry smile. 'I should thank you for my life by the sound of it. But this Committee of yours decided to keep me under restraint, I take it.'

'That's it, sir. There was some as reckoned you did ought to be put in the cutter with Mr Searle and the others, but I says it wasn't a matter o' you changin' sides, just a try to stop 'em killing. Besides, you was wounded an' spark out.' Garbutt paused. 'Mr Searle, he did ask why the surgeon wasn't in the cutter – just as they was shovin' off, it was – an' Meyer shouts "McMullen's got a berth with us." '

McMullen digested this in silence, recalling his impression, when Searle had visited his cabin, that the gunner suspected where his sympathies lay. If Searle ever got back to Jamaica he would report that *Hermione*'s surgeon had been one of the mutineers; that was true enough and the idea of denying it to save his neck had never entered McMullen's head. But now anyone hearing of it would adjudge him guilty of brutal murder. It was not easy to resign himself to that.

On deck there was an interchange of shouts, followed by the sound of the ship's bell.

'Four bells?' he said, frowning.

'That's it.' Garbutt's tone was an odd mixture of pride and shame. 'The old Hermy's back to ship routine of a kind. Meyer and me saw to – '

'Four bells of what watch?'

'First dog, sir. An' today's the twenty-third.'

The professional physician in him rose to overtop McMullen's other troubles for the moment. Eighteen hours since he had visited his patients!

'Who's in charge of the sickbay?' he demanded sharply.

'Solly Crump was,' said Garbutt, 'but he's took over as cook now. That soup you've just had was Solly's brew with a dash o' rum from his own ration, an' I can see as how it's done you a power o' – '

'But Zadowa, and Ayers! I must – '

McMullen tried to get to his feet. His legs gave way before he had achieved erectness and Garbutt steadied him down onto the seachest again.

'You just take it easy, sir,' he admonished. 'You're a sickbay case yourself for a while. There's no one else in it – Ayers is back in his mess, a bit tottery-like but none so bad. Zadowa – well, Solly reported to me a bit after dawn and said he reckoned Zadowa was dead. I took a look and he was.'

Remembering the man's condition when he had last examined him, McMullen was not surprised. It seemed highly unlikely that he could have done anything to save him.

'We gave him a right an' proper burial,' Garbutt went on, with significant emphasis. 'Likewise Carver an' Brady that had to be shot. Meyer, he read a bit o' the Service. He's had more'n a touch of education, has Fred. It's him as has charge of our navigation now.'

McMullen remembered something. 'I thought you'd planned to keep the master on board to navigate you.'

'Aye – but the Committee decided he was to go in the cutter with the rest. We made Mr Southcott give us the course before he went, though – south by west forty-eight leagues to the Grand Cayo passage, an' with the wind fair and steady like it is we did ought to sight Cayo island by noon tomorrow. After that' – Garbutt's thick grey eyebrows drew together in a frown – 'it's sixteen leagues south by east for La Guayra.'

'*La Guayra?*' McMullen repeated incredulously. 'But that's the – '

'The chief Spanish navy base on the Main,' Garbutt took him up quickly. 'It's decided we're to turn over the ship to the Dons. Strike a bargain, like. They to give us our freedom an' a fair chance to make a livin' ashore or in coasters – '

McMullen ceased to listen. The possibility of such a sequel to the mutiny in *Hermione* had not occurred to him; he had vaguely imagined a landing on some deserted shore or island, the mutineers attempting a new and primitive life or scattering inland to seek their fortunes. Perhaps illogically, in view of what had passed, the handing-over of the frigate to the enemy seemed to him a crime of the blackest hue.

'By God, Harry Garbutt!' he broke in on the seaman's explanations. 'I'd not have believed this – you, a man-o'-war's man, to give a King's ship to the King's enemies! Shame on you for a traitor, a – '

'Now see you here, Mr Surgeon McMullen!' Garbutt rasped, turning on him a face like granite. 'I'll take no such talk from you, d'ye see? I'll tell you this – I don't much like turning over the old *Hermy* to the Dons. I voted agin it. But I'm standin' by what the Committee's decided on.'

'And your duty to King George? That goes by the board, does it?'

'Duty, sir? What's you an' me got to do with duty now? I've turned my coat once and I'll not turn it again. I stick with the lads from now on, whatever chances.'

'Then we part company,' McMullen said angrily. 'I refuse to countenance any damned bargain with the Spaniards. I'll have no part in it, do you understand?'

Garbutt laughed, short and harsh. 'I've little choice enough but you've none.' He stood up. 'I've to go on deck. If you need to make water afore I go you'd better let me help you, sir. You'd never make the quarter-gallery and there's a can in the corner yonder.'

In smouldering silence McMullen allowed himself to be raised and supported above the can. Afterwards he was picked up and deposited on his cot again. Garbutt found a blanket and spread it over him.

'The sun seems to have left these waters for a spell,' he remarked conversationally. 'We're sailin' into cloudy weather and it'll get colder, maybe.'

He turned to leave the cabin. McMullen, his wrath exacerbated by the man's calm tone, shouted at him wildly.

'Mark what I say, damn you! If this vessel puts into La Guayra I'll not be in her – I'll jump overboard first!'

Garbutt gave no sign of hearing this futile utterance.

'I'll send Solly down to change them bandages,' he said evenly. 'You'll get soup an' grog at two bells o' the first watch, Mr McMullen.'

The cabin door closed behind him and the key grated in the lock.

2

Half-an-hour later McMullen was easier in body though not in mind. He had been able to inspect his wound, when Solly had removed the bloodstained bandaging, and found as he had expected that the knife slash was not a serious injury, Lynch's blade having missed the muscle by a hairsbreadth. It was a four-inch cut, all the same, and it was the profuse veinous bleeding that had caused his present weakness. Under his direction, Solly got the flask of oak-gall styptic from his seachest and bathed the oozing slit with it before swabbing it and applying a long plaster with a light bandaging to hold it in position. McMullen had the bandaging done three times before he was satisfied; he wanted to ensure that he had the full use of his left arm and at the same time to guard against the reopening of the wound. A notion that he might be involved in some sort of desperate action shortly was already in his mind, though he had no idea as yet what form it might take.

There was little to be got out of Solly Crump concerning the mutiny and its aftermath. The loblolly-boy had remained in the sickbay with the dying Zadowa during the bloody events on deck, and his imperfect wits seemed not to have grasped what had happened.

'I'm cook now, thir – cook'th a promotion.'

This, as far as Solly was concerned, was the most important transaction of the past twenty-four hours.

'How d'you like your new officers?' McMullen asked him, and was answered with an uncomprehending stare.

He was sorry for Solly Crump. Like the rest of them, he would walk in the shadow of the gallows for whatever of life remained to him; when it came to dealing with mutineers His Majesty's Courts Martial made no more distinction between halfwits and men in full possession of their senses than they made between foremast hands and surgeons – or between those captains who used flogging as a just punishment and those who made it the servant of a madman's lust.

Solly had brought a pitcher of water and McMullen took a long drink from it before the loblolly-boy left him, slaking a raging thirst. There was a guard on his cabin still, for the door had been locked after Solly entered and he had to shout for it to be opened before he could get out. McMullen heard the key turn and two pairs of footsteps departing along the alleyway. His wounded arm burned like fire but the pain in his head was gone and he could move his head with only trifling discomfort, he found. But he was tired, very tired. Too tired to care about his hopeless future, let alone assess the chances of escape from his present predicament. Above him on deck there was intermittent shouting and sometimes a snatch of song – *Hermione* was no longer a ship of inhuman silence. But in spite of this and the sting of his wound he fell into a deep sleep.

He woke, reluctantly, to find Solly at his side with a mug of soup and two thick slices of bread. He raised himself, with a wince as the weight came on his wounded arm, and ate his supper in silence, with no more than a word of thanks to Solly and a sleepy comment, as he handed him the empty mug, that the soup was good soup.

'I'm cook now, thir,' said Solly, beaming. 'No one in thickbay now – no more flogging now, thir.'

He blew out the cabin lantern and departed. No more flogging, McMullen echoed to himself as he lay back on his cot. Whatever was lost, that was gain. Lucy Preston at least would account it so. Would she think the price that had to be paid too great? Would she grieve that John McMullen, in paying his share, would never see her again? But even on this theme his thoughts lost coherence, and before he knew it sleep had overtaken him once more.

The next time he woke it was to find grey daylight peering through the crack of the doorjamb from the alleyway and the frame of his hanging cot rasping against the bulkhead. Overhead there was the stamping and yo-ho-ing of men hauling on sheets or halyards. Evidently the wind had strengthened; and at once McMullen was asking himself whether it was still a fair wind for the course to La Guayra. Gone now were the confused reflections of last night. He could set the ugly past behind him and coldly sum up his present situation: a proscribed outlaw by his own act, he was prisoner in a ship which was to be handed-over traitorously to the enemy – an event which, since he hadn't the slightest chance of preventing it, he was determined neither to take part in nor to witness. Escape was his immediate concern. If he could only effect that he cared little for what the future might hold, dark though it must be. And escape seemed on the face of it to be impossible.

He lay for a few minutes flexing his muscles and trying the movement of his wounded shoulder, his mind working clear and fast. Escape when *Hermione* was alongside in La Guayra port was a possibility that could be dismissed at once; not only would he have to evade the ship's company but there was also the problem of hiding or running in an enemy town of which he had no knowledge. It must be before that, then. And before the frigate entered harbour, if he wanted to get away unseen. He set himself to recollect as best he could the chart of the south-eastern Caribbean, wishing he had given it more attention when he and Edward Hamilton had studied it months ago in the captain's cabin.

He could make a fair mental picture, he found. The long chain of the Windward Islands stretching down from the north to Trinidad and the coast of the Main, and that coast – all the territories of Imperial Spain – running away westward in great bays and promontories for a thousand miles and more behind its protective fringe of islands large and small, Margarita and Tortuga, Grand Cayo and Curaçao and Aruba. On the mainland of Spanish America (about due south of Grand Cayo, he thought) was the mountain city of Caracas, capital of the province that Christopher Columbus had named Venezuela. Below it on the coast was La Guayra, its port. According to what Garbutt had told him yesterday, *Hermione* would pass through the chain of islands by the Grand Cayo passage, with fifteen leagues still to go to La Guayra; Garbutt had hoped to sight the island of Grand Cayo, he remembered, by noon of this present day, so the frigate might well pass within five or six miles of it. McMullen was a strong swimmer, but even with a calm sea he couldn't swim that distance. And there was his wounded arm.

Suddenly conscious of urgent need, he moved himself gingerly to the edge of the cot and slid to the deck, with some difficulty because of the frigate's steep heel. His legs supported him this time, though the few steps he had to take to the can in the corner were made a trifle shakily, and his spirits rose as he stood over the can. A sore arm and a stiff neck wouldn't stop him from taking a chance of escape, however desperate, if it came.

Footsteps sounded in the alleyway and he scrambled back onto the cot in a hurry, finding his left arm fully usable despite the pain. By the time the door was unlocked, admitting Garbutt, he was lying motionless with his eyes closed.

'Mr McMullen!' said Garbutt. 'You awake, sir?'

'Yes.'

He spoke in a faint voice. It would be foolish to admit to his recovered strength. He remembered making some silly threat about jumping overboard; likely enough a light fever caused by his wound had led to that.

'Your breakfast's on the way, sir,' Garbutt said awkwardly. 'Solly brought it at eight bells but you was fast off an' he let you lie. Feelin' a mite better, I hope?'

'I feel very weak,' McMullen lied, in a whisper.

'Aye? Like me to help you over yonder?' Garbutt jerked his head towards the corner of the cabin.

'No.'

Garbutt went to the can and seemed to inspect it. McMullen hastily forestalled any comment with a question.

'What's the time now?'

'Comin' up to four bells, forenoon watch.' The seaman hesitated. 'Maybe it's no good news to you, sir, but Grand Cayo's two leagues off the larboard bow, a'ready. The wind shifted northerly in the middle watch, blowin' half-a-gale,' he went on. 'It's fallin' off now an' we've run through a couple of rain squalls, but we're like to come into La Guayra before nightfall.'

'And what then? Am I to remain a prisoner on board?' McMullen inquired bitterly.

Garbutt rubbed his chin with a rasping sound. 'See here, sir,' he said slowly. 'I mislike puttin' you under lock an' key, you an' me havin' been shipmates in the old *Lion*. But it's been decided and that's that. The lads know you've turned agin 'em an' you're to be kept close.'

'Why?'

'Why, sir, 'cause there ain't one among us as can speak the Dons' lingo. You can. We need you to speak for us in La Guayra, to the admiral or the governor or whatever he calls himself. But there's this I'll do. If you was to give your word not to make a run for it – '

'I shall do nothing of the kind!'

'But you stood in with us at the start, sir,' Garbutt pleaded. 'You're with us now, for good or ill. Your word would help you, as well as us, spoken to the governor.'

'I shall give no parole and I shall speak no word to the governor.'

McMullen was aware that he was lessening his already slender chances of escape, but though he had no scruples about feigning weakness he could never bring himself to break his parole, if his life depended upon it. He raised himself on his right elbow and spoke sternly, forgetting his pretended lack of strength.

'Hear what I say. I stood in with you – yes, because there was to be no shedding of blood. That, Garbutt, I had on your own assurance. Whether willingly or not, you betrayed me and murder was done. I owe you and your companions nothing, nothing at all, and you, Harry Garbutt, owe me reparation for that betrayal. I think you're an honest man. If you were a just one you'd have me put ashore, at the least, before we reach La Guayra.'

He had been watching the man's face in the half-light as he spoke; but Garbutt, with a sudden movement, had turned away when he spoke of betrayal. In the short silence that followed his words there came from overhead a dull roar like the rolling of muffled drums; the beat of a tropical rainstorm on the deck.

'You know that ain't possible, sir.' Garbutt spoke without looking round. 'Even supposin' I – ' He checked himself and swung round, his lined face hard as stone. 'You can walk as far as that there can, you've told me you'll jump overboard, you won't give your parole.' Someone banged on the cabin door. 'That means you're locked in here till a way's found o' bringin' you round to our side, d'ye see?'

He went to the door, unlocked it to admit Solly Crump, and was gone without another word.

Solly brought in with him a waft of cold salt air and a shower of spattered drops from the officer's boat-cloak he had thrown over head and shoulders. From beneath the cloak he produced, with a wide grin, a steaming bowl of burgoo and a mug half-full of grog. McMullen sat up and made himself eat the burgoo slowly, between sips of grog; there was a possibility – he would have liked to call it a certainty – that this was the last meal he would eat on board *Hermione*. That it was likely to be the last he would ever eat he accepted with grim resignation. Desperate was a mild description of the plan he had determined upon, and it had to be put into action within the next hour.

When Solly had gone, taking with him the empty bowl and mug, he listened to the footsteps – Solly's and those of the man on guard who had let him out of the cabin – as they went the short distance along the alleyway. No footsteps returned; the guard had stopped, either at the foot of the ladder leading to the after-deck or on deck at its head. Probably he was doing a double sentry-duty, for the liquor store where the rum casks were kept was on this deck and the prudent Meyer would post a reliable guard near it. There was perhaps one chance in ten that the man would be standing at the head of the short ladder, round a corner and out of sight of the quarter-gallery, when McMullen made his attempt; but he must be prepared to deal with him if he was closer at hand. The quarter-gallery on the larboard side of the stern, where below the small heavily-glazed windows was the square hinged port used as an officers' privy, gave his only hope of escape.

He slid from the cot to the deck and stood, this time without any tremor of the leg-joints. Between him and the quarter-gallery the only barrier apart from the guard was the locked door, and he knew the lock to be a stout one. He put his ear to the door-jamb, but the ceaseless drumming of the rain on the hollow deck prevented him from detecting sounds in the alleyway and he knelt instead to open his sea-chest. From among his surgical instruments he took his largest knife, of finest steel by Huntsman of Sheffield. The lock was an ordinary mortice lock and time and the working of the ship's timbers had widened the jamb, so it was easy to insert the steel point well in against the flat of the bolt and obtain a modicum of leverage. Cautiously, pausing to listen between each essay, he worked the blade until at last he felt and saw the bolt begin to slide back. He withdrew the knife without springing the lock and before replacing it made a quick inspection of the sea-chest's contents. Nothing here heavy enough for a stunning blow – but the silk handkerchief would be quieter and more certain. He put the handkerchief in his breeches pocket and sat down on the sea-chest to make a mental rehearsal of his plan.

The *rafale* of the downpour filled the cabin with sound. McMullen had experienced the autumn rains of these waters before; he remembered Edward Hamilton's theory that the nearness to the coast of the Main of the Cordillera, as the Spaniards called the great range of mountains, caused the clouds that gathered at this season of the equinox to discharge above the coastal seas. More to the point of his present intention, such discharges might last for days at a time, which added to his chances of evading pursuit if that should be put in hand. But first he had to leave the ship. He set forth in his mind the detail of that.

A blanket on the cabin deck for a start, to muffle the noise as he emptied the sea-chest, which must then be securely locked, empty. It was a solid box of seasoned oak, not brassbound as some others were, and should have a good margin of buoyancy. Then the knife to the lock, the bolt drawn carefully and the door opened sufficiently to allow a quick look into the alleyway. If the sentry was invisible, pick up the sea-chest and – in stockinged feet as he was now – dash round to the quarter-gallery. The privy port unbolted, the chest flung down, and he himself would drop the dozen or so feet into the sea. Swimming with an arm over the chest –

He stopped suddenly in his scheming, aware of a high-pitched cry just audible over the rain's drumming – the masthead lookout's hail. Land in sight? Or a sail? If it was the latter, she must have come close to be sighted in the poor visibility of heavy rain. Much shouting on deck followed the

hail, and McMullen felt the slow lurch and shudder of the hull
as the frigate turned into the wind – she was heaving-to. Now
there sounded above the other noises the yells and yo-ho's of
men hauling on ropes, and a few moments later a shout whose
words came clearly to his ears: 'Lower away!'

It was another ship, then, and a boat was putting off to her.
A Spanish vessel for a certainty, this near the Main. The
attention of everyone on deck would be drawn by this
encounter – should he make his attempt *now*? No. The boat
had been lowered on the larboard side and the oarsmen in her
were more than likely to see him as he plunged from the
quarter-gallery. And while a boat was in the water his
recapture was a probability. Moreover, his rough calculations
had persuaded him that he must wait another hour before
Hermione's course brought her within swimming distance of the
island.

Finding that excitement had set his heart pounding fast,
McMullen took a deep breath and sought to resume his
methodical planning, not without distraction from the gabble
of voices on deck – the whole ship's company, he thought,
must be gathered there to stare through the pouring rain after
their boat. Assume, then, that his luck was out, that the glance
into the alleyway discovered the guard alert and close at hand.
Back into the cabin, a shout or a scream to bring the man
rushing in, and then from behind the open door the lightning
move with the silk handkerchief, throttling him into
insensibility. It was an operation, he reflected wryly, in which
he had had no practice; but it would have to be done with
deftness and precision. Given its success, the quarter-gallery
and the plunge followed, the sea-chest – he was confident he
could hold on to it with his injured arm and swim with the
other – and the beginning of a watery journey which he had
only the slenderest chance of completing.

Judging by the frigate's movement as she lay hove-to, there
was only a very slight sea running; but this might rise during
his long swim and overwhelm him. Grand Cayo, if memory
served him, was ringed by coral reefs; the breaking surf might
pound him to pieces. But his worst enemy, he told himself, was
a thing for which medicine had no name. On more occasions

than one McMullen had tended men hauled out of the sea after prolonged immersion, unscarred by any wound, only to have his revivifying ministrations frustrated by simple cessation of the heartbeat. And this in Caribbean waters, whose comparative warmth he had himself measured as between 75 and 80 degrees on Herr Fahrenheit's scale. Doubtless the falling rain was considerably lower in temperature –

The rain! In it the visibility would be mightily reduced – for a swimmer at wave-level perhaps no more than a few yards. How could he hope to steer himself blindly, without chart or compass, to an island several miles away?

He stood up, appalled at this tardy perception of an obstacle that appeared to end all chance of survival. As he did so there came a renewed shouting from the deck overhead and then a slight thud as something struck the frigate's hull amid a chorus of jubilant yells. The boat had returned, and quickly. By the outburst of cheering that followed it seemed she had brought good news for the mutineers. A voice bellowed orders and the cheering was superseded by a babble of excited talk accompanied by a rush of feet across the deck. Someone growled a command in the alleyway outside the cabin, the door was unlocked, and Garbutt stepped in with a single quick stride.

'Not a second to waste – you're leavin' now,' he snapped; his glance swept the cabin. 'Got anything to force a lock?'

Amazement held McMullen rigid for a moment only. He stooped, whipped open the sea-chest, and produced his knife.

'That'll do.' Garbutt took it and dropped it just inside the door. 'That's how you got out o' here.'

'But how – '

'Listen!' Garbutt gripped his wrist and spoke with fierce intensity. 'A Spanish *guarda costa* – nearly ran her down. We h'isted a white flag and sent away the gig. She's goin' to lead us into La Guayra. We're gettin' under way now.' The frigate's hull began to tilt slowly as he spoke. 'The lubbers have left the gig alongside, painter made fast to the mizen shrouds. I'm goin' for'ard now and I shall cast it off as I pass – they'll think it worked adrift. You'll count twenty, slowish, and then overboard. Better drop from – '

'From the quarter-gallery privy. Garbutt – come with me.'

'No, sir. I'm tryin' to pay off a debt. Mast an' lugs'l lashed under the thwarts. Wind's still due north an' course for land is south. They'll h'ist her inboard any minute so I'll go now. Good luck, sir!'

His grip shifted to McMullen's hand and loosed it.

'My thanks,' McMullen said quickly. 'Garbutt – '

But Garbutt was gone, leaving the door open behind him. McMullen never saw him again.

3

... *eighteen – nineteen – twenty*. McMullen peered out into the alleyway, saw that it was deserted, and bolted to the right along it. The inward-slanting windows of the quarter-gallery were almost vertical because of *Hermione*'s list as she came round to starboard, and his stockinged feet slithered on the tilted deck. He drew the bolt of the square port and it swung open above swirling grey-green water a dozen feet below. In the infinitesimal moment of time before he let himself drop ugly presentiments flew through his mind. Garbutt would be intercepted before he could cast-off the gig's painter – or he would be too late and they would have started to hoist her inboard – there would be no boat, then, and he would drown. He struck the water feet first and the sea closed over his head.

Underwater, his body was pushed strongly sideways and he was aware of some large dark mass thrusting past him – *Hermione*'s rudder, that would be. He kicked himself upward and broke surface. The chill of the sea-water had been hardly perceptible, but the densely-falling rain felt icy cold on his head. Its heavy drops raised a multitude of tiny fountains as they hit the long smooth swell on which he rose and fell peering anxiously for a sight of the gig. Above him the frigate's stern, a towering wall, seemed to shrink and fade as she drew away, soon vanishing altogether into the grey veil of rain. And still there was no sign of her boat; McMullen felt the utter indifference of Nature to his fate, alone here in the heaving seas and blinded by the rain, and had to fight down a rising panic. Treading water, he raised himself as high as he could, turning his body through a full circle to scan the few fathoms' radius of his restricted horizon. A streak of darker grey yonder – a trick of the light on a wave-crest. Or – was it? He swam a few strokes in its direction and raised himself again. It was the boat. In thirty seconds he had his hands on the gunwale, edging round to the stern with no little hurt to his wounded arm. A heave and a kick and he was sprawling in the sternsheets. He got himself onto the stern thwart and sat for some moments to collect his thoughts and consider his position.

Hermione's gig was primarily a pulling boat; a stout clinker-built sea-boat capable of carrying sixteen men and pulling eight oars. Like *Surprise*'s gig, in which McMullen had made many a short passage, she carried a stumpy mast which could be stepped for'ard to bear a lugsail of no great area and so could enlist the wind's help when it blew from astern or on the quarter, though being keel-less she would make more leeway than headway when it came from any other direction. *Mast an' lugs'l lashed under the thwarts.* They were there, as Garbutt had said they would be. And where was Garbutt now? Still at liberty among *Hermione*'s new masters, or shot – maybe hanged – for conniving at a prisoner's escape?

McMullen, rain streaming down his face as he adjusted the soaking bandage on his arm, spared a moment's thought for the man who had given him the chance of escape. He had liked Garbutt and could sympathise with his dilemmas of loyalty; and though it had probably been his own accusation of betrayal that had brought the man to the point of aiding him Garbutt had taken grave risks in doing so. No doubt he had ordered the sentry to leave the alleyway and no doubt the man would report that, as soon as the evasion was discovered. And even if he had managed to cast-off the gig's painter unobserved, the coincidence of the boat's going adrift just as the prisoner broke out of his cabin was not likely to go unremarked. It looked as though Garbutt's fate was sealed. McMullen saluted him mentally as an honest man caught in a web of perverse circumstances; and reflected with half a smile that the same terms could fairly be applied to himself.

He shivered suddenly. The northerly breeze that drifted the rain across the mottled waves was chilling his wet body, light though it was. *Wind's still due north an' course for land is south.* It sounded simple enough. If that wind held steady and the sea rose no higher the veriest lubber could hardly avoid making landfall somewhere on the thousand-mile-long shoreline of South America's north coast. But how far was he from it? Fifty miles, a hundred? The distance was as uncertain as the hazards of wind and weather he might encounter. What was certain was that many long hours of sailing in an open boat lay before him. It was most unlikely, he thought, that the frigate would put about and beat back to look for him, and if she did she would hardly locate him in such thick weather. He had better get under way without delay, all the same.

The knife-slash in his arm had reopened and bled a little but the tightened bandage had amended that and he could use the arm freely. The mutineers had left the oars lying carelessly across the thwarts. He laid these together, and when he had unlashed the mast with its rolled sail and yard used the lashings to secure the oars. Even in her brief passage to the *guarda costa* and back the gig had taken in so much rainwater that it lapped back and forth across the bottom-board as the boat rocked on the swell. He knelt and scooped some up in his palm to taste it; it was slightly brackish but drinkable. A continuance of the rain would at least free him from fear of thirst.

Rudder and tiller were stowed at the side of the small locker beneath the stern thwart. He shipped the rudder and then investigated the contents of the locker. It held only the sea-boat's canvas bag, with the customary items: marline-spike and hammer; palm and needle and spunyarn; leadline and tallow; a square of copper for a tingle with a square of fearnought to go with it, and a little bag of copper nails. These, the shirt and breeches and stockings he wore, and the gig (he could regard her as a prize taken from the Spaniards) were now all he possessed in the world. The thought brought a grim smile to his lips as he took the mast and its gear for'ard.

With the halyard rove and the backstays in position, he stepped the mast and secured the stays. He led the sheets aft before hoisting the flapping brown sail, then stumbled back to the sternsheets and drew in the sheets. The sail filled, the gig answered to her rudder. With the wind right aft she began to forge steadily forward, lifting and descending over the grey-green furrows. Raising his face to the falling rain, McMullen drew a deep breath that was an inarticulate prayer of thanks. He was free and in control of his fate again. That the future was an utter blank seemed, for the moment, a small thing compared with this.

As he had expected from the mast being stepped so far for'ard, the gig had no weather-helm at all – he could loose the tiller and she would hold her course without any tendency to turn into the wind. While this was an excellent quality in her for his present purpose of running free, it meant that in effect he could do nothing else; if the wind by some freak shifted to the south he would be blown northward, out to sea again. His only hope in such a case would be to take to the oars. McMullen very much doubted whether his injured arm would hold out for long under such a strain, for the oars were long and heavy, being of course intended for single-oar pulling. It was comforting to know that the prevailing winds in these waters were the north-east Trades, and that if they veered or backed (as now) in unsettled weather it would not be for long. Moreover, a shift of the wind from north to north-east would not prevent him from reaching the coast but merely ordain a longer voyage and a landing farther west.

And still the rain poured down, its close forest of silver stems ever retreating before the gig's thrusting bow. McMullen's lank black hair was plastered to his head and discharged runnels of water inside his drenched shirt as he sat with an arm on the tiller and an eye on the sail, but though he felt the chill of the falling rain he was not excessively cold; the following wind was almost lost in the gig's forward progress and the light waft that blew past him was if anything warmer than the rain. The sail, intended as no more than an aid to the oarsmen when the wind chanced to come from astern, was a loose-footed standing lug and inadequate for a heavy boat like the gig. As she dipped and rose over the long smooth swell he tried to estimate her speed and decided she might just be making three knots. Take the distance as a hundred miles and assume these conditions unchanged, he meditated, and he was going to spend a day and a half at the tiller with no opportunity for sleep. The hours of physical relaxation enforced by his injuries could perhaps be counted among his blessings, as could Solly's last ample mess of burgooo.

On, steadily on, over the long hillocks of sea into the grey opacity of rain. McMullen's watch was with all the rest of his possessions, in the sea-chest aboard *Hermione*, and he could only guess at the passage of time. Two hours, perhaps, had gone by when he noticed the perceptible increase in the amount of water swilling about on the bottom-boards. He was reasonable sure that the volume of rain was responsible and that the hull was staunch, but if this shifting ballast much increased it could be an extra hazard in the event of worsening weather. There had been no baler or panikin in the locker or under the stern thwart where it would usually be kept but he might have overlooked it in the bows. Using the sheets to lash the tiller amidships, he scrambled for'ard, peering beneath the thwarts as he went; but there was no baler, nor anything that could be used as one.

The gig had sailed herself comfortably during his absence from the helm – another blessing to count, no inconsiderable one for a single-handed mariner. He watched her for a while, leaving the tiller lashed, and then took off the sopping bandage and replaced it more to his satisfaction. By now the chill of continuous drenching was penetrating to his bones and he was shaken by bouts of shivering; but he took little account of these, remembering a remark of Doctor Hunter's that violent shivering was merely the body's way of renewing lost warmth. His thoughts, as the long minutes flowed on with the heaving rollers, dwelled on the past; on William Hunter and the Great Windmill Street lectures, on his first ship as a naval surgeon, on *Surprise* and Edward Hamilton – a good friend, never to be seen again – and on Lucy Preston, who also could be no more than a memory now. But the future he resolutely declined to consider at all. Such consideration had no basis to work on and so could only be idle speculation. He would face the future when he could see something of it. There was a good deal of the pragmatist about John McMullen.

But if he denied the future access to his thoughts he could not bar the immediate past. The events of two nights ago and of the days that led up to them passed through and through his mind as he crouched at the tiller, his teeth clenched to stop their chattering. The few yards of shifting water ahead of the gig, the hanging screen of rain that retreated before her advancing bows, were stage and backdrop for the vivid re-enactment he projected upon them again and again. The floggings, the deaths by falling from the yard, the horrid scene in Pigot's cabin when the dying captain was thrust bleeding out of the stern window, all passed before him in endless succession. And always it was upon the figure of the ship's surgeon – an actor taking part at short notice in this drama – that his critical faculties were bent. Should he, or could he, have acted otherwise than he did? Again he saw himself confronted with the reality of impending mutiny and facing the decision it involved. It was here that he needed reassurance. The verdict of the Navy in which he served he knew already, and accepted it; the verdict of his own conscience was, to McMullen, the one that mattered, and this he must have clear and definite before he could face the unknown future.

The grey veil ahead of him darkened. Imperceptibly the rain slackened, the silver lances dissolving into a fine mist that slowly merged into the gloom of dusk. Night had fallen when McMullen, raising his head, shook the water from his wet locks and with it the last of his doubts. He had been at fault indeed – in accepting Garbutt's judgment of the men's temper unchallenged. But with that set aside he had no cause to blame himself. He had made the only decision possible in the circumstances, had obeyed dictates of humanity that stood above those of Their Lordships at the Admiralty, had kept faith with his conscience. Freed from this burden, he could give more attention to his present predicament.

Night had fallen, a blackness made more absolute by the encircling mist. Such wind as there had been had dwindled to intermittent puffs that flapped the nearly invisible sail on its creaking yard. The gig rose and fell as though suspended in the mid-air of some viewless Acheron, and the surge of the waves along her sides was like the breathing of unseen monsters.

McMullen had to force himself to dismiss such fancies and initiate some sort of physical action, for the chill of continuous drenching had taken insidious hold of his body. With arms and fingers benumbed by wet and cold he succeeded in dragging off his sopping breeches and stockings and wringing them out, afterwards doing the same with his shirt. They would hardly dry in the all-pervading dampness of the mist but at least the heat of his body might warm them a little. It was then that he noticed with some concern that there was little or no warmth emanating from his body. The wind had dropped completely now and the gig wallowed in the shallow troughs and over the low crests without any steerage way. A spell at the oars, he thought, should restore the flagging circulation of the blood.

It was astonishingly difficult to make his fingers fasten on the knots of the wet lashings and casting-loose two oars took an unconscionable time. When at last he had the oars free it took almost as long to insert the thole-pins in their sockets and lift the oars into place, and he found the effort so exhausting that he had to rest for some time before he could attempt to grasp the handles of the heavy looms. It came to him that he had no idea of his direction; the wind, his sole guide, was gone and the bows might now be pointing north for all he knew – he might well be heading for Puerto Rico. This discovery struck him as so amusing that he laughed out loud.

McMullen regained control of himself with a violent effort of will. The crazy sound of his own laughter had shocked and startled him. A few score yards one way or the other, he told himself, could make little difference to his position and the primary need was to warm himself with exercise. A shadowy fear stirred in him. Was this the onset of the nameless enemy he had wondered about when he planned to escape by swimming?

The mere taking-hold of the oar handles demanded all his will-power to achieve, and to raise the heavy blades, push the looms forward, dip, and pull seemed a labour for Hercules himself. He set his teeth and succeeded, but knew with a sinking heart that there was little strength left in him. As he lay back on the stroke, his face upturned, he saw that the black void of the mist had opened overhead to reveal a circle of sky thronged with brilliant stars. Edward Hamilton, he reflected dully, would instantly have obtained his bearings from those sparkling constellations. He himself, a stranger to celestial navigation, was more at home with the circulation of the blood than with the circulation of the stars. This whimsy brought an impulse to silly laughter which he fought down angrily. What was happening to him?

He set himself to pull. Each stroke seemed feebler than the last and the enforced pauses between them grew longer. The mist vanished from the sea's face, leaving an undulating plain of blackness spangled with starry reflections. But the starlight was dimming. A mass of cloud spreading across the heavens erased the twinkling points one by one, reached and passed the zenith, cloaked sea and sky in utter darkness again. The gig's lugsail flapped once, twice, and streamed out with the sheets rattling against the thwarts.

McMullen, slumped across his oars, roused himself from a torpor of exhaustion, dimly aware of pain in his wounded arm and of the need to do something about the flapping sail. The boat was swaying wildly under the impact of the rising wind and in attempting to get his oars inboard he lost both of them overside. He crawled clumsily aft and managed to haul in both sheets through their fairleads, though twice his lifeless fingers let them slip. His mind seemed to be working as ineptly as his fingers but it could grasp the possibility that he might soon be unable to control either, so with infinite toil and using his teeth for the knots he secured the sheets at the fairleads and used the slack to lash the tiller amidships. As he fell limply across the tiller, totally exhausted by this final effort, rain slashed down out of the darkness; a cold rain that yet brought no sensation of cold because his labour at the oars had failed to warm him in the slightest degree.

And now the gig was lurching and leaping through waves that showed white teeth alongside in the darkness and at intervals lopped over the swaying gunwales to add to the considerable flood that seethed across her bottom-boards. It would take only a little more wind, a sea only a trifle higher, to send her to the bottom. Whither she was being driven or how long it would be before she foundered McMullen neither knew nor cared, for he was beyond fear as he was beyond pain and cold. He realised without emotion that he was very near to death; his failing senses, he thought, must mean that. As a man sinking in a slough strives desperately upward he strove to retain a hold on consciousness, and for a brief moment gained sufficient control of his mind to think rationally. It was characteristic of John McMullen that his last thought was an attempted diagnosis of his malady. The heart continuously pumping blood to outer surfaces continuously chilled. The blood returning chilled to the heart, minute after minute after minute, for hour after hour. And each time colder. Each – time –

The diagnosis remained incomplete. The gig drove on before the wind until the squall blew itself out. Slowly the sky cleared and the revealed stars grew paler before the approach of dawn. The huddled figure in the sternsheets knew nothing of the long black bar of land that rose over the horizon, fine on the gig's larboard bow; or of the white line of surf that flashed, as she drew nearer, in the first rays of the sun. Yet some spark of awareness must have lingered in John McMullen, for he dreamed a dream.

In his dream he could not see but only hear and feel. There were voices and the touch of hands, a sensation of being lifted and laid down. Then voices very close to him and again the touch of hands, this time stripping his clothes from him. The voices reminded him of Salamanca, somehow. There seemed to be an interval in his dream before he felt the slow growth of warmth in him, warmth that came from a source pressed close against him. He found he could move limbs and head with this returning warmth. His hands groped across naked flesh, his cheek rested against a woman's breasts.

This much only he remembered afterwards, for a dreamless unconsciousness rose over him like a flood.

CHAPTER FIVE

A Man Called Juan

1

Captain Hiram Dinneker of the schooner *Martha Phelps*, lounging in a hammock-chair on his after-deck, ejected a thin brown stream of tobacco-juice overside. His chair was placed close to the lee rail so that he could do this at intervals without endangering his spotless planking.

'Why I'm leaving all this,' he observed, breaking a long silence, 'I'm goldarned if I know.'

With a gesture of a hand the colour of teak he indicated the dazzling blue sea-plain of the Caribbean, smooth as silk, that spread away beneath a cloudless sky to the horizon on the larboard hand, a horizon rimmed with a thin line of brilliant green.

'A man kin stay away from his home city just so long, mebbe,' suggested Captain Hornback, slumped in a second hammock-chair beside him with a straw sombrero tilted over his long nose and the long cigar that stuck out beneath it.

'Aye,' said Captain Dinneker. 'But – back to Boston, with winter in the offing, Tom. Snow driving over Copp's Hill and the sleds grinding slush in Washington Street.' He sighed. 'Well, I guess I'm plumb crazy. Keep her full-and-bye, you black rascal,' he added over his shoulder to the man at the wheel.

'Yassah – full-an'-bye, sah,' said the negro with a wide grin.

The schooner was closing the Venezuelan coast at an angle, with a light but steady breeze filling her sails. Though the morning sun was far short of its full height it was already hot enough to justify Captain Dinneker's costume, which was merely a pink-striped shirt and a belt with a clasp-knife; his companion wore a white shirt and loose cotton trousers. Both men sported a fringe of whisker reaching from the ears round the bottom of the chin, but whereas Captain Hornback's whiskers were blond and fluffy Captain Dinneker's were grizzled and bristly.

The anomaly of a vessel with two captains aboard was explained by the fact that Hornback was a passenger, or more accurately a temporary unofficial supercargo. His trading schooner *Mystic* had reached Puerto Cabello from Hispaniola two weeks ago and was now there refitting, a hurricane encountered west of Aves Island having badly damaged her spars besides drowning several of her crew. When his repairs were completed he proposed to transfer his trading activities to the coast of the Main; and Captain Dinneker, who had traded along that coast for five years and had now decided to return to his native Boston, had agreed (for a consideration) to place him in touch with his trading contacts.

'This Irico we're heading in for,' said Hornback now, swivelling his cigar from one side of his mouth to the other. 'It'll be logwood there, I calc'late?'

'Logwood mainly, but there's boucanned meat from the *llanos* to be had, and fresh fish too if you're sailing direct to Guayra.' Dinneker dispatched a brown stream neatly into the Caribbean. 'A little gold even, now and again.'

Hornback sat up. 'Gold?'

'No call to get in a sweat, captain. No reefs in Irico, just the dust. The *mestizos* pan it, up on the Tocaru rapids, and they work darned hard for every grain. There ain't much.'

'First time I heard of *mestizos* working hard,' Hornback said. 'Some Don Diego stand over 'em with a whip?'

Dinneker shook his head. 'There's nary a Diego in a hundred miles from Irico. It's the man they call Juan, and he don't use whips.'

'The man you say is English?'

'That same.'

'Plenty of deserters from British warships around this patch of ocean,' said Hornback. 'Likely he's one of 'em. Or mebbe worse,' he added suddenly. 'How long's he been at Irico?'

'Two years to my knowledge.' Dinneker glanced sharply at him. 'What's on your mind, Tom?'

Hornback drew on his cigar and blew out a cloud of smoke. 'The big frigate that came into Cabello two days afore we sailed – you went on board of her. *Nostra Senora de* something they're calling her but she was the *Hermione*, wasn't she? British frigate that mutinied just about two years ago. You remember?'

'Sure I remember. I was in Guayra when her crew brought her in. She had a dead man hanging from her bowsprit-end, some fellow who'd been caught helping one of their prisoners to escape.' Dinneker shook his head. 'Dirty business, mutiny, for all it meant one less fighting-ship for the goddam Britishers.'

'What happened to her crew?'

'The Governor would have naught to do with 'em – sent 'em packing every man.'

'And that was two years ago,' Hornback said slowly. ''Bout when this Juan turned up at Irico. I heard in Castries there's two or three dozen of the *Hermione* mutineers been taken. Hanged at Kingston. And the British are offering a bounty for any more that's –'

'There'll be no truck with the British!' interrupted Dinneker, sitting up and glaring at his companion.

Hornback looked surprised. 'We ain't at war no longer,' he said a trifle querulously. 'We licked 'em and it's done with. Last I heard, President Adams had sent a note to Bonaparte to say he don't like the way he's behaving.'

Captain Dinneker seemed about to make an angry reply but checked himself. Instead he removed the quid from his mouth, inspected it critically, and tossed it over the side.

'Captain Hornback,' he said solemnly, 'you and me's got on pretty well so far and I'll be sorry if we disagree over the British. I'll tell you straight I hate 'em like poison. 'Twas a British frigate raiding into Boston roads back in '77 that sank my father's schooner with my father in her. The *Martha Phelps* never touches at a British port, I never touch a penny of their trade, and the more seamen that mutiny and desert from their vessels the better I'm pleased.'

'Why, sure. But –'

'Hear me out. I'll not lift a hand to help the British, bounty or no bounty. What you do's your own affair. But I'll be very considerable disobliged – to put it no stronger – if you let out a word to anyone, British or Spanish, consarning this man Juan. English or Dutch or Eskimo, he's a good friend of mine. He's worked up the trade at Irico and it's good trade. You've heard of killing the goose that lays the golden eggs. And what the British Admiral at Jamaica don't know he can't grieve over. Let sleeping dogs – '

'Yay, yay, yay!' Hornback broke in hastily. 'I read the signal, captain. My oath on it, I won't drop a word about Juan. But how in the creation does he come to be at Irico?'

Captain Dinneker did not immediately reply. He had got to his feet and was gazing ahead along the deck, where the men of the deck-watch, all negroes or mulattoes, lay or squatted up in the bows. The schooner's long bowsprit slowly rose and fell as she slid smoothly across the almost imperceptible swell, the tapering jibs dazzling white in the strong sunlight. She was steadily closing the coast now and the green horizon was discernibly a long strip of tropical forest, ending far to the right in an olive-green rise of higher land devoid of trees. The darker blotch that interrupted the even greenery of the forest showed where mangroves attended the outflow of a river, and the sapphire of the intervening sea was discoloured with broad tendrils of muddier water. The captain went for'ard and up the foremast shrouds, his shirt-tails flapping in the breeze, and vanished above the curve of the fore-mains'l, returning after five minutes to speak a brief word to the helmsman and settle himself again in the hammock-chair.

'No leading-marks,' he explained, 'and a couple of reefs, coral, awash at low water. They're marked on that chart I gave you but you want to get your own two eyes on 'em, coming in. There'll be buoys there some day, when Irico's a port and Juan the harbourmaster,' he added with a chuckle.

'I was asking how he came here in the first place,' said Hornback.

'Aye, you were. Well, it's a mighty queer yarn.'

Captain Dinneker fumbled in a leather pocket on his belt, drew out an oblong of black plug, and bit off a chew.

'A body might as well question an oyster as Juan,' he said, working his jaw luxuriously, 'but I got it out of an old *mestizo* who had about as much Spanish lingo as me. Souzel was his name. He's dead now, and his daughter Quita, last year. Marsh ague – they all die of it, soon or late.'

He paused to work his quid into a position more conformable with speech.

'Well, now. Seems it was a morning two year ago – in '97, 'twould be – when Souzel and his girl was out early along the shore. Just where the mangroves end there's a fair stretch of beach with fair-sized breakers a-smashing on it. Out of the breakers come pitching a big boat with a man in it.'

'What sort of boat?' Hornback put in quickly.

'Ship's boat – a gig. And the man's dead, or so old Souzel reckons. Fishbelly-white and cold as marble. His daughter wouldn't have it so. They carried him up to their hut and stripped off what clothes he had on. Souzel was for pouring a lot of *ava* down his throat – that's the spirits they distil out of coconut, Tom, and you want to steer clear of it. Quita, she had another plan. She strips off too, stark, and claps herself down on top of him where he was lying.'

'Hi-*hi*!' crowed Hornback delightedly.

Dinneker nodded without smiling. 'Aye, I dare say. But the girl – I call her that but she was ten years older than him and big with it – the girl showed uncommon sense. I've seen it done north of the Banks, Tom, when a man was took off an ice-floe as near dead as makes no matter. Four Greenlanders of the crew stripped and packed round him close, for a good hour by the clock. And he was taking his spell at the wheel next day.'

Hornback raised his eyebrows but made no other comment. 'So she saved his life – Juan's life, eh? 'Cording to the story-books he ought to've married her.'

'The *mestizos* don't take much stock in marrying,' Dinneker said. 'The Jesuit missionaries have given Irico a miss, seemingly. But Juan took her for his woman until she died and I never heard that he looked at another wench.'

'Well, it sure is a ro-mance,' Hornback's close-set eyes flickered in a quick glance at his companion. 'I'll admire to see this Juan of yours.'

'You'll see him in thirty minutes. – Mister Castro! I'll have a lookout at the mainmast head.'

The mate, olive-skinned and mustachio'd, turned from the midships rail where he had been lounging and gave a yell that sent a black-skinned seaman up the shrouds.

'Juan knows I'm doo third week in September,' Dinneker explained. 'He puts a man on watch up on the hill above the village. We can load and sail inside of an hour.'

'You seem mighty confident he'll have a cargo for you, captain,' remarked Hornback.

'He's never let me down yet,' Dinneker got up from his chair. 'I've gotten the copies of the Irico manifests in the cabin.'

'Manifests?'

'Sure. Juan can read and write and we do business right and proper. You'd best take a look at 'em – get an idee of the barter values. Though you'll never find Juan trying any jiggery-pokery.'

Hornback tossed his cigar-butt over the rail. 'For a feller that riles so easy when a body mentions the British,' he remarked as they went below, 'you seem mighty taken with this Englishman, captain.'

'A good man's a good man, English or American,' Dinneker retorted sharply. 'It's kings and governments that riles me.'

When they came on deck again ten minutes later the place where the flat-topped wall of jungle gave way to bare hills above the shore was broad on the larboard bow and little more than two miles away. Through the heat-haze that danced above the water they could make out the line of white surf along the beach, and Dinneker pointed out the just-visible dots of the Irico huts on the hillside.

'Juan should have seen us by now,' he said. 'Mister Castro! You got a dead man at the masthead?'

Castro funnelled his hands to shout aloft but before he could do so the lookout hailed.

'Deck! Boats puttin' out from shore, sah!'

'What sort of boats, goldarn ye?' Dinneker shouted.

'*Canoas*, sah, big boat an' four raffs, sah.'

'That's better.' The captain turned to Hornback. 'That'll be logwood on the rafts.'

'And the big boat, that'll be the gig Juan come ashore in?'

'Aye. We'll take a stroll for'ard. Bear up a point,' he added to the helmsman.

The schooner's bows swung slowly to starboard until she was creeping along parallel to the coast. The two captains stood together right for'ard, staring ahead with eyes narrowed against the sun-glare.

'You don't want to come in any nearer than this,' Dinneker said; he spat overside. 'Fifteen to twenty fathom down there but inshore the coral banks come up. There's deep water off the river-mouth but you can get bitten to death by the devils they call mosquitoes as much as a mile off shore. There's the boats now. Reg'lar flotilla.'

The cluster of craft had attained a point right ahead of the *Martha Phelps*. As she came nearer the cluster resolved itself into a large boat with four laden rafts towing astern and half-a-dozen *canoas*. Dinneker gestured to the waiting mate.

'All right, mister – hatches off the main hold.'

At Castro's yell the hands set noisily to work knocking out wedges and stripping off the canvas hatch-cover.

'Not more'n five or six cords of logwood there,' Hornback commented, shading his eyes to study the rafts.

'Logwood's fetching a good price in Cabello. See here, Tom,' Dinneker added, 'I'd like a private word with Juan. When he comes aboard I'll introduce you, see, and then maybe you'll stay on deck to see the cargo taken in while we're in the cabin. I'll give you a hail. Then it's drinks for the three of us before we sail.'

Hornback nodded. 'You're the skipper. While you're jawing, why don't you tell him about the *Hermione* in Cabello – watch his face? I'll lay you five to one he was in her two year ago.'

'I'm not taking you.' Dinneker swung round abruptly to face aft. 'Stand by the sheets, fore and main. Helm a-lee.' The schooner came gently round into the wind, the sails on her two masts flapping and banging. 'Let go!' The anchor plunged and the cable rattled out through the hawse-hole. 'Veer – veer – bitt her there, mister.'

The *Martha Phelps* curtseyed to the pull of her cable and lay rolling lazily with the light breeze rippling her canvas, a long pistol-shot from the boats.

'Fifteen fathom and good holding-ground,' said her captain complacently. 'The current sets west a couple of knots so it ain't much good just heaving-to.'

Hornback's gaze was on the boats, now closing in with the gig and her tow escorted on either hand by *canoas*. A British warship's gig for certain, he was thinking.

'And that'll be the man called Juan,' he said aloud.

The man who stood erect in the gig's bows was naked except for a loincloth and his skin was the same dark golden colour as that of the *mestizos* in their little craft, whose blood was Spanish and Indian in varying proportions. Alone of them he had a beard, short and cut to a point, and his shoulder-long black hair was bound with a cotton fillet round his forehead.

'*Buenas dias, señor Juan,*' Dinneker called as the gig approached.

Juan raised a hand, palm outward. '*Buenos dias, señor capitan.* Did you bring the oak-galls?' he added in English.

'I've got 'em,' Dinneker shouted back, 'and one hell of a job I had to find 'em. What d'you want 'em for?'

'For the care of my people,' Juan answered; his lean face showed a fleeting smile. 'A styptic solution.'

He turned and spoke to the oarsmen in their own language, a mixture of Spanish and Indian dialect, and they ceased pulling. The gig and her tow drifted slowly towards the schooner's side.

'*His* people?' Hornback said, low-voiced. 'And what's this styptic?'

'He's a kinda mayor in Irico,' Dinneker muttered. 'Does some doctoring on the side, I reckon. – Fenders outboard, you there!'

'He don't talk like a foremast hand,' frowned Hornback. 'An officer, mebbe?'

Dinneker, intent on the business of getting the rafts alongside, made no reply. Ropes were thrown and made fast, the *canoas* under Juan's direction nosed the rafts against the side of the *Martha Phelps*. Juan swung himself over the rail to the schooner's deck and briefly grasped the hand Dinneker held out to him. His body was lean almost to emaciation; against the uniform golden-brown of his skin the raised cicatrice of a long scar on his left forearm stood out in pale relief.

'Thisyer's Captain Hornback, Juan,' said Dinneker. 'He'll be trading on this coast 'stead of me.'

Juan, about to shake hands with Hornback, checked the motion and faced the older man. 'You mean that?' he demanded. 'You're leaving the Main?'

'Aye. Back to Boston. Cabello to unload and take on stores, then away quick for the Windward Passage.'

'I'm sorry to hear it, captain.'

'But Captain Hornback here will take your trade same as I've been doing,' Dinneker assured him. 'His schooner – *Mystic*'s her name – will be off Irico in six weeks' time. That's so, captain?'

'Certainly, captain.' Hornback extended his hand a second time. 'Pleased to meet you, Mr Juan.'

Juan was slow to answer, as if he had to search memory for a forgotten formula.

'Your servant, sir,' he said as they shook.

'Same here,' said Hornback. 'Here's to a prosperous 'sociation, as they say. You're better equipped for trade than some along the Main, I notice. That gig, f'r instance. Ship's boat, I'd say. I've been in the Caribbean three year and I've only seen one vessel as might carry a boat like that. In Puerto Cabello it was, three days ago.'

'What vessel was that?' Juan inquired, displaying no more than polite interest.

Hornback stared hard at him. 'A captured English frigate, by name *Hermione*.'

There was perhaps a momentary flicker in the steady gaze that met his but the angular brown face was without expression. Juan was given no opportunity to speak, for Captain Dinneker, with a ferocious scowl at Hornback, broke in hastily.

'Business, Juan, business. I've little time to spare this morning. We'll go below – Captain Hornback'll keep an eye on the lading.'

Juan, without another glance at Hornback, followed him down to the cabin.

2

It was not the first time that John McMullen had been in Captain Dinneker's cabin, and on this occasion as on the others he experienced a painful emotion akin to homesickness. It was a small cabin lit by a skylight in the deckhead, with barely room for table and chair and the long locker-chest whose top made a seat. A sort of alcove in one side accommodated the captain's bunk, lockers along the bulkhead housed his belongings (including, as McMullen knew, some bottles of good Madeira) and there was a shelf of books high up on the after bulkhead. His gaze fastened avidly on that shelf. How long since he had opened a book! It was as if, in seating himself on the chest, he returned for a brief space to his native land from exile; to a place where men lived and thought and spoke as he had been used to do long ago. A prisoner allowed out of gaol to visit his family might feel as he did now. He tried without much success to thrust such fancies out of his mind as the captain, having taken down a thin ledger from the shelf, sat down facing him across the table.

'You got a reli'ble man to take charge?' he inquired, taking ink-horn and quill from a drawer.

'Tola's in charge,' said McMullen.

'That lad? Still in his teens, ain't he?'

'Tola's very intelligent for a *mestizo*. I'm teaching him to speak English. He's mastered enough of the language to deal with trading already.'

'Aye?' Dinneker dipped his quill and ran a finger down the ledger page. 'Well now, what's your will and what have you got?'

'Six cords of logwood, two quintals beef,' said McMullen briskly. 'There's fresh-caught fish if you can take it, about one and a half quintals.'

'No gold?'

'Not this time, captain. The river's been running too high

for panning. As for our needs – ' McMullen ticked them off on
his fingers – 'powder and shot, fish-hooks and line, two good
sheath-knives, a bolt of canvas.'

'Going to rig a sail on the gig, maybe?'

'No. We're constructing a new hut for a hospital. I want the
canvas for screens.'

'A hospital!' Dinneker was scratching little sums in the
margin of his ledger. 'You was a doctor once, I reckon,' he said
without looking up.

'I was a ship's doctor once,' McMullen said evenly.

There was a short pause while Dinneker, his lips moving
soundlessly, totted-up his sums. From the deck came shouts
and clattering as the logwood came aboard, and the schooner's
hull quivered as successive loads were shot down into the hold.
The captain took a sheet of paper and began to write on it.

'You'll get a keg of powder and one bag of scatter-shot.
Fishing-tackle, knives, canvas – I can supply 'em all but it'll
leave me short on the deal.' He pushed ledger and paper across
the table. 'Cast your eye on my figgers.'

'I'll take your word for it, captain. How much short?'

Dinneker pursed his lips. 'Half-an-ounce of dust would
cover it.'

'I've got that much ashore. I'll send a *canoa*.'

'Can't wait.' Dinneker took the paper and stood up. 'It's
past high water and by noon your goldarned current 'll be
setting westward two knots faster.' He mounted the steps of the
companionway and shouted for Castro to come and get the list
of Juan's requirements. 'Your oak-galls is in the bag with the
shot,' he went on, returning. 'Don't mix 'em up. – What I'm
aiming at is a quick passage back to Cabello. But see here,
Juan. I'll 'low you four days' credit for the dust, 'cause I'll be
off Irico again in four days time.'

McMullen showed surprise and pleasure. 'There'll be a
lookout on the hill and I'll have that half-ounce waiting. But I
thought you were homeward bound next voyage, captain.'

'So I am – and maybe I'm a darned fool.' The captain shook
his grey locks and fetched a sigh. 'It's just that I hanker after
the old place. Feel I want to walk across the Common again,
down past Frog Pool. Can't seem to sleep o' nights, thinking of

it. So it's across the Caribbean and out by the Windward Passage and the Bahamas. The *Martha Phelps* sails from Cabello two days from now. I shall take her out past Cape San Roman, which is west of Aruba, so it's but a long spit out of her way to call at Irico.' He paused. 'And maybe I've got another reason too.'

He seemed to deliberate within himself, rubbing his chin and frowning at the table. McMullen broke the short silence.

'You're going to make a quick turn-round at Puerto Cabello, then,' he remarked.

'Sure,' replied Dinneker absently. 'Everything on a split yarn – stores paid for and waiting to come aboard. Hornback's going to deal with the cargo when I've unloaded.'

'Hornback,' McMullen repeated. 'Captain Hornback's a friend of yours, captain?'

'Not to say a friend. We get on so-so. Tom Hornback's mighty sharp in the trading line. Hails from New Haven,' Dinneker added as if that explained Captain Hornback.

'He spoke of a – a vessel in Puerto Cabello. I believe he said she was called *Hermione*.'

The captain nodded slowly, his gaze steady on McMullen. 'She was the frigate *Hermione*, took from the British. I should know her – saw her brought into Guayra two year ago, crew in charge after a mutiny. Thisyer crew, Juan, had hanged one o' theirselves as he had helped an officer get clear away.' He paused. 'And I reckon you can tell me the name of the man they hanged.'

McMullen had let his head sink on his breast. Now he raised it and met the captain's hard stare coolly.

'His name was Garbutt,' he said. 'I was the man he helped to escape. I think you guessed I was from *Hermione*, captain.'

'Maybe. But what licks me now is why you're staying hid at Irico. If you was an officer and got away from the mutineers – '

'I condoned the mutiny,' McMullen broke in. 'I sided with the mutineers on condition that there was no bloodshed. They murdered the captain and a dozen others. They proposed to hand over to ship to the Spaniards. I protested and was held prisoner.'

'So there's a noose waiting for you same as for the others.'

Dinneker seemed to find an odd satisfaction in this. 'That's what I thought. Now hear me, Juan.' He leaned forward urgently. 'What happens to King George's ships is no consarn of mine. If the Dons use a British frigate agin the British Navy it suits me fine. But you're another matter – I've done business with you and I reckon you're square.'

'Thank you, captain,' McMullen said with a faint smile.

Dinneker ignored this. 'Take note, now. What I've just told you, Tom Hornback knows nigh as much as me about it. I've told you I'd rather see the *Martha Phelps* founder than touch at a British port or handle British trade in these waters. Hornback ain't so partickler. Where the money is, there he'll go after it – Castries, St George, and like enough Jamaica.'

'You don't think he'd – '

'Nothing. I don't think nothing – I'm telling you so's you can do the thinking. 'Cording to Hornback the British at Kingston have rounded-up some of the *Hermione* mutineers and they're offering a reward for the others – dunno how much but I reckon 'twould be more for an officer.'

It was very hot in the cabin. The captain passed a hand across his forehead and flipped the sweat from his finger-ends. McMullen, immobile as a figure in bronze, seemed not to feel the heat.

'I see,' he said slowly after a moment.

Dinneker set his elbows on the table and leaned forward, his eyes beneath their bushy brows intent on the other.

'In case you're thinking Irico ain't just as comfortable as it might be,' he said deliberately, 'here's a proposition for you. I could do with an extra hand for the Boston v'yage. Ship with me when we call in four days' time – '

'No!'

The interjection was involuntary and Dinneker ignored it.

'There'll be no questions asked in Boston,' he went on. 'I reckon you'll find our citizens more your kinda folks than a lot o' brown savages. You can make a fresh start – '

'No,' interrupted McMullen again, but this time more gently. 'It's a generous offer, captain, and I'm truly grateful. But I've made my life here and I'll live it out here.'

'It could end in a noose,' the captain muttered.

'I'll face that danger if and when it comes.'

'You're missing a chance. 'Tain't likely you'll get another.'

'I know it.' McMullen shook his head as if to rid it of some insidious doubt. 'My mind's made up. Let's change the subject. Did you learn what *Hermione* is doing in Puerto Cabello?'

Shrill cries and solid thuds from the deck told of hatch-covers being lowered into place. Captain Dinneker tugged at his whiskers, shrugged, and accepted the rebuttal of his plan with obvious dissatisfaction.

'I'd ha' thought you'd have had enough of that vessel,' he said gruffly. 'Aye – I can tell you a deal about *Hermione*. Went on board of her looking for my agent Hernandez. Hernandez is agent for the Spanish navy in Cabello and he had all the noos of her. Seems they're aiming to make her the strongest warship this end of the Caribbean.'

'How so?' McMullen demanded, frowning.

'They'll pierce her for six more guns, making her a forty-four. She'll carry four hundred men and that's with soldiers and artillery-men. She's to be called the *Nostra Senora de* something and a Don by the name of Raimond de Chalas takes the command.' Dinneker wagged his head, not without relish. 'Looks like King George's ships 'll get a walloping, up along the Windward Islands and thereabouts.'

McMullen's lean brown face had lost its stolidity. His eyes were bright with excitement and he sat erect and tense.

'When will she sail?' he asked sharply.

'Completes her refit middle of October, so Hernandez says. The buzz is she'll sail for the Havana.'

Captain Dinneker, a man of no great imagination, was none the less aware of the change that was taking place before him. The naked black-haired *mestizo* was looking and speaking as an officer in the Royal Navy might look and speak. Jacket and breeches, a clean shave and a neat queue tied with black ribbon, would have completed the transformation. At the back of his mind McMullen was mistily conscious of the same thing; he was thinking now as Edward Hamilton or Forbes Wilson might think.

'A forty-four-gun frigate, by God!' he exclaimed. 'And fast

with it. She has the heels of *Surprise* – Captain Hamilton told me so. We'll have nothing to touch her.' He drummed with his fingers on the table, his face frowning and intent. 'The Admiralty will have replaced *Hermione* but the Channel and Mediterranean Fleets have first call on the fast frigates. Captain, do you chance to know our current force on the West Indies station?'

'I don't know and I don't care,' Dinneker said roughly. 'It ain't *my* force.'

'But that matters little.' McMullen, ignoring the captain's retort altogether, brought his fist down on the table with a thump. 'It's the news that's important. It must reach the Admiral in Kingston at the earliest – ' He checked himself suddenly, realising his own impotence, then stabbed a forefinger at Dinneker. 'You could take it, captain! Jamaica's not far off your course to Boston.'

Captain Dinneker rose from his chair without replying, reached up to lay a hand on a small black book on the bulkhead shelf, and turned to glower down at McMullen.

'Thisyer book,' he said slowly and emphatically, 'is the Bible. For reasons you know of, I've sworn on this Bible never to set foot in a British port. I'd not lift a finger to – '

'Below there, captain!' 'A shadow darkened the companionway. 'Cargo aboard and hatches on.' Hornback came down into the cabin. 'What's keepin' you – business or the bottle?'

He spoke jovially but his little eyes swept suspiciously from one to the other. Dinneker stooped and opened a locker.

'Just onto the drinks, Tom,' he said, setting a bottle and glasses on the table. 'We'll up anchor soon as maybe.'

He poured Madeira. Hornback raised his glass.

'Here's to the gold you'll have for me next call, Juan,' he said.

McMullen's face had resumed its former impassivity. 'I will see what can be done, captain,' he said gravely.

There was little further talk, for Dinneker seemed anxious to get away. He contrived to leave Hornback in the cabin looking over the cargo list while he went on deck with McMullen.

'Heave the cable short, mister,' he said to the mate as they went to the rail.

The *canoas* lay waiting some little distance out, the gig with her tail of empty rafts was alongside. The young *mestizo* who held the gig in below the schooner's rail had fixed his eyes on McMullen as soon as he appeared.

'Call Pablo to come into the gig, Tola,' McMullen said in the Irico dialect. 'I shall return to the shore in his *canoa*.'

He turned and briefly gripped Captain Dinneker's outstretched hand before throwing a leg over the rail.

'Four days' time, then, captain,' he said, 'and half-an-ounce of gold dust to come.'

'My offer's still open,' Dinneker said. 'Think on it.' He turned away as McMullen dropped into the gig. 'Heave her in, mister! Back the jib, for'ard! Ease your sheets, main and fore!'

The huge booms creaked slowly over, the canvas flapped and filled. Before the anchor emerged dripping under her bows the *Martha Phelps* was gathering way on her eastward course to Puerto Cabello.

3

Between the sky's pearly blue and the deeper blue of the sea the level horizon shimmered uncertainly in the heat of a Caribbean noon. The north-east Trade breathed gently across the vast plain of water, scarcely flawing the surface of the long lazy swell. Far to eastward a sliver of white hung on the blue, slowly diminishing and fading. The man called Juan, sitting solitary in the *canoa* with his two-bladed paddle across the gunwales, watched the *Martha Phelps* until she was lost to sight in the haze of distance.

For two years he had been called Juan and the name had become part of himself as it had become part of his life in Irico. To be wrenched back into the personality of John McMullen, ship's surgeon, had left him greatly disturbed, brief though the experience had been. When, after the first few weeks, he had realised that fortune had brought him to a hiding-place as safe as any in the Caribbean he had deliberately set himself to merge into this new life; the old life, since he could never regain it, he had striven to forget, and with some measure of success. The brief contacts with the *Martha Phelps*, recurring as they did at long intervals, had brought their moments of nostalgia but he had been able to dash them aside. The use of English to simplify his bargaining with Captain Dinneker had been incautious; but the captain had accepted without comment his story that he was a wanderer who had chosen to make his home with the little settlement of *mestizos*. After these rare visits of the schooner he had always found it easy enough to revert to the ways of Irico, to live the life and speak the tongue of the semi-primitive folk who were his friends and companions. This morning in early September (he was oblivious of dates these days though he knew the year was 1799) had brought home to him the inescapable fact that he was still an Englishman, with an Englishman's loyalties and responsibilities.

No one, not excepting a ship's surgeon, could serve in a vessel commanded by Edward Hamilton without being infected with the captain's single-minded devotion to his Service. Under his aegis John McMullen had not only learned to hand, reef, and steer like any of his seamen but also to think as he and his lieutenants thought: that to defend England against revolutionary France and her allies it was necessary to strike fast and hard wherever the enemy was to be found. The tenets of the Navy remained in him unchanged, a hard core within the shell of Juan the *mestizo*, laid bare when the shell was cracked open as it had been this morning by Dinneker's news. The old feeling of guilt was still there too – the knowledge that by defying a basic rule of naval discipline he had aided in the capture of a British frigate by the enemy. For it was not, now, the deaths that had resulted from the mutiny that lay on his conscience; he had done what he believed to be right and if the course of affairs had gone awry it was not by his doing. It was the ship he thought of, *Hermione* in Spanish hands arming against his country. He was responsible for this, in part at least, and it would be in some sort a partial reparation if, through him, the news of her whereabouts and intentions could be got to the Admiral at Kingston.

The *Martha Phelps* had disappeared some time ago. The *canoa*, a light thing of wicker framework covered with the inner bark of a jungle tree, had gradually turned until its bow was pointing straight out to sea. As always, there was no white speck of sail on the empty expanse of blue. Jamaica, McMullen knew, was 700 miles to north-westward beyond that sea horizon; between him and Jamaica lay the islands of Curaçao and Aruba, fifty or sixty miles out, islands belonging to France's Dutch allies; eastward and farther out still the line of Spanish islands stretched. Close at his back was the long coastline of Spain's empire in the Americas; so that he was hemmed in by enemy territories. Doubtless there was much coming and going of ships between the islands but none of them passed within sight of the mainland, and those vessels sailing from La Guayra or Puerto Cabello for the Venezuelan gulf or Cartagena kept well below the horizon on their course to clear Cape San Roman. Captain Dinneker's two-masted schooner alone ventured to close the coral-rimmed coast west of the Tocuyo river.

With a deft stroke of his paddle McMullen spun the *canoa* so that he faced the line of the shore nearly two miles away. From here, looking across the smooth undulations of iridescent water, it appeared primeval, untrodden by the foot of man. Only an eye that knew what to look for could have discerned the moving specks at one point in the line of white surf, where gig and rafts were being hauled up on the beach, or the dots of paler brown on the hillside above that were the palm-thatched huts of Irico. For the watcher in the *canoa* everything he saw had a history and a meaning.

Reaching away to the left until it was lost in distance was the low green line of the forest, supplier of fruits and (latterly) meat, blotched along its foot by the darker mangroves where the marshy delta of the little Tocaru river met the sea. Fifty miles beyond that were the swamps of the much larger Tocuyo; and a further forty miles of similarly impassable terrain lay between the Tocuyo and the new naval seaport of Puerto Cabello. It was small wonder that no traveller by land ever reached Irico. McMullen's gaze returned to the place, nearly opposite to him across the water, where the forest thinned and ended in a rise of treeless ground. That was where he had been flung ashore from the gig, a carcass with no more than a faint spark of life in it. Quita had kept the spark alive with the warmth of her body, had brought him back from the threshold of death; and since he had nothing else to give her to show his gratitude he had given her the physical love she craved for. It must be nearly a year now since she had died, he reflected.

She had been a big woman, older than himself; coarse-featured, stolid, unintelligent. He remembered the animal smell of her, the roughness of her skin under his hands. Yet she had made a home for him, a stranger, in that squalid hut where the wizened old man her father lived with them, and in taking her for his woman he had won a rapid assimilation into their little community. It was the most primitive of human societies.

How the fifty-odd men, women, and children who composed the settlement of Irico came to be in that isolated place he had never discovered; they seemed to have no history or tradition, not even a religion. Their Spanish-Indian dialect was simple and easy to master for a man who had a working knowledge of Spanish, but there was far more Indian than Spanish blood in these *mestizos* and their way of life showed nothing of the cultures of either race. Fishing was almost their only occupation and on fish they chiefly lived, preferring a certain fish that was to be found in the waters off the river outlets, where the forest sent its sprawling mangroves down to the sea's edge. This, he had concluded, was why they had built their ramshackle village in the swampy verges of the forest at sea-level, subjecting themselves to the onslaughts of the myriads of stinging insects.

From the first he had exercised his medical skill among them, limited though he was by total lack of instruments and medicines. His first successful cure, a fever-stricken child for whom the grave had already been dug, won him respect and, as the weeks passed, a popularity that was not diminished by his failure to save others of the community who sickened and died of the marsh ague. Deaths from this ailment were frequent and accepted by the Iricoans with a mixture of stoicism and apathy. McMullen's medical learning told him that there was no specific to cure this particular fever but he knew that in the parts of southern Europe where it was

endemic they called it *mal aria*. He began to wonder whether
the 'bad air' of the river marshes, from which there did indeed
emanate an unpleasant fetor, might not be responsible.

Then old Souzel had died. He had been a sort of counsellor
or sachem to the little tribe, and by common consent his dingy
mantle fell upon McMullen. He recalled (smiling a little as he
sat reflective in his *canoa*) Quita's pride in his new status, and
how she had domineered it over the other *mestizo* women –
poor Quita, who was herself to die of the marsh ague within a
few weeks. He had felt real sorrow at her death but also a kind
of shamefaced relief. It came back to him now how the
memory of Lucy Preston, which he had thought to have
banished for ever, had suddenly flashed into his mind as they
scraped the soil over Quita's grave.

But Lucy and the rest of his irrecoverable past had been
forgotten again in the building of the new Irico. It had taken
all his new authority, and days of argument, to persuade the
apathetic Iricoans that they must escape from the *mal aria* of
the swampy shore and shift their village to the hillside. He
would never have won his case, he thought, had it not been for
the wider horizons he had won for them. For by now a
periodical barter had been opened with Captain Dinneker's
enterprising schooner; he had a musket, and the fish diet was
supplemented by meat, though this was usually monkeys or an
occasional peccary. With Casado and the lad Tola, his chief
friends among the Iricoans, he had made a two-day journey
inland over the boundless *llanos* that extended behind the
coastal hills and made contact with their nearest neighbours, a
tribe of Indian *llaneros* who lived by hunting wild cattle. A
subsequent journey had taken them to the rocky barrens where
the Tocaru sparkled in cascades before losing itself in the
swamps and forests, and here in the fine gravel at the water's
edge McMullen had discerned the tiny glittering grains of gold
which had ensured regular visits from the *Martha Phelps*. The
old life was already changing.

The *canoa* had swung its bow sideways. McMullen paddled it
round so that he could comfortably face the new Irico on its
hillside. The distance was too great for much detail to be seen
but he could make out the cluster of huts which was his only

home, and even some vertical marks that must be the upright supports of the half-built 'hospital'. He had created the place, he had made its people his people. And now he was going to abandon both.

For although he had not consciously made any such resolution McMullen knew in his heart what his decision must be. Three things impelled him to it and one of them was, for him, imperative – the need to get early news of *Hermione*'s present situation to the Commander-in-Chief on the West Indies station. He saw no possible way of doing this, except that he himself must take it, but some way he would find. If this had been the only reason for leaving Irico he might have taken longer to consider it, but Captain Dinneker had brought two other impulses to bear, lesser ones but carrying weight enough to tip the scale. He knew that what the captain had said was true: the return of the *Martha Phelps* to Boston afforded him his last chance of making a fresh start among folk of his own speech and kind. And brief though it had been his acquaintance with Captain Hornback had convinced him that his continued safety at Irico had become at best precarious.

So he would leave. There were thorny problems to be solved but he had four days for considering them. For the moment he put them from his thoughts and set himself to paddle the *canoa* towards the distant shore.

The gap in the surf that marked the place where boat-landing could be effected opened ahead. Away to the left seven or eight *canoas* were out fishing, and the brown-skinned fishermen waved in response to the greeting of his upraised paddle. Then he spun his light craft into the opening between the white roar of the surf on either hand, rode the smooth crest of a racing wave, and swung agilely overboard to run the *canoa* up the shingle away from the receding undertow. The gig was pulled up well above high-water mark, under the miniature cliff at the foot of the hillside. Tola had waited for him and came down the beach to help him carry up the *canoa*.

'The others have carried the things from the schooner to the houses,' he said in Iricoan.

McMullen smiled, nodded, and spoke in English.

'Where are the goods from the schooner, Tola?'

'Gone,' Tola said, knitting his brows in effort of thought. 'Men – carry – up.'

'Good. We will go to the village.'

They climbed the zigzag path, now well trodden, up the steep hillside. Lizards scuttled on the rocks, columns of ants crossed the path here and there; behind them the blue floor of the sea widened as they climbed. They overtook old Ester toiling up under a wicker basket of bananas gathered from the palms that fringed the forest, and she returned their greetings with a cackle and a toothless grin. Ester, McMullen reflected, must be at least sixty and the oldest member of the community; she had escaped the marsh ague and if she continued to do so it might be postulated that age gave some protection against the disease, though indeed Souzel had died of it. A record of the incidence of the ague in Irico, kept over the years – but he would not be here to keep it, he remembered with a small pang of sorrow.

They came up to the village, a triple rank of huts built on the slope with short poles supporting the floors and a rough thatch of palm-leaves bound with lianas covering the low-pitched roofs. Brown babies rolled naked in the dust while their mothers squatted nearby gossiping and plaiting mats from dried reeds. The women smiled and raised their hands in salute as McMullen passed. A girl with a large earthenware water-pot supported on her bare shoulder was coming along the narrow path that traversed the hillside from the spring, and he didn't have to look behind him to interpret Tola's wishes.

'I have no need of you just now,' he said over his shoulder; and Tola loped away to meet the water-carrier.

The bolt of canvas had been laid on the flat rock below the floor of his hut and the other things placed inside. He stepped up into the shade below his roof and reached for the water-jug that hung in the inner corner above his musket. The jug was crudely made of baked earth from the river-bank, but its porosity had kept the water reasonably cool and he took a long draught before stretching himself on the rush matting. Tola and Lali would have children, would take the marsh ague or escape it, and he wouldn't be here. There had been three deaths in the past six months but it was too early to assess the beneficial effects of moving the huts up here from the forest edge. These things would have to pass out of his life, as *Surprise* and Lucy Preston had gone from it before them. His concern now must be for the immediate future.

If he himself was to take the news of *Hermione* to Kingston – and he could see no alternative – he must obviously seize the fortunate chance of the *Martha Phelps*'s voyage to Boston, which would take her within a hundred miles or so of Jamaica on her course to the Windward Passage. Somehow Captain Dinneker must be persuaded to put him ashore. This, he thought, might be done, provided that the schooner was not required to enter Kingston harbour and that the captain's oath to avoid stepping on British soil was not held to bind a temporary member of his crew. Once ashore – and it should be somewhere whence he could reach Kingston on foot – he could merge himself with the motley swarms of ragamuffins, black and brown, that idled along the waterfronts between the old port and Kingston. And then, how to deliver his message?

It was out of the question, of course, that he should attempt to deliver it verbally. To approach any British authority, or a naval officer, and state his information in English would be to invite questioning, arrest, and subsequent identification. Were the news he brought to prove never so important, it would not win his escape from the hangman. It crossed his mind that the one person in Jamaica who, if he revealed his identity, might not instantly deliver him to justice was Lucy; but he could not involve her in so dangerous a concealment. No – he must act quite alone; and his information must be conveyed by written message. It would have to be anonymous but as authoritative and convincing as he could make it, and be got into the hands of someone who would realise its significance and inform the Admiral. An officer of one of the British warships would be the man. If he could reach a naval officer he had only to slip the package into his hand and make himself scarce before he could be detained.

With this much firmly settled in his mind he could consider details. Materials for writing and sealing his message would be found on board the schooner – assuming that Dinneker the Anglophobe would allow him to use them. For his landing, the cove six miles west of Spanish Town where he and Wilson had gone botanising – aeons ago, it seemed now – would serve the purpose; again, if the captain agreed to come in close enough. And if he could take his little *canoa* in the schooner he would not have to ask Dinneker for one of his own boats to reach the hated shore.

As to escape when his mission was fulfilled, there was a chance – not to be counted upon – that Dinneker might agree to remain off the coast for a short time, so that he could regain the schooner. Failing that he would have to take what steps he could to evade or delay capture. Juan the ragged *mestizo* might perhaps ship as deckhand on a lugger or a fishing-boat – But this was profitless speculation, as useless for practical purposes as forebodings of the rough weather that could altogether prevent his landing. His purpose was clearly defined and fortune could take charge of the rest.

For the next three days McMullen was very busy. Under his direction, himself taking an active part, the building of the hut that was to act as hospital was finished and the roof thatched. The canvas screens made by the women were hung in position and the only patient under McMullen's care at this time, a man recovering from snake-bite, was placed in it. To Tola, who had received some training as surgeon's assistant, McMullen gave meticulous instructions for the treatment of this and other ailments; to Casado, an older man of some authority among the Iricoans, he repeated the basic rules of sanitation which he had succeeded in introducing to the community. At sunset of the third day he called Casado and Tola into his hut and the three of them squatted cross-legged in close conference.

'First,' McMullen said, 'you shall swear that what I now tell you will not pass your lips before tomorrow's sunset.'

He held out his hand palm downwards and they each placed their right hands upon it.

'So. Then I tell you that when the schooner comes tomorrow I shall sail in her. I return to my own people.'

Apart from a brief widening of the eyes Casado's brown face remained impassive, but Tola's displayed great distress.

'This I must do,' McMullen went on quickly, 'for reasons I cannot explain to you. Let there be no questions. Casado, you will take my place in directing matters in Irico. When Captain Hornback's schooner comes you will go out to her, taking Tola with you, and manage the trade as I have shown you. Tola, you will be the doctor – remember what I have taught you.'

'I will try, Juan,' said Tola in a whisper; two tears had forced themselves from his lowered eyes and were rolling down his cheeks.

'Tomorrow I shall go out alone in a *canoa* to Captain Dinneker's schooner.' McMullen turned to Casado. 'It is yours now to speak as leader. Send a man to keep lookout on the hill at first light in the morning.' He stood up, the others with him, and laid his hands on their shoulders. 'I am sad to leave my friends. Farewell.'

The two Iricoans turned away and vanished in the gathering dusk. McMullen lay down on his mattress of palm-fronds and rushes and reflected with some surprise that his last words had been perfectly true; these were his friends, and in parting from them he felt a genuine sorrow. That a man of some cultivation should be sorry to escape from an exile among savages was clearly unreasonable; yet it was so. Perhaps tomorrow, with the deck of the *Martha Phelps* underfoot, he would feel differently. He turned on his side and went to sleep.

Some fourteen hours later Captain Dinneker, gazing from the rail of his schooner as she closed the coast, emitted a loud grunt of satisfaction and followed it with a stream of tobacco-juice.

'One *canoa*,' he said, breaking a rule by voicing his thoughts to the mate. 'Likely he'll sail with us. Stand by to bear up and heave-to, mister.'

It was a morning of sun and wind and the tiny *canoa* tossing in the waves ahead was intermittently visible. The *Martha Phelps* held to windward of the *canoa* and came round with much banging of sails and shouting from the black crew to lie head-to-wind while the solitary paddler drove his craft across the heaving water into her lee.

'*Buenos dias, señor capitan,*' called McMullen.

He had donned a sleeveless canvas smock in addition to his loincloth, and there was a small canvas-wrapped bundle in the *canoa*. Holding on to the edge of the scuppers with one hand while the *canoa* rose and fell against the hull, he held up a little snakeskin bag for the captain to take.

'Half an ounce as near as I can judge,' he said, 'with my thanks for past trading.'

Dinneker stared down at him, frowning. 'Never mind your thanks – are you coming with me to Boston?'

'Listen, captain. Somehow I've got to get ashore on Jamaica. If you'll put me off in this *canoa* within reach of the island I'll ship as deck-hand now. If not, I'll go back to Irico.'

Captain Dinneker clutched his grizzled locks, stamped a pace to the left and a pace to the right, and whirled round to roar at his mate.

'Lines and tackles here amidships, mister! Get this goldarned cockle-shell aboard and sharp about it!'

CHAPTER SIX

The Shadow Of The Noose

1

The *Martha Phelps* had sailed from Puerto Cabello, with water and provisions for three weeks, on September 23rd. It was ten days before she sighted the Morant Cays 50 miles south-east of Kingston, this slow passage being chiefly due a long period of windless calm following a violent thunderstorm. There were lesser delays, too; and these played their part in furthering McMullen's plan.

The schooner was less than a hundred miles north-west of Irico when she was intercepted by a Spanish *guarda costa* of 16 guns and summoned to heave-to. Captain Dinneker thereupon hoisted his flag of red stripes with thirteen white stars on a blue canton and fired one of his guns – the *Martha Phelps* carried six brass 4-pounders – to call attention to his neutrality, without deigning to heave-to. On this the *guarda costa* sent a shot across his bows. Beside himself with rage and roaring oaths, the captain himself laid his gun and fired it to such good effect that the ball passed a mere two fathoms from the Spaniard's bowsprit. Prudence and the appeals of the mate then induced him to heave-to. The angry Spanish lieutenant who came aboard with the laudable intention of discovering whether the *Martha Phelps* carried any goods destined for enemy ports met with so fiery a reception, such thunderous threats of vengeance on a nation that fired on the flag of the U-nited States, that he departed again in a hurry with a flea in his ear. And when, off Aruba two days later, the schooner was similarly accosted by an armed sloop belonging to the navy of the Batavian Republic, Captain Dinneker's fury knew no bounds. His brandished fist impelled an arrogant Dutch officer back into his boat with such precipitation that he sent his stroke oarsman sprawling and lost his hat overside.

Undoubtedly these incidents inclined the captain more favourably towards a scheme which involved deviating from his course in order to assist the enemies of Spain and Holland. Their influence might indeed have been undone had he encountered, as was quite likely, a British warship cruising to intercept suspicious neutrals off Jamaica. But the *Martha Phelps* sighted only three other vessels, all traders, before she raised the Morant Cays and altered course westerly to approach the Jamaican coast east of Portland Point.

McMullen had from the first insisted on working his passage in full, standing his watches and messing with the cheerful negroes who constituted two-thirds of the schooner's crew, despite hints from Dinneker that he might voyage more comfortably if he chose. The captain's liking and respect for Juan (as he still called himself) were if anything increased by this. Before a week was out he had so far acquiesced in the Englishman's plans that he had committed himself not only to landing McMullen wherever he wished but also to waiting to pick him up afterwards. The *Martha Phelps*, he said, would stand off-and-on for twenty-four hours; but McMullen would not hear of this. If he did not regain the *canoa* in much less than twelve hours it would mean that he had been taken. It was arranged that the schooner should wait for twelve hours, and if there was no sign of the *canoa* by the end of that time she would continue on her way to Boston. There remained the unpredictable factor of the weather.

The steady Trades had held while the *Martha Phelps* made her seventy or eighty miles of westing from the Cays. When she turned northward, close-hauled, to head in for the Jamaican coast she came gradually into the lee of the Blue Mountains, and the wind became fitful and brought with it repeated rain-squalls. The coastal waters hereabouts were unfrequented by shipping; there was no harbourage west of the old port that had served Spanish Town, the ancient capital, and this was used only by small craft. Moreover, the shore all round this southern corner of the island was wild, rocky and deeply indented. It was also defended by inshore reefs, and had it been a lee shore Captain Dinneker would not have ventured so close as he did in the early afternoon of October 5th. As it was, he had the leadsman working in the bows when the schooner was within two miles of the coast.

As she crept in closer under jib and reefed mains'l McMullen studied the coast with the aid of the captain's glass. He could see a long line of broken rock thickly clad with trees and bushes, but everything above thirty feet from sea-level was hidden in the low canopy of mist. There were dozens of rifts and coves to be discerned or imagined, and seen from seaward any one of them might be the cove he and Wilson had visited more than two years ago. He tried to visualise again what they had seen when they had scrambled down to the narrow beach of the cove. Hadn't there been a pinnacle of fantastic shape standing up from the sea just off the cove?

'Deep nine – by th' mark ten – deep eight,' chanted the leadsman.

There could be no doubt that Wilson and he had come to the shore somewhere west of the promontory that showed a sheer cliff. It might have been anywhere in the half-mile of coast. But for the mist he could have identified the place by the gap in the hills above it, where the exiguous path – a goat-track, they had thought it – penetrated from above the old port. There was certainly a pillar-like shape to the right of a dark patch that could be an inlet –

'Found your bearings?' demanded the captain gruffly, at his elbow.

'I believe so.' McMullen snapped the glass shut and handed it to him. 'I'm ready when you are, captain.'

'Deep eight – by th'mark seven, sah.' There was a note of anxiety in the leadsman's voice. 'Deep six – '

'I'm ready now,' snapped Dinneker. 'Helm a-lee! Bring her to the wind!'

The schooner swung round to lie hove-to, swooping and dipping on the long swell. McMullen picked up a canvas wallet on a leathern sling from the deck at his feet; the bundle he had brought on board had contained this, as well as the canvas drawers and rawhide sandals he was wearing and two or three strips of boucanned meat. Now the wallet also held a carefully-written document wrapped in tarpaulin, and a little box containing flint and steel.

'Not much above a mile, I reckon,' Dinneker said, scowling at the shore. 'Look out you don't broach-to in them rollers.'

'I won't.'

Held by slip-lines, the *canoa* was being lowered over the side.

'I'll be on lookout for smoke or flames ashore until eight bells o' the morning watch,' said the captain; he held out his hand.

McMullen grasped it. 'Thank you, captain – and for all your help.'

'And may the good Lord watch over ye,' growled Captain Dinneker, harshly and unexpectedly.

McMullen bestrode the rail, waited his moment, and dropped neatly into the *canoa* as it rose on a wave-crest. A few seconds of furious paddling took him clear of the schooner's side and as he brought her stern-on to the long smooth waves that swept in towards the shore a rain-squall blotted out all but the few yards of water ahead. He heard the faint receding shouts as Captain Dinneker headed his vessel out to sea; but when the squall had passed over him and he turned to look back the *Martha Phelps* was lost to sight behind the grey veil of rain.

He had slid the precious wallet under his thighs to keep it as dry as possible. Now he paddled strongly, the *canoa* lifting buoyant as a cork on the crests and obedient to his expert stroke, peering ahead for his landing-place. The long wall of vegetated rocks loomed closer under the mist, its clefts and inlets slowly taking shape as he approached. He heard the muted roar of breaking waves, but there was no heavy surf as there was on the north coast; landing should present no greater problem here than on the Irico beach – how far away now in time and space!

A cove, rock-walled, was opening straight ahead and hardly a musket-shot away, and to the right of it was the formation he had taken to be an outstanding pillar of rock. But it was not a pillar at all, only the vertical nose of a miniature headland. McMullen's heart sank. Where was the cove he needed, the only one (so far as he knew) where he would find a path to lead him through the tilted wilderness of crag and thicket? Should he cast to larboard or to starboard? He swung the *canoa*'s bow to starboard at a venture, cursing himself for the folly that had thought to locate from seaward a place he had visited only once before, and that two years ago and by land. The *canoa* was rolling now in the troughs and difficult to control. Another cove opened on his left beyond the waves; a sheer promontory next; a steep of tangled tropical vegetation; and then, sliding gradually out as he passed the steep, a queer-shaped rock-tower with the waves breaking at its base. It shape struck no chord of memory – but there was indeed a little rocky bay on its hither side, with a shelving beach. He made for it, bringing the *canoa* stern-on to the shoreward-racing waves; rode into the narrow entrance on a curling crest; and plunged in waist-deep as it broke, to splash through the backwash to dry land dragging the *canoa* with him. At least he had landed on Jamaica.

'Dry land' was very much a relative term here, he soon saw. The cove, not much larger than the stern cabin of a 74, sloped up between rock-walls that for all their steepness were covered with green plants, and from their upper ledges larger shrubs and small fronded trees arched overhead, dripping with moisture from the recent rain. It was a gloomy place and very wet. McMullen, settling the *canoa* well above the litter of decaying driftwood that marked the line of high water, reflected that it wouldn't be easy to light the signal-fire he had arranged with Captain Dinneker.

A glance round him brought no sense of having been here before. Even the rock pinnacle looked no more familiar than it had looked from seaward. The little path through the tangle of forest, he remembered, had brought them to the inner angle of the cove where they had found a slanting ledge by which they had come down to the beach. And the ledge – or a ledge – was there, at the cove's upper end! He slung the wallet on his shoulder and clambered up the ledge, his sandals slipping on the wet rock. At its top, where the low cliff eased its angle, he was confronted by a dense mass of stems and creepers and branches that appeared as impenetrable as a stone wall. He groped and peered from left and right but there was no path or sign of any way through.

There was a cold fear at McMullen's heart as he slid down again to the shingle. If he had landed in the wrong cove after all, how was he to find the right one? It was impossible, as he had seen, to scramble along the shore in either direction, and if he launched the *canoa* to continue his search along the coast he might well exhaust the remaining hours of daylight in vain landings and puttings-off. He turned to survey the big waves surging into the entrance to shatter in foam on the shingle, resting a hand against the slimy wall on his left as he did so. It might even prove impossible to launch the *canoa* again. There was a chance that he could edge out, supporting the *canoa*, along the rocks at the side –

His thoughts came to a dead stop. It was the feel of the rock beside him that had arrested them. His hand was on the edge of a small flat-bottomed concavity in the rock, a hole of precisely the size and shape to take the toe of a man's boot. And recollection rushed upon him like a flood.

He saw Forbes Wilson's eager sharp-nosed face uptilted to peer at a tiny star-shaped plant in a cranny high above; saw himself assisting the amateur botanist to get his foot into just such a hole. He looked up, and there was the little plant – Wilson had given it some long Latin name – solitary and just where it had been when his friend identified it. The small blue flowers were there too, though now they were withered on their thin stems. He was sure of it now – this was the cove they had visited, and the path must be there.

He climbed swiftly up the slippery ledge again, again faced the impenetrable thicket. Two years had passed, he remembered; in these latitudes that was more than long enough for a path a few inches wide to become totally overgrown if it became disused, and the goats – if it was they who had made it – might have found new pasturing. *Tomorrow to fresh woods and pastures new.* Milton's line buzzed absurdly in his head as he tore at the intertwining creepers and stamped the leafy stems until he could stand upright on the easier slope under a canopy of dripping branches. Beneath his feet he could feel a narrow band of ground harder than the yielding soil on either side of it. The path.

It climbed steeply, straight up the slope of forest. Parting the branches and fronds before his face, feeling his way with his feet, he started slowly up it, his spirits high once more. In twenty paces he had lost the path and no amount of searching with eyes and feet could locate it again. He was still confident, however, remembering that the open ground from which he and Wilson had descended into the forest was not far above – not more than half-a-mile, he thought.

It might have been half-a-mile but the distance was no measure of his labour. Now he was climbing through tropical forest on a line that had never been opened by a path, treading among the vegetable wreckage of centuries and thrusting through living screens that had renewed themselves since the first saplings had grown here. In some places it took him five minutes to win five yards. The green gloom in which he toiled blurred with mist as with infinite pains he gained height, and though the saturated air was clammy on his cheek he sweated continuously. If there were animals and birds here he saw nothing of them, nor even a snake; perhaps the noise of his strenuous progress had sent them into hiding. But the plants themselves attacked him, knife-edged blades and boughs spiked with thorns, drawing blood from his bare legs and arms. He pressed steadily on, now and again feeling for his wallet to make sure it hadn't been torn from him by some grasping branch.

How long it took him to reach the place where only a fringe of palms stood between him and open ground he could only guess. But the mist overhead, which had lifted as he climbed, was already tinged with a deepening gold that hinted at the westering sun above its upper surface. McMullen took five minutes of much-needed rest, sitting at the foot of a grey rock as big as a cottage that stood at the edge of a sloping wilderness of similar rocks. From his wallet he took one of his pieces of sun-dried meat and chewed it (though he would have infinitely preferred a draught of water) while he surveyed the limited prospect before him. He had mounted a short distance on the rocky slope so that he could see above the forest's upper trees, and between the line of treetops and the underside of the mist he could see a strip of silver-grey sea with a few small fishing-craft moving slowly on it. The boats would be out of the old port on the coast below Spanish Town; from the old port ran a coastal track which ended close to the Apostles Battery in the western end of Kingston harbour – he had come that way with Wilson on their excursion to the cove. If he kept along the slope just above the forest rim he should be able to strike the goat-track where it emerged and follow it down to the coastal track.

Thought of Kingston brought home to him the fact that he, an outlaw, was soon to encounter other men. In the labours and anxieties of route-finding he had temporarily forgotten that he was a fugitive from justice deliberately thrusting into danger. A moment's consideration gave him confidence. The motley crowd of fishermen and beggars and thieves that haunted the Kingston waterfronts were of all shades of colour and very variously clad; a brown-skinned fellow with a black beard, wearing tattered smock and drawers, would hardly attract even a passing glance. Had *Surprise* been still on the station, and in port, he might have feared recognition by some member of a shore party, but she had gone home two years ago. He stood up somewhat stiffly in his drenched clothing and resumed his journey.

It was hard going traversing along the tilted chaos of boulders and spiky plants and his progress was little faster than it had been in the forest. But at last he paused on a rocky eminence and saw a deep valley at his feet, with the forest rim curling away down the slopes on his right towards the sea. And not far below him, twisting downwards between the rocks, he discerned the pale thread of the path.

Half-an-hour later McMullen was crouched in a thicket close above the broad track that wound up from the old port towards Spanish Town. The few buildings of the port and the gleam of the bay were just visible down to his right and there were two men coming slowly up the track. The two passed below him without a word spoken between them; one of them was smoking a rank-smelling *cigarro* and the other – a lean fellow clad much as he himself was dressed – carried a long thin fishing-pole across his shoulder. When they had passed from sight round a bend higher up the track McMullen scrambled down and into the bed of the ravine on the other side, where the spray of a tumbling stream splashed the stems of the tall bamboo-grass growing on its banks. First he drank long and avidly from the stream; and then, selecting the longest bamboo cane he could find, he broke it off at the base and removed the feathery tip. Dragging the cane behind him he climbed out of the ravine on its further side and made a laborious route through rocks and thickets to gain the coastal track some quarter-of-a-mile clear of the old port. There was no one to be seen on the narrow stony road. He set out at a brisk pace, assuring himself that he was the very picture of a poor fisherman with his rod and wallet trudging homeward to his hovel on the outskirts of Kingston.

Dusk was fast gathering now. The forested steeps on his left soared almost black into the darkening cloud, and across the sea that glimmered between trees on his other hand an orange-red bar of sunset glowed strangely between the rain-squalls that drifted in the south-west. At first he met no one. The way seemed longer than he remembered it, and it was nearly dark when he encountered the first wayfarers, a man and two women perched on mule-back. They passed him without a greeting, and some way farther on, as a few lights in the distance ahead caught his eye, he was overtaken by a man driving a horse and cart who took no notice of him. He came at length to the first dwellings, a cluster of huts below the roadside whence came the gleam of firelight and a smell of cooking. When, in a few hundred yards, the square outline of a stone fortress rose on the right above lesser buildings he dodged aside by foul-smelling alleyways to pass clear of the walls of Fort Passage and ten minutes later found the stones of the quay underfoot and the harbour waters close on his right. Lights shone from the shipping moored off the quay or tied up alongside, and from the windows of the long row of buildings standing back from the quaystones. It was too dark now to make out the nature of the vessels lying farther out at the naval moorings, and while he was vainly straining his eyes into the distances of the wide harbour the rain came driving to obscure everything. He turned away from the quayside towards the houses, making his way across the wet stones past piles of casks and coils of old rope and steering clear of the few other dark figures who like himself were heading for shelter. His plan for the final stage of his mission was already decided upon.

Among the houses fronting the quay was a sizeable stone building whose lower windows glowed with welcoming lamplight through the rain. This was Roald's tavern. McMullen had been inside it more than once. Its proprietor, son of a Danish father and a mulatto mother, had maintained it in so clean and respectable a state that it had become a meeting-place, almost a club, for naval officers coming ashore. It had been a common practice in McMullen's *Surprise* days for any officer having business on shore to pause at Roald's for a glass of wine or a dram before proceeding with his affairs, and he had resolved that his best chance of getting his packet into the right hands was to lurk near the open door of the tavern. It was perhaps no more than an even chance that a ship's boat would put an officer ashore this evening, but he would explore it before considering an alternative way.

He gained the corner of the tavern and entered the dark mouth of the alleyway beside it. Here, laying down his bamboo on the cobbles, he set his back against the rough stone of the wall and prepared to wait, with the water from the tavern's eaveshoots splashing on his toes. It was a long wait. The rain dwindled and ceased; from somewhere on his right half-a-dozen figures hurried across to the quayside; raised voices, a stave of a song, sounded faintly from inside the tavern. Then another squall of rain blew across the stones, and through the spatter of heavy drops he heard the crisp orders and rattle of boated oars as a boat came alongside the steps opposite him. Peering from his lurking-place, he saw a man hooded and muffled in an officer's boat-cloak step onto the quay and begin to walk across the stones towards him. His moment had come.

McMullen took his packet from the wallet and stripped the tarpaulin from it. The sealed missive was superscribed in his best copper-plate hand: *Most Urgent – to the Commander-in-Chief, West Indies Station.* He waited until the officer, a slight erect figure, was within a few paces of the open door and then darted out packet in hand. The foot of his quarry was on the broad step of the porch and he had to come into the light that streamed from the door before he could tug at the man's boat-cloak, holding out his letter.

Instantly his wrist was caught in a grip of steel. He shrank away, jabbering in Iricoan dialect, but with another swift movement the steely fingers shifted, grasping and feeling the raised cicatrice of that old knife-wound. The movement shook back the hood of the cloak and the officer's startled features showed plainly in the lamplight.

'John McMullen, by God!' exclaimed Edward Hamilton.

2

Captain Edward Hamilton's capacity for lightning thought and decision, which his light-hearted manner concealed, had long been known to his surgeon friend; but McMullen was afterwards to marvel at the speed with which he acted in this moment at the porch of Roald's tavern. McMullen himself, at that moment, was too stunned by the unexpected turn of events to think or act. As from a distance he heard Hamilton's quick command spoken in his ear: 'Follow me close – you're a dead man else!' As in a dream he entered the low-beamed lamplit room at the captain's heels and heard his curt speech to the landlord.

'Roald, attention here – I've private business with this fellow. A room above stairs, lights, a bottle of your cheapest wine.' Hamilton paused and sniffed loudly. 'And a cigar to mitigate my ragged friend's stink.'

McMullen was dimly conscious that the half-dozen men in the room laughed at that and resumed their drinking; that he then climbed some narrow stairs behind Hamilton and a negro bearing a lighted candle; and that when the servant had left them Hamilton closed a door and locked it. The room was a small one and furnished with a truckle bed and a table and two chairs. He felt, suddenly, completely exhausted.

Hamilton tossed cloak and hat on the bed, shot a keen glance at his friend, and pushed him into a chair. Then he poured wine from the bottle the man had carried up and set the glass before McMullen.

'Drink that,' he said crisply, 'And not a word till I've read this *billet-doux* of yours.'

McMullen gulped the wine thirstily, feeling the slow return of normal perception. The captain ripped the cover from the inner document without hesitation and read the careful script. His quaintly boyish features were set in unusual sternness; but as he read his eyes sparkled and he seemed to repress an excited exclamation. When he came to the end he made no comment but refilled McMullen's glass before starting a second and more deliberate perusal, frowning as he tilted the paper towards the candle's light. The frown persisted while he carefully folded the letter, placed it in his pocket, and turned a penetrating stare on the man opposite him.

'You're aware, I suppose, that it's my plain duty to have you put in irons?' he said; his voice was totally devoid of expression.

'Then you'd better do it, sir,' said McMullen dully.

'You know, then, that your name is on the list of men proscribed for mutiny in the *Hermione*. I saw the list myself at the Admiralty in London and there's a copy here in Kingston, but you can have seen neither. How do you come to know of it?'

McMullen showed momentary surprise. 'I assumed it,' he said after a pause. 'The master and four others were sent away in a boat off St Vincent. There was little doubt they'd get safe to land and make their report.'

'They did. I've seen their report. They say you took part with the mutineers. Is it true?'

'I – yes, it's true.'

Hamilton bowed his head and covered his eyes with one hand. 'I cannot credit it,' he said in a low voice. 'Pigot was a brute – there's evidence been given as to that. But that you should join in slaughtering him and his officers – '

'I had no hand in it!' McMullen broke in angrily. 'I fought to save Pigot – I was wounded trying to defend him!'

'What's that?' The captain sat up with a jerk. 'This is beyond my comprehension, Mr McMullen. Tell me, if you please, your whole story. You may have to tell it to a court martial,' he added, 'but what you say for my ear alone goes no farther.'

'I know it, sir. Permit me one question first. What brings you back to Jamaica?'

'His Majesty's frigate *Surprise* – what else?' Hamilton answered with a fleeting touch of his old humour. 'When *Hermione* was – lost, the Admiral badgered their Lordships for a replacement frigate. They sent the *Peterel*, sloop, but she was snapped up by a thirty-two gun Frenchman off Madeira so they raked *Surprise* away from the Channel Fleet and sent her instead. We've been back on this station four months. Now – your tale.'

His stiff manner a trifle relaxed, he filled a glass of wine for himself, replenished the other glass, and lit his cigar at the candle-flame. Through the curling strands of smoke his steady gaze remained fixed on McMullen's face while he told his tale; nor did he once interrupt, long though it was in the telling.

McMullen had no wish to make a long story of it. He set himself to relate the facts as he had seen them and acted them, shunning self-excuse and accusation of others. The details of the mutiny two years ago were clear and vivid in his mind and he gave them without shirking any of the part he had played in it. In his account of his long stay with the people of Irico he was far less exact, and he contrived to compress it into half-a-dozen sentences. Even so, the candle was two inches lower, and Captain Hamilton's cigar a cold butt-end on the floor, when he told of his landing from the *Martha Phelps* and his journey to Kingston.

'I've questioned Hiram Dinneker concerning his information about *Hermione*,' he ended, 'and I believe it to be sufficiently accurate.'

Hamilton nodded. Then he reached a hand across the table and after a moment's hesitation McMullen grasped it.

'The hand of a mutineer, Captain Hamilton?' he said quietly, with a wry smile.

'But not of a murderer, John.' Hamilton stood up, frowning down at him. 'All the same, by my tenets – those of the navy – you're a guilty man condemned out of your own mouth. By yours, I believe you're innocent. I know you, John, and I know you couldn't have acted otherwise than you did. But this – ' he tapped his pocket – 'important as it is, won't save your neck.'

'I'm ready to pay the penalty,' McMullen said wearily.

The captain clenched his fist and let it fall on the table with a bang, rattling the glasses.

'By God, it's the damnedest thing!' he burst out. 'The King's justice to be done on a man for standing up for his principles!'

He began to walk up and down the room with short quick steps. It was a small room and he turned at every five paces, the skirts of his gold-braided coat flying, his brown eyes quick with thought even while he spoke in jerky sentences.

'News of the mutiny reached London while *Surprise* was refitting. Of course I went to the Admiralty to find out what had happened to you. They had the signed testimonies there – the Admiral has copies of 'em here. The statements of the master, Southwell or some such name – '

'Southcott.'

'Aye. His statement and that of the gunner put it beyond doubt that Pigot exceeded all bounds in his floggings. That business of the men falling from the rigging, their bodies pitched overboard – pah! – that's on record too, though they didn't print it in the *Gazette*. But it makes no difference.' Hamilton halted in his pacing. 'Twenty-seven mutineers have been caught so far, John, and hanged on that evidence, here in Kingston.'

He sat down with a thump, set his elbows on the table, and rested his head on his hands. McMullen could find nothing to say and so said nothing. It was a full two minutes before Hamilton spoke and then it was as if to himself and without removing his hands from his eyes.

'The testimonies. Scrutton has them. Sir Hyde's on board the flagship. There's a chance. By God, there's a chance!'

His odd countenance was working with sudden excitement as he lifted his head and reached across to grasp McMullen's wrist.

'Listen, John – this letter of yours shall reach the Admiral tonight, by my hand. But first I'm going to see Charles Scrutton, Admiral's secretary. He has his house and office behind the port, not ten minutes away, and I was bound there in any case to put in my report of prizes. I want a look at those testimonies. You'll remain here until I return – an hour or a little more.'

'The innkeeper may suspect – '

'He won't. Roald has his secrets and I know one of 'em – concerning an illicit cargo of rum. He'll do as I say.' He sprang to his feet. 'Lock the door when I'm gone and let no one in unless he gives a password – *Surprise*, it shall be.'

'And suppose I choose to make a bolt for it?'

Hamilton had snatched cloak and hat from the bed and was at the door. He turned at McMullen's words and bent a stern glance on him.

'If you did,' he said, 'you'd be God's own damned fool, John. It's all Lombard Street to a China orange you'd be caught. You see, it'd then be my duty to hunt you down – and I know where you'd head for.'

The door closed behind him. McMullen got up and locked it, telling himself as he did so that he was sealing his own fate. He could feel no faith in whatever ingenuities Edward Hamilton was planning; to a court martial he must come and its outcome was inevitable. To make the hopeless bid for freedom while the opportunity offered – surely that was better than to wait supinely here while another made an equally hopeless attempt to save him.

He sat at the table and stared unseeing at the guttering candle-flame. He thought of Captain Dinneker waiting for him, watching for the signal-fire in the cove. The *Martha Phelps* would have to sail for Boston without him now, for his route of escape was known and even with an hour's start he would be overtaken by horsemen before he gained the goat-track. Abandon that, then, and strike through the twisting alleys behind Kingston to climb into the steep forest that rose behind the port? They would hunt him down with dogs, as they did with slaves that escaped from the plantations. He was still revolving unlikely modes of escape in his mind when there came a knock on his door and an unfamiliar voice spoke Hamilton's password. He unlocked it and admitted Roald's negro servant carrying a bowl of water, a towel, and a fresh candle.

'With Mistah Roald's compliments, sah,' said the man with a deferential grin; and went out again to bring in a tray with a platter of food.

McMullen turned the key when the man had gone and sat down in some bewilderment; there had been no hint of gibing in the negro's obsequiousness. This was surely strange treatment for the captain's 'ragged friend', an Indian to all appearance and stained with mud and blood. He gave it up and bestirred himself to make a rudimentary toilet before he fell to on his meal. He was very hungry.

He would have been less puzzled had he overheard Captain Hamilton's brief conference with the innkeeper before he left the tavern. The fellow upstairs, the captain had confided in a conspiratorial whisper, was none other than one of Mr Pitt's most trusted spies, cleverly disguised and just arrived from Spanish territory with important news; he was to remain *incommunicado* in his room until tomorrow, when he would go aboard the flagship to divulge his news to Admiral Sir Hyde Parker in person. The innkeeper, much impressed, had readily agreed to send up food and toilet materials and was impressed still further by Hamilton's insistence on the use of a password.

Unaware of his new rôle, McMullen made short work of the cold roast chicken and yams which was the best Mr Roald could do, at such very short notice, for a trusted agent of Britain's prime minister, helping it down with the remains of the wine. When he had finished he found he had recovered something of his old pragmatical philosophy. Escape was out of the question now and he could dismiss all thought of it; he could do nothing at all about his future and it was therefore pointless to consider it. It was enough that he now felt strong enough to face whatever was to come.

The coarse blankets on the bed seemed reasonably clean and he lay down on them, in his mind a line of Ovid remembered from long-ago days of schoolboy construing: *My present blessings exceed any apprehension.* For two blessings at least he could give thanks – he had done what he set out to do, and he had not lost Edward Hamilton's friendship. He had always envisaged the possibility that he would be taken when he ventured into Kingston, so he must not complain when that possibility became accomplished fact. For some time he lay watching the steady flame of the candle and thinking of past days; of London and Salamanca, of *Surprise* and her ship's company, of his successes in healing and surgery. And of Lucy Preston. He would have liked to see Lucy again. Was she still in Jamaica, he wondered? It was two years ago, and it was not impossible that she had married and gone to England. If she was still on the island he might indeed see her again – on the day of his death. For a condemned mutineer, he supposed, would be hanged from the flagship's yardarm with the crew ceremonially assembled and a crowd watching from the quayside, and Lucy might be in the crowd.

McMullen had achieved a mood of melancholy resignation to death that amounted almost to equanimity when his thoughts took this turn. Now another self rebelled against equanimity. He was twenty-seven, a man in his prime and possessed of special skills for helping his fellow-men – skills that he could have exercised for another two-score years. Had he indeed deserved to die the most shameful of deaths? True, he had transgressed a man-made law and incurred the penalty, but he had nowhere transgressed the laws of his own conscience. He had stood up for his principles – he remembered Edward Hamilton's exclamation – and for that, and because circumstance had betrayed him, he was to suffer the King's justice. That could not be called just.

He flung himself off the bed and began to pace the floor, setting the candle-flame a-quiver as he passed to and fro. He could not, now, resign himself to die, to be blown out like a candle. The rights and wrongs of his case, considerations of justice and injustice – these were as nothing to the instinct that rose in him like a resistless wave. He wanted to live!

His pacing brought him close to the door at the moment when someone outside knocked upon it. Edward Hamilton's voice muttered the password and McMullen, controlling the animal emotion that gripped him, admitted him. The captain had a leather satchel under his arm and his brown eyes glittered as he marched to the table and threw himself into a chair.

'Sit down,' he said peremptorily. 'We've little enough time.'

He drew a thin sheaf of papers from the satchel. 'I go to the Admiral with these tonight. I believe I can persuade him to see you in private tomorrow. But first, John, I want your assurance that you'll tell a lie – just one lie – to save your neck.'

McMullen, who had sat down opposite him, scowled and lifted his head. 'I'm not ashamed of my actions, sir. And I'm not accustomed to lie.'

'No?' Hamilton's face, thrust close to his, wore a fierce frown. 'You told me tonight, in this room, that you lied to Mr Searle, *Hermione*'s gunner. You told him you had neither knowledge nor suspicion that any mutiny was brewing.'

'That was to save – '

'I've heard your reasons. The reason for telling it a second time is that it may save your life.'

'Repeat that lie to the Admiral? I won't do it, Edward.' McMullen bit his lip. 'He'll ask other questions – he'll see that I'm lying. And nothing can counter Southcott's testimony and Searle's, if that's what you've got there.'

Hamilton repressed an angry retort. 'Listen to me, John,' he said with restraint. 'I'm asking you two things – to leave the management of this to me, and to support me by making a single untrue statement. As to the Admiral, you don't know Sir Hyde and I do. At this moment I'm in high favour with him – our last cruise put a fine lump of prize money in his pocket. The testimonies – but we'll consider those in a moment. The crucial point is this. From the instant that Mr Reid was struck down all your actions were against the mutineers. Before that – this is what you'll maintain – you knew nothing of what was to happen.'

'I can't say that. I've told you I knew – '

'God damn and blast your scruples!' Hamilton burst out. 'Did you know Reid was to be cut down, Pigot and the rest slaughtered?'

'No, but – '

'But you'll stick to this tale of suspecting that a mutiny was toward, so that you can get yourself hanged from the yardarm. Is that it? You won't pay the price of a twice-told lie to save your own life. Is that it?'

McMullen was silent. The captain, who had leaned far across

the table in the intensity of his argument, sat back and passed a hand across his brow.

'If you want to die, John,' he said wearily, 'I can't save you. But consider this. Here's a man – think of him as a stranger – who'll lie to save a parcel of murderous rogues from flogging or worse. When he's asked to do the same thing to save the life of a man of integrity and courage, one John McMullen, he refuses. Would you call him madman, knave, or fool?'

For a moment McMullen eyed his friend without speaking. Then, despite himself, he grinned.

'Of all the jesuitical counsellors a man ever had,' he said, 'you're the most devilishly ingenious, Edward Hamilton. But – I don't want to die. I'll do as you ask.'

'Well, praise the Lord for that.' Hamilton took a watch from his fob and glanced at it. 'Five minutes for a look at these testimonies and then I must up anchor.'

They bent together over the papers.

3

Morning sunlight flashed from the rippled water of Kingston harbour, gilding the upper spars and rigging of the swarm of craft alongside the quay or lying at moorings beyond it and winking from the steaming puddles left on the quaystones by last night's rain. It glinted on the epaulettes of Captain Hamilton's blue coat and on the hilt of his sword as he walked briskly from the door of Roald's tavern towards his waiting gig. Half a pace behind him stalked a taller man plainly dressed in dark-blue coat and breeches, wearing an ill-fitting hat which the lively breeze threatened to lift from his head.

John McMullen had been roused two hours earlier by Roald's servant bringing a breakfast of cold beef and ale. The man brought also a large bundle which proved to contain clothes and hat and a razor. Pinned to the coat was a curt note: *Do what you can with these. Be ready at half-past nine and keep your room till I come.* It was thus a clean-shaven man, very dark of skin but with an odd pallor about the lower face, that crossed the quay behind the captain. Little had been said between them except for Hamilton's muttered comment (the negro was within hearing) that all went well and the Admiral would see them at four bells of the forenoon watch.

Surprise's cutter was at the steps in charge of a diminutive midshipman. As McMullen, at the captain's gesture, stepped down into the sternsheets a big seaman at the stroke oar stared wide-eyed and open-mouthed.

'Well, blow me to buggery!' he ejaculated. 'If it ain't – '

The midshipman's outraged screech of 'Silence, there!' cut him short. McMullen had recognised Seaman Bragg but he was careful not to look at that large and rapidly crimsoning face.

'You have that man's name, Mr Viney?' Captain Hamilton seated himself on the stern thwart. 'Then give way, if you please – to *Abergavenny*.'

The flagship, an ancient two-decker of 54 guns, came in sight two cable-lengths away as the boat pulled out from among the quayside shipping. The much smaller frigate lying astern of her McMullen knew instantly for *Surprise*.

'The seventy-four over by Fort Nugent is *Cerberus*,' said Hamilton beside him.

He spoke casually, as one making polite conversation; but McMullen, glancing at him, saw the jut of lower lip and tenseness of jaw that showed inquietude tightly reined. He felt a sudden wave of affection for his friend. Only now did he realise that Hamilton was jeopardising his naval career by seeking to aid him, and he resolved that the lie they had agreed upon should be told with all the conviction he could muster.

'*Surprise* has retained some of her ship's company, I gather, sir,' he remarked.

'I have all my senior officers save one,' Hamilton replied absently, 'and nearly half the lower-deck ratings signed on with me a second time. – Larboard side, Mr Viney.'

The gig shot round below the flagship's stern and came neatly alongside. Hamilton went up the entry-port ladder to the shrill piping of the boatswain's mates, and McMullen, following at a respectful distance, halted two steps inboard of the rail while the captain exchanged a word with the officer of the watch. Then Hamilton beckoned him and they walked to the door below the quarterdeck, where a marine came noisily to attention and stood aside. The big cabin into which they advanced was bright with ceaselessly-moving lozenges of light, reflections from the water beneath the wide stern windows. The Admiral, who was standing with his hands behind his back looking out of the windows, turned as they entered and came round the end of the long table that occupied the after end of the cabin.

Sir Hyde Parker, Vice-Admiral of the White, was a small plump man of sixty. There was something old-lady-like about his prim self-satisfied countenance and the similitude was increased by the old-fashioned wig he saw fit to wear, which sat on his head like a widow's cap. He glanced briefly at McMullen and then at the captain, who had halted to stand stiffly with his hat under his arm.

'Good morning, Hamilton,' he said, lending the words a certain pomposity. 'Perhaps your – ah – companion will be so good as to see that the door is properly closed. A chair, Hamilton – here, if you please. And another – there.'

McMullen, returning from the door, found that he was to sit facing the Admiral and six paces from him, while the captain was seated rather to one side. Sir Hyde took some papers from the table, sat down with his back to it, and directed a frown towards the captain on his left.

'I repeat, Captain Hamilton,' he said somewhat querulously, 'that these proceedings might be called irregular – indeed, highly irregular.'

'But rendered necessary, sir, by unusual circumstances,' said Hamilton respectfully.

'Precisely so, precisely so.' Sir Hyde's little eyes fixed themselves on the man in front of him. 'Mr – ah – McMullen, Captain Hamilton has represented to me that you may have been the victim of – um – unusual circumstances. This, together with the fact that valuable information has reached me through your – um – endeavours, has disposed me to make personal inquiry into your case.'

'Thank you, sir,' said McMullen as he paused.

The Admiral frowned. 'You will be silent until I require you to answer questions,' he said severely. 'You are aware, of course, that you are deemed to be one of the mutineers in that dastardly affair of the *Hermione* two years ago?'

'Yes, sir.' McMullen had been warned by his friend to volunteer no explanations.

'Very well. I am told that you deny this, despite the signed testimony of two of *Hermione*'s officers to the – ah – contrary effect. Is that true?'

'Yes, sir.'

'Very well. You maintain that subsequent to the mutiny you escaped in one of *Hermione*'s boats, were cast up on a desert shore, befriended by a tribe of savages, and remained with them two years. Two years is a long time, Mc McMullen. You didn't think of attempting to make your way back to Jamaica?'

'No, sir. I had no means of building a craft large enough.'

'You had *Hermione*'s gig,' snapped the Admiral.

'By your leave, sir,' Hamilton interposed quickly, 'a ship's surgeon can hardly be supposed to have the ability – '

'Thank you, Hamilton,' Sir Hyde interrupted irritably, 'I am conducting this inquiry, if you please.' He returned to his questioning. 'So you were incapable of sailing the gig?'

'I believe I could have sailed her along the coast and reached Puerto Cabello, sir,' said McMullen truthfully, 'but that would have meant giving myself up to the Spaniards.'

'Um,' grunted Sir Hyde; he rustled the papers on his knee. 'I shall proceed, then, to your behaviour prior to escaping from *Hermione*.'

The October sun had not reached its height and it was quite cool in the big cabin, but McMullen felt the sweat standing on his brow. The Admiral was peering closely at one of his papers.

'The fourth paragraph, sir,' murmured Hamilton.

'Eh? Ah, yes. Mr McMullen, this is the statement of William Southcott, master. He says, "the mutineers rushed past me into the captain's cabin. Among them was the ship's surgeon." ' He looked up. 'Is that a true statement, Mr McMullen?'

'Perfectly true, sir. I was using all the force I could to reach the captain and save him.'

'In which you failed.'

'I was one against twenty, sir. I saw Captain Pigot, severely wounded, being thrust out of the stern window. Then I was stabbed and knocked unconscious.'

The Admiral stared hard at McMullen and then nodded. 'Very well. Mr Southcott adds that he had no further sight of you and that he was surprised that you were not put into the cutter with him and the others.' He took up another paper. 'The statement of Mr Searle, gunner, appears to throw some light on that. Let me see – um – yes. "On the cutter putting off, I hailed the mutineers asking why the surgeon was not put off with us. Meyer, one of the ringleaders, replied in these words: stow your gab, you old bugger, McMullen has taken a berth with us." What do you say to that, Mr McMullen?'

'In a sense, sir, the man was speaking the truth,' McMullen answered; he was feeling slightly easier. 'I was lying on my cot at that time, wounded and weak from loss of blood. My door was locked and there was an armed guard outside it. This had been my situation since my attempt to defend Captain Pigot.'

'Indeed.' The Admiral eyed him stonily. 'Am I to take it that you had taken service with the mutineers?'

'Good God, no!' exclaimed McMullen hastily. 'I mean certainly not, sir. I was – '

'Then pray restrain your attempts at levity, sir! This man Meyer was *not* speaking the truth in any sense. Can you explain why you were thus kept on board instead of being murdered or set adrift like the other officers?'

'I beg your pardon, sir,' said McMullen, abashed. 'I speak the Spanish language. I was to be forced to interpret for the mutineers when they handed over the frigate to the Spaniards at La Guayra.'

'Um. Now as to the manner of your escape, Mr McMullen.' The little eyes fixed upon him intensified their scrutiny. 'According to your story as told to me by Captain Hamilton last night, you were aided to escape by one of the mutineers. I find that difficult to believe.'

'I also, Sir Hyde,' Hamilton put in with a frown; throughout the interview his expression had been as stern as a Grand Inquisitor's. 'And yet,' he went on, 'if Mr McMullen were lying he would hardly invent so unlikely a tale.'

'That may or may not be so,' said the Admiral shortly. 'Well, Mr McMullen? Why did this man act as you say he did?'

McMullen hesitated for the fraction of a second. The reason

he had to give must be considered a lame one.

'It was a seaman whose broken arm I'd set when we were shipmates in the *Lion* seventy-four,' he said, not very hopefully.

'The old *Lion?*' For the first time the Admiral's face relaxed its severity. 'D'you hear that, Hamilton?' he went on, turning to the captain. 'The *Lion* – I was second in her in '58. And,' he added as an afterthought, 'how often have I said the tie of shipmates in the Navy is the strongest on earth?'

'I've heard you say it often, sir,' Hamilton said with answering enthusiasm. 'And now here is proof that you're right.'

'Precisely so, Hamilton, precisely so.'

For a few seconds Sir Hyde's plump features were almost benign. He seemed to be contemplating bygone days in the old *Lion*, for he sighed and wagged his head.

'Ah well, Hamilton,' he said at last, 'we must bring this present affair to a close.'

'Yes, sir.' The captain was quick with his rejoinder. 'And it appears to me, with respect, that Mr McMullen has very satisfactorily accounted for the points cited against him.'

He sat forward on his chair and made as if to stand up. The Admiral flapped a hand at him.

'Wait, wait. If I mistake not, we found a second reference to Mr McMullen in the gunner's statement.' He frowned at the paper. 'Yes – first paragraph. "Suspecting that trouble was brewing on the lower deck, I visited the surgeon" –

The sweat broke out again on McMullen's forehead. Here it came. So far he had been able to keep to the literal truth, but now there was nothing for it but to lie. In spite of the assurance he had given Hamilton he baulked at it.

' – "and acquainted him with my suspicions." ' The Admiral looked up from his reading. 'Did you yourself harbour any such suspicions, Mr McMullen?'

'Sir!' Hamilton interjected suddenly, sitting up with a jerk and speaking very fast. 'Here's a plain case of dereliction of duty – it didn't occur to me last night – when Searle, an executive officer, sees fit to divulge his suspicions of the coming mutiny to a civilian warrant officer, a surgeon. Why didn't he go at once to the captain or first lieutenant? He was in duty bound – '

'Captain Hamilton!' Sir Hyde cut him short. 'Whether or not Mr Searle was at fault is not – ah – germane to our purpose. It should be plain to you, moreover, that the matter is no concern of mine, nor of yours. If Mr Searle chose – but let it be, let it be.' He glanced up and down his paper. 'You've made me lose my place, confound it!'

'I beg your pardon, sir,' said the captain remorsefully. 'It merely occurred to me – '

'Ah. Mr Searle says, "I asked him did he find that the men under his care showed sign of discontent or rebellion." ' Sir Hyde looked up. 'What, Mr McMullen, did you reply to that question?'

McMullen let out his pent breath as unobtrusively as he could. 'I told him frankly, sir, that I'd observed much discontent because of Captain Pigot's action in throwing two bodies overboard without due ceremony,' he said carefully.

'Yes, yes. Pigot was – ' The Admiral checked himself. 'Well, Hamilton?'

'If I may say so again, sir, the fault here lies rather with the gunner than with the ship's surgeon. As to the whole of Mr McMullen's story – well, sir, I don't possess your competence to pass judgement on that.'

The Admiral nodded. He looked thoughtfully at McMullen, pursing his lips. Then he shrugged his shoulders, turned to place his papers on the table, and stood up.

'Very well, Mr McMullen,' he said with no relaxation of gravity. 'I shall inform their Lordships that you have returned to duty. Your name will of course be removed from the list of those concerned in the mutiny of the *Hermione*.'

McMullen and the captain had risen with him.

'Thank you, sir,' said McMullen.

Hamilton nodded briefly at him and addressed his senior. 'There remains, sir, the finding of a berth for Mr McMullen. My present surgeon, Attwood, rates assistant surgeon merely, having only two years' service. If I may take Mr McMullen on the books of *Surprise* – '

'Yes, yes, yes. You have my authority for doing so.' Sir Hyde had begun to walk towards a door in the larboard bulkhead.

'Come over here, Hamilton. With regard to your orders – '

The two halted by the door and conversed in lowered voices. McMullen remained standing in the centre of the cabin trying without much success to realise the fullness of his good fortune. He was not to die. He was to return to *Surprise*. It was nearly too much for him and he had to gulp down his emotion. He had scarcely regained his composure when the Admiral went out through the door and Hamilton came running to grasp his hand, a delighted grin on his face.

'I'm to wait five minutes for my orders,' he said. 'John, I felicitate you – *persona grata* once more and ship's surgeon in *Surprise*. By God, the wardroom will rejoice to have you back!'

'It was your doing, Edward. I don't know how – '

'Nonsense. You kept your end up, as the cricketers say.'

'And, after all, I didn't have to lie.'

Hamilton burst out laughing and clapped him on the shoulder. 'You called me jesuitical,' he said, 'but damn me if you aren't the most pedantical, puritanical – but let that be. Listen. I go straight to *Surprise* and you with me. We sail tomorrow – '

'Whither bound?'

'Sealed orders, but it must be the eastern Caribbean – it must be.' Hamilton lowered his voice. 'I asked the old – I asked the Admiral last night to give me twenty more men and an extra boat and let me cut out *Hermione* from La Guayra, but he wouldn't have it – said twenty-eight carronades had no chance against forty-four long guns. But he'll have to act on your information and *Surprise* is the only frigate on the station just now.' He wagged his head deprecatingly. 'Sir Hyde may have been a dashing officer when he served in the old *Lion* – you played a trump card there, by the way – but he's a bit of an old woman now.'

'I've a feeling he wasn't too well satisfied with my story, Edward.'

'I daresay he wasn't. He's sharp enough to sense that all was not – by your leave, John – totally above-board. But never mind that. You'll have to live under something of a cloud with the Admiral, that's all. If you were an executive officer, now, you could disperse the cloud like a shot, by cutting a dash at the head of a boarding-party or something of that sort. Of course,' Hamilton added, 'Sir Hyde might be in hospital with Yellow Jack and you save his life.'

'If it's Kingston hospital he'd be dead before I could lift a finger,' observed McMullen drily.

Hamilton laid a hand on his arm. 'That reminds me. You no doubt recall Lucy Preston?'

'She is still here?' McMullen said sharply.

'Very much so, and her plantation hospital a veritable institution. The Governor himself has visited it, I'm told. But if you visit her, John, I must prepare you for trouble.'

McMullen frowned. 'How so?'

'Well – ' Hamilton hesitated for a second – 'knowing that she and you were acquainted, I made it my business to call on Miss Preston when *Surprise* reached here in July.'

'She knew of the mutiny?'

'Of course. And of Pigot's misdeeds too – she'd picked up a few tales of those. But I had to break the news that you were accounted one of the mutineers, and d'you know what she said, John? "I'm glad," she said – to my face, mind you! – "I'm glad he stood up for humanity!" What she'll say when your exoneration comes to her ears I – '

He checked himself quickly and went towards the Admiral, who had re-entered the cabin.

'Your orders, sir,' said Sir Hyde curtly, handing him a sealed package. 'May good fortune attend you.'

'Thank you, Sir Hyde.'

Hamilton bowed stiffly and turned. McMullen followed him out past the marine sentry into the warm sunlight of the flagship's after-deck.

CHAPTER SEVEN

A Feat of Arms

'A Feat of Arms unsurpassed
in the annals of the Navy.'

– *Dictionary of Naval Biography*

1

*You are to proceed, with the vessel under your command, to Cabo de la
Vela west of the Gulf of Venezuela, and to cruise off the Cabo de la Vela
for as long as your stores will allow, and in particular to look out for the
frigate Hermione now in enemy hands.*

Captain Hamilton was not at all pleased with these orders,
which he opened as directed as soon as *Surprise* had cleared
Kingston harbour. It was true that if *Hermione* was to sail for
Havana, as Captain Dinneker's information suggested, she was
bound to pass Cabo de la Vela; but the cape was 200 miles west
of Puerto Cabello and the orders precluded his going there. Sir
Hyde's self-protective caution was plainly displayed in his
careful abstention from directing what was to be done if
Hermione was encountered. If *Surprise* attacked a frigate of twice
her force and was lost the responsibility would be her
captain's.

Wind and weather favouring her passage, *Surprise* reached
her cruising station on October 8th and there remained,
patrolling back and forth, for nearly a fortnight. In this time
she chased and took three Spanish merchantmen, sending their
crews ashore in the boats and burning the ships; Captain
Hamilton, aware that every officer and man might be needed
for a fight with *Hermione*, was not going to waste them in

161

sending back prizes. So much he set forth plainly to his men, summoning all hands aft for the purpose, for the destruction of three valuable cargoes meant a not inconsiderable loss of prize-money. But the only grumbling on the lower deck was at *Hermione*'s slowness to appear and give battle. The whole ship's company, from the half-dozen ship's boys to the captain himself, was possessed with the idea of vengeance, the more urgently desired because the honour of the Navy was involved. Not only did they regard the mutiny as a stain to be wiped from the record of the Service, but there was also the sorry fact that a British frigate had remained in Spanish hands for two years.

Apart from the general impatience to come to close quarters with *Hermione*, *Surprise* was a happy ship. Captain Hamilton kept his men busy with gun-drills and practice musterings of boarding-parties, and on calm days of steady breeze the pipe of 'Hands to dance and skylark' set Mulroney the fiddler scraping away while bronzed seamen demonstrated their various versions of the hornpipe. One day towards the end of the fortnight he ordained a relay race, watch against watch: up and down fore, main, and mizen masts, right to the truck in each case, and back again for'ard. It was during this contest that Seaman Bragg, in an excess of zeal for the larboard watch, slid down a backstay at such imprudent speed that he removed a great deal of skin from his forearms and had to be treated in the sickbay.

'Don't put 'em on too tight, sir, please,' said Bragg as McMullen applied bandages. 'I don't want no handicappin' when we comes board-an'-board with *Herminey*. Will there be any o' the old Hermys on board, sir,' he added, 'them as killed their captain?'

'I hardly think so,' said McMullen, tying-off a bandage.

Bragg's large ugly face creased in a scowl. 'I'm right sorry for that,' he said. 'I'd give a year's pay to beat the guts out o' them murdering bastards.'

Ten days ago McMullen would have felt a guilty pang; his uncomfortable conscience would have reminded him that he had calamitously associated himself with those murdering bastards. But time and practice had made it easy to forget the few hours during which, in ignorance of its outcome, he had condoned a mutiny. Indeed, he felt that but for the continual reminders of *Surprise*'s present purpose the whole episode – not the mutiny only but Irico and Captain Dinneker and Sir Hyde's inefficacious interrogation as well – would have faded from his mind like a dream at waking. He had taken up his life on board the frigate where he had left it on that fateful night two years ago.

The wardroom gave him a hero's welcome (which brought him many a twinge of conscience) and of course he had to recount his adventures over and over again, finding it easier each time to forget his action, or lack of it, in the twenty-four hours preceding the mutiny. Three new midshipmen had replaced the three he remembered, but with the exception of Rieu, now commanding a sloop in the Channel, the familiar wardroom faces were all present. Forbes Wilson and the jovial William Hamilton were first and second lieutenants, the frigate having at present no third; John Maxwell the warrant-officer gunner, Lieutenant Turpin of the Marines (as plump and cherubic as ever) and little Hathaway the sailing-master with his hooked nose and bushy eyebrows – they were all undoubtedly glad to have him in their friendly company again.

From them he learned the latest news of the war, how Rear-Admiral Nelson had smashed the French fleet at the Nile and how Abercrombie's expeditionary army in Holland had been driven from the country with heavy loss; and, too, of the triumphs of the Corsican general, Bonaparte, the rising star of the revolutionary Directory. But – as he quickly discovered – these topics were secondary to another and overwhelming interest: they were all dedicated heart and soul to their present mission, which they considered to be the retaking of *Hermione*. When interest in McMullen's tale had somewhat abated the talk at the wardroom table was all of *Hermione*; not whether she could be taken but how it could best be done. Everyone was agreed that if the two ships met at sea *Surprise* would have to cram on sail and come to close quarters with all speed, running the gauntlet of *Hermione*'s forty-four long guns until she could bring her twenty-eight short-range carronades into effective action; that she was more than likely to be pounded to matchwood before she could fire a gun seemed to worry nobody. But the general opinion was that the more certain way to take her was by a cutting-out operation using all the boats. It had somehow become known (though the captain had said no word on the subject) that *Surprise*'s orders did not allow of any such expedition. Against this, however, was the additional cutter that Captain Hamilton, by some means known only to himself, had contrived to take aboard on the evening before he sailed. With a pinnace taken from a Dutch ship off Aruba two months earlier, and counting the little jolly-boat, this gave *Surprise* six boats. What, demanded the wardroom, was all this deck-hamper for if the captain wasn't thinking of a cutting-out? And what did McMullen think of *Hermione*? Was she such a flyer as they made out? Would she really have the heels of *Surprise* in a chase?

In ardent debate of this sort McMullen was deeply glad to take part. It consolidated his feeling of having come home. Moreover, he was as ardent as the rest in his desire that *Hermione* should be restored to the Navy, for he still nursed the uncomfortable sense of personal responsibility for her being in Spanish hands. If *Surprise* succeeded in taking her against what would be tremendous odds it would give him (he felt) at least some satisfaction in having made amends, even though his own part in it must be no more than coping with the casualties of the encounter.

The familiar surroundings of his sickbay added to his sense of homecoming. The faithful Attwood showed no sign of resentment at being superseded by his old chief and was glad to consult him concerning a mysterious outbreak of ulcers among the starboard watch. One of the patients, a gaunt beanpole of a fellow named Tillotson, turned out to be brother-in-law to that Dobson whose foot had been amputated in '77, and from him McMullen learned that Dobson with his wooden stump had been nimble enough six months ago to dance at his sister's wedding.

During this fortnight of the surgeon's mental and physical re-integration he saw less of Edward Hamilton than he had done in the old days. Though the captain retained all his good temper and cheerfulness he seemed to hold himself more aloof from his officers than heretofore and to spend more of his time on the quarterdeck pacing in solitary reflection. McMullen, who knew his single-mindedness of old, felt sure that his friend had set his heart on bringing *Hermione* back to Jamaica, a prize – that he was considering not only how to achieve this but also his responsibility for his ship's company, outgunned and outnumbered two to one as they would be in a fight. Hamilton, he told himself, must be seething with impatience at having to hang about here with no certain knowledge as to his prey's whereabouts. The only sign of impatience Captain Hamilton showed, however, was to promise five golden guineas to that one of his masthead lookouts who should first sight *Hermione*. The only sign – until the morning of October 20th.

The sky before sunrise, that morning, was cloudless, a dome of clear green glass with a spreading stain of orange colour above the eastern horizon. Captain Hamilton, who had come on deck at daybreak, was slowly pacing up and down the weather side of his quarterdeck in lonely meditation. Except for a curt 'Good morning' to the first lieutenant and Joyner the senior midshipman, who had retreated to the lee side on his arrival, he had not spoken a word. Suddenly the pallid canvas of the frigate's upper sails glowed with resplendent light, and as the first dazzle of the sun's rim flashed on the horizon the captain came to a halt.

'Mr Wilson!'

'Sir!' The first lieutenant crossed the quarterdeck.

'I fancy you're something of a Latinist?'

'Botanically, perhaps, sir. In other respects I fear – '

'But you can construe one line of Ovid for me, I'm sure. *Quae fugiunt, celeri carpite poma manu.* What d'you make of that?'

Wilson considered a moment. 'Why, sir, I make it "With quick hand, pluck at the fruit which passes away from you".'

'Just so, Mr Wilson – thank you. I'll have her on the larboard tack, if you please, topgallants and royals hoisted. Mr Joyner, please to carry my compliments to Mr Hathaway and ask him to step up here.' Hamilton glanced at the two eager faces and nodded. 'You may tell Mr Hathaway that I wish to lay a course for Puerto Cabello.'

Through that day and most of the next *Surprise* sailed eastward, making long reaches close-hauled and short northerly tacks to hold her course. Her captain's decision was based on more than a Latin tag, for she had but one week's supply of stores remaining; also there was the possibility, no very unlikely one, that *Hermione* had sailed days ago and had slipped past her in the night. Orders or no orders, Hamilton argued, it was his plain duty to look into Puerto Cabello before returning to Kingston. Had he needed support for his argument he could have had it wholeheartedly from any one of his 196 shipmates.

So in the late afternoon of October 22nd John McMullen had his first sight of the Cordillera foothills, humped shapes hovering in the blue haze above the distant coastline of the Main. Hamilton sent his men to quarters as the frigate closed the land and placed his best lookouts at fore and main, but there was no *guarda costa* to oppose her swift approach. Steep wooded shores rose and spread, the waters under them dotted with fishing-craft, and then the harbour of Puerto Cabello opened right ahead below its forested hills. Now indeed there were sails in sight – small craft, a brig, a two-master that might be a *guarda costa* – all intent on racing back to the harbour mouth and out of reach of the stranger warship. Hamilton held his course, steering for the right-hand promontory of the two that flanked the entrance to the bay. Sunset light flooding from below the cloud-wreaths on the hills picked out the squat buildings of forts on either headland and the movement of a ship's upper spars between them.

Surprise was little more than a mile from the nearer headland when a puff of smoke appeared against the walls of the fort and a short column of water, dyed pink by the sunset, rose a musket-shot off her starboard bow. The helm was put over and she came round to speed across opposite the harbour entrance. Hamilton, who was about to climb the shrouds for a look into the harbour, used his glass from the quarterdeck rail instead. For *Hermione* was in full view from the deck, moored head-and-stern between the forts with her broadside presented, her yards crossed and sails bent ready for sea, and her decks – as his lens showed him plainly – swarming with men.

A second gun boomed from the same fort, the shot falling

well astern of *Surprise* as she drew past the harbour. Captain Hamilton snapped his glass shut and turned to his first lieutenant with a smile.

'So the fruit is still on the tree, Mr Wilson,' he said. 'We must consider how to pluck it.'

'It looks ripe enough, sir,' Wilson returned with a grin. 'Maybe it'll fall into our hands.'

Hamilton laughed. 'It's a damned poor analogy anyway. But if you mean she may come out to teach us a lesson, it's certainly a possibility. And we'll give her the chance. For the present, we'll bid the Dons *hasta la vista*.'

He had the frigate brought round on the starboard tack and with the wind on her quarter she headed out to sea. Astern the fort-crowned headlands of Puerto Cabello and the darkening hillsides behind the port dwindled and faded into twilight and distance.

At first light of the next day the watchers on shore and on *Hermione*'s decks saw the impudent intruder coming in from northward, to strip to topsails and jib as though she was preparing for a fight. Under this reduced sail, and keeping well beyond gunshot from the forts, she cruised slowly back and forth all day, scaring all the local craft from their legitimate sailing and fishing-grounds and puzzling the watchers by sending up one signal-hoist after another to her yardarm.

'Now, Mr Leigh,' Hamilton had said to his signal midshipman, 'you're in need of practice as you and I very well know. Compose suitable insults and hoist them for the Dons to see – there may be some among 'em who understand English. Pray don't be more coarse than you can help.'

But whether or not Don Raimon de Chalas, the Spanish captain of *Hermione*, or any other of the Dons could read English signals, they remained unprovoked by *Surprise*'s coat-trailing and Mr Leigh's insults. *Hermione* was not going to be tempted out of her completely impregnable position.

Once again the British frigate sailed away at nightfall. And Jukes, captain's steward, divulged to his particular mates (who of course spread the news through the ship) that Captain Hamilton spent the whole of that night working in his cabin and using up a deal of paper and ink.

The following day at noon, *Surprise* being seven miles north of Puerto Cabello, the captain invited all his wardroom officers to dine with him in his cabin.

2

John McMullen long remembered that dinner-party of October 24th in the last year of the old century. The food indeed was not especially memorable; the ham (which the captain required his surgeon to carve, as a skilled anatomist) had been long in pickle and the wine they drank with it was thin Jamaican stuff. But he had never seen Edward Hamilton in so blithe a mood or so resourceful in quips and questions designed to draw out his companions. Joyner the senior midshipman, a tall youngster afflicted with pimples, was with them so there were eight at table and a cheerful company they made.

The stern cabin in *Surprise* was by no means large and the table filled most of it. The frigate, moving slowly under easy sail, gave only a slight list to the board and there were none of the more usual discomforts of sliding dishes and spilt drink. Bright flakes of light, reflections from her wake, chased themselves across the deck-beams overhead and flashed across the gold-hilted sword (presented to the captain by the grateful planters of Jamaica) that hung on the bulkhead. Not until Jukes and his attendant boys had drawn the cloth and retired was *Hermione* even mentioned. As the steward closed the cabin door behind him Hamilton was concluding a mildly scandalous story concerning a nameless admiral and a dockyard commissioner's lady, and William Hamilton, who had an endless fund of anecdotes, chipped in eagerly on the ensuing laughter.

'Good, sir, good. But have you heard the tale of the bishop and the chamber-pot? It seems that this chamber-pot – '

'Sit on it, I beg you,' the captain interrupted with a grin. 'Forgive the crudity, Mr Hamilton, but I'm sure it will keep until, say, this time tomorrow. At this moment I ask your closest attention.' He filled his glass from the decanter of port which Jukes had left on the table and pushed the decanter to his left. 'Pray charge your glasses. I intend now to consider *Hermione*.'

McMullen's heart began to beat faster. He knew from the dancing light in Edward Hamilton's eyes that some audacious project was in his mind; and he knew also that no project, however ingeniously planned, could alter the heavy odds that faced him. *Hermione*'s guns had a range four times that of *Surprise*'s carronades and it was rumoured that the heavy guns in the two forts numbered more than two hundred. Once or twice in the past he had wondered whether the trepanning he had performed on his friend's skull (with a silver plate inserted to protect the brain) had left a residual tendency to slight madness on occasion. The captain's first words – he had paused while he took a paper from his pocket and laid it before him – seemed almost to support this idea.

'That hour, of night's dark arch the keystone,' he said, smiling faintly. 'Midnight, gentlemen, is our time. At eight bells of the middle watch tonight the boats will be engaged in cutting-out *Hermione*.'

A deep murmur of satisfaction ran round the table. Hamilton quelled it with a slight gesture and consulted his paper.

'Six boats in two divisions, one to board from starboard and one from larboard. Tow-ropes will be rigged to keep each division together until we close the enemy. The starboard division as follows – the pinnace, with myself, Mr Maxwell, Mr Viney, and sixteen men. The launch, Mr Wilson in command with Mr Leigh and twenty-four men. The jolly-boat commanded by Mr Joyner with Mr Ritchie and eight men. It seemed to me very proper,' he added gravely, 'that Mr Joyner should have the carpenter to support him.'

Chuckles ran round the table and Joyner's blush hid his pimples.

'The leading boat of the larboard division will be the gig.' There was no change in Hamilton's tone as he went on. 'Mr McMullen will command her, with my coxswain and sixteen men. The two cutters will follow, Mr Hamilton in command of the first with Lieutenant de la Tour du Pin and sixteen marines – '

McMullen ceased to hear him. He was taken completely by surprise. It was surely quite unprecedented for a ship's surgeon to be given command of a boat in a boarding operation. He had fired a pistol once or twice, had – long ago – had some instruction in fencing, but he had never grasped a cutlass in his life; was not altogether sure, indeed, whether he could bring himself to strike a man with intent to kill. What was Edward Hamilton about, thus to thrust him in among the fighting-men? Recollection of something the captain had said gave him a clue: *If you were an executive officer, now, you could disperse the cloud like a shot, by cutting a dash at the head of a boarding-party or something of that sort.* And that was probably it. Edward was giving him his chance.

'Mr Wilson, you'll take three axes in the launch,' Hamilton was saying. 'Your first task is to cut the bow cable and set the foretops'l, so you'll board at the starboard bow. You, Mr Joyner, will also take three axes – see they're razor-sharp – and board at the quarterdeck to cut the stern cable and set the mizen tops'l. Mr McMullen boards at the larboard bow and Mr Hamilton and the marines at the larboard gangway. The rendezvous for all will be *Hermione*'s quarterdeck.' He sat back and looked round the circle of eager faces. 'What say you to that, gentlemen?'

What they said individually was lost in the general roar of approval. Turpin sprang up and insisted on shaking William Hamilton's hand, Maxwell gave Midshipman Joyner a congratulatory slap on the shoulder. Ham freed himself from the marine lieutenant and stood up glass in hand, his rubicund face one large grin.

'A toast!' he vociferated. 'I give you a toast, gentlemen all! Here's to the health of our captain, success to tonight's venture, and a hot seat in Hell to the bloody Dons!'

They drank that with acclamation, McMullen (inwardly shaking his head at himself) with as much enthusiasm as the rest. Captain Hamilton looked at them with affection.

'I see I've no need to ask for your support,' he said. 'I'll ask instead for comments and suggestions.'

Wilson's red head came forward. 'I don't doubt you've

thought of this, sir, but we can hardly hope to take the Dons by surprise. They'll be well prepared, with guard-boats rowing patrol at night, I imagine.'

'Certainly they will, Mr Wilson. But we may still surprise them with the speed of our attack. Straight in and board all together – that's our watchword. *Magno cum impeto strepituque* is the Latin of it,' Hamilton added with a smile.

Hathaway, the sailing-master, wagged his grey head ruefully. 'You've no such Latin motto for me, sir, I take it,' he said. 'I'm to stay with the ship?'

'I'm afraid so, Mr Hathaway. You're the only officer I have left. And if – which is very unlikely – I should find myself in a Spanish gaol ashore I'll sleep the sounder for knowing *Surprise* is in safe hands, as safe as any in the Navy.'

'Thank you, sir. Then the motto for me is one we have in Oxfordshire – patience is the poor man's remedy.'

Hamilton laughed. 'I can give you a better one, coined by an Oxfordshire man by name John Milton – they also serve who only stand and wait. But I trust you won't have to wait long, Mr Hathaway. Our business should be concluded before eight bells of the first watch.' He hesitated briefly. 'In the event of my not being on board to give orders, you will make sail for Kingston at sunrise tomorrow.'

'Aye aye, sir.'

McMullen had an instantaneous vision of failure; of half the cutting-out party killed or wounded and the rest taken prisoner. A glance at the faces round him banished it. It was surely impossible that such confidence should fail.

'Any further comments, gentlemen?' said the captain. 'Yes, Mr Joyner?'

'S-s-sir,' said Joyner, stammering in his embarrassment, 'the b-boats, sir – shouldn't they rondyvoo at the bows? I mean, after we've got aboard her? Then they'd be ready to tow her out if there ain't enough wind.'

'A very good point, Mr Joyner, and thank you. I had it in mind, with some other matters which I shall put to the hands themselves.' The captain stood up, his officers doing the same. 'And now, gentlemen, I must indeed ask for your support – on the quarterdeck, if you please, while I address the crew. Mr

Wilson, pray pipe all hands aft.'

They trooped out after him into the blazing sunshine of the after-deck and up the ladder to the quarterdeck. The shrill piping of the boatswain's mates was bringing the men tumbling up from below to join the watch-on-deck in the rush aft, Mr Turfrey the boatswain was waving them into position with his big brown hands, Lieutenant Turpin was hurriedly aligning his twenty marines at the rail below the quarterdeck; and in the midst of all the bustling movement was the helmsman at the wheel, motionless except for the slight movement of his hands on the spokes and the glance of his eye from the swelling sails to the binnacle in front of him. Then, suddenly, there was stillness. The faint high thrum of the wind in the rigging could be heard, and the wash of the waves along *Surprise*'s flank as she moved steadily across the empty sea under main and topsails. A memorable picture, McMullen thought; white sails against the blue sky overhead, and below them the blue and gold and scarlet fronting the crowd of brown eager faces massed athwartships. He felt his plain borrowed coat to be a trifle out of place on the quarterdeck, which had turned into something like the stage of a theatre.

Captain Hamilton stepped – it might almost be said that he swaggered – forward to the taffrail. His cocked hat was set jauntily to one side on his dark curls, his chest was well thrown out, his chin uptilted. He set both hands on the rail and sent a long glance across the expectant throng, commanding their attention without a word spoken. Then he made his voice ring.

'Well, my lads! A couple of leagues over yonder – ' he pointed dramatically to the southern horizon – 'there's a fine forty-four-gun frigate that belongs to us by right. She won't come out and fight us and I can't wait for her any longer. We're short of victuals so I shall sail for Kingston tomorrow.'

There was a short and stricken silence and then some muted but very audible groaning. Hamilton allowed a few seconds for this to subside before continuing.

'We've had the trouble of running her to earth. When she breaks cover she'll be a fat prize for the lucky ship who takes our place.'

He paused again and this time the groans were louder.

Someone (McMullen thought he recognised the voice of Seaman Bragg) shouted 'Shime!'

'And shame it is!' Hamilton cried swiftly. 'I feel it myself, lads. And I see a way out of it.' He struck an attitude. 'I shall cut out that frigate this very night!'

The sudden roar of cheering was like an explosion. Hamilton raised his hand to check it and kept his arm extended like a man holding a sword aloft.

'I shall lead the boats myself!'

This time the cheers were deafening.

'Lads, will you follow me?'

And now they yelled themselves hoarse in their eagerness to impress him with their devotion. The captain turned from the rail and McMullen, meeting his eye, was somewhat shocked to see him wink. He swung round again and flung up his hand.

'Still!'

It was surprising how he could make his voice resound, and the uproar ceased as if by magic. Hamilton leaned confidentially on the taffrail, his face now serious and intent.

'Hear me, every man!' he said solemnly. 'I know you'll fight like heroes but there's more to it than that. Each of you must know his duty. First, we need challenge and answer for recognising a friend in the dark of midnight, which is when we go into action. The challenge will be "Britannia" and the answer "Ireland". Second, every man going in the boats will wear dark clothing – not a rag of white or light colour.' He paused briefly. 'I except Bobadil – he may go naked.'

This brought a shout of laughter, Bobadil being a Jamaican negro as black as coal.

Hamilton lifted a finger and the laughter stopped. 'Pay attention, now. I'll tell you precisely what I intend. I shall close the coast after nightfall and lie well out to avoid discovery, so you can prepare for a long pull. The boats – '

And he proceeded to repeat in detail all that he had told his officers. There were no histrionics now, but had he been Garrick speaking Hamlet's soliloquy at Drury Lane he could not have had a more attentive audience.

'If I had enough boats you should all go,' he ended. 'As it is, I've made my selections and you'll be told which boat to go in.

Only do your duty, lads – as I hope I shall do mine – and
Hermione is ours. That's all I have to say.' He turned from the
rail. 'Pipe down, Mr Wilson, if you – '

'Three cheers for the cap'n!' someone yelled, and the triple
shout seemed to McMullen to shake the frigate.

Hamilton responded by going to the taffrail and doffing his
head. When he turned again his face had gone very red.

'I'd never do on the stage, John,' he muttered as he passed
McMullen. 'I find the applause disconcerting.'

The pipes squealed, the hands departed for'ard in an orderly
crowd. Captain Hamilton dismissed his officers but beckoned
McMullen to him.

'I shall be obliged if you'll look to the sickbay and orlop
yourself, John,' he said in a low voice. 'See to it that Attwood
has plenty of room for casualties – and elbow-room to handle
that bone-saw.'

McMullen frowned. 'But if an amputation's needed I'll do it
my – '

He checked himself abruptly. Hamilton grinned and
nodded.

'This time,' he said, 'the surgeon might have to suffer a
surgeon's attentions – a salutary experience, I should think.'
He clapped his friend on the shoulder. 'Forgive my
gruesomeness. Judging by your past record you'll come
through without a scratch.'

McMullen's answering smile was achieved with some
difficulty.

3

There was no moon, but the reflections of the brilliant stars
overhead winked bluely on the black undulations of the sea,
sparkling on the wakes of the two lines of boats. There was less
than an hour to go to midnight when Captain Hamilton's
low-spoken order came across the water to the three boats of
the larboard division. In McMullen's gig as in all the boats
there was a subdued bustle of movement as oarsmen changed
places; the captain had prescribed that the men specially

detailed for boarding should take first spell at the oars, changing with the regular boat-crews halfway to their objective.

'Oars!' said Antonio, beside McMullen on the stern thwart. 'Give way together!'

There was a jerk as the towrope to the cutter astern came taut, and then the creak and plash, creak and plash of steady pulling began again. The breeze, light but steady, was blowing off the land ahead, so that sounds would hardly be carried landward. Nevertheless, McMullen found himself holding his breath, so close did the humped black shapes of the hills above Puerto Cabello appear and so bright the few scattered points of light near the shore. When they pulled away from *Surprise* he had thought the night a dark one, propitious for the task in hand, but now he was astonished at the clarity of his vision in the starshine. He could plainly see Hamilton's movements as he stood erect in the bows of the pinnace, half-a-cable-length away to starboard, now and then raising his night-glass to his eye, and by turning round on the thwart he could make out the cockaded hats of Turpin's marines and the rhythmically jerking pigtail of the man who was pulling the bow oar in Ham's cutter. The marines' scarlet coats looked black by night, and their white crossbelts had been removed until the order came to cast off the tows.

Hamilton, reflected McMullen, had thought of everything, from the bandages and tourniquet he was carrying in a pouch strapped to his waist to the hook-ropes in each boat for towing out the frigate. If care and foresight could give them a chance in the desperate business confronting them they had a chance; but it depended on all six boats boarding simultaneously – and nothing could lessen the odds of more than three to one against them.

McMullen felt an inner and physical discomfort as he thought of those odds. With it came remembrance of a walk on the Chiltern Hills with his uncle the doctor, long ago. 'Observe yonder sheep,' his uncle had said. 'She is frightened and wishes to run from us yet she waits to empty her bladder first. It's instinct, my boy, not the reaction of fear – she will run the better lightened of her load.' He grinned at the recollection and bestirred himself; if instinct had to be obeyed it was now or never. Kneeling on the thwart, he contrived to relieve himself overside and felt the better for it.

From this position he could look above the heads of the men crowded in the gig and see the dark coast that seemed suddenly much nearer. The twin yellow sparks widely separated and at some height above the water must be lights in the headland forts, and the space between them the harbour entrance. Midway between them and lower down there was a duller light on what might have been an island just inside the harbour mouth but was – as he now perceived – the prey they had come to seize, *Hermione* herself. The forts were awake, the frigate probably equally so. He remembered that Hamilton had from the first discounted the possibility of taking the enemy unprepared; remembered also Wilson's prophecy that there would be guard-boats rowing patrol outside the harbour. As yet he could see no sign of the latter.

Sitting down again, he felt with his foot for the cutlass he had laid on the bottom-boards, and touched the pistol stuck in his belt (for the third or fourth time) to make quite sure it was not cocked. At this business of hand-to-hand fighting he was indeed the veriest novice. It had been a relief when Antonio, as befitted a captain's coxswain, had taken charge of the tiller and boat-handling; but the time was fast approaching when he must take command. He would have to get himself for'ard into the bows, be the first to face the muskets and boarding-pikes as he tried to clamber up the side. He swallowed hard as he thought of it, but he found himself more excited than apprehensive.

Nearer they crept across the starlit water, the two lines keeping meticulous distance and the leading boats abreast. The headlands on either side of the entrance rose slowly higher and opened their black arms; the lights in the forts were now so near that it seemed impossible that some watcher on the ramparts should not espy the flotilla below. A voice, loud above the creak of oars and the rustle of water, spoke suddenly from the starboard boats. Immediately afterwards a brief glare of light beyond them showed the boats in black silhouette for a moment and the report of a gun shattered the stillness.

'Gunboat!' Antonio rapped. 'Four-pounder in the bows.'

Hamilton's shout rang out. 'Cast off! Cast off and carry on!'

McMullen started to fumble at the lashing of the tow-rope but Antonio's razor-sharp knife severed the hemp.

'It's seconds as counts now, sir.' The coxswain raised his voice. 'Pull, ye buggers, pull! Send her along, now!'

The gig began to foam through the water. From starboard came three breathless cheers and McMullen's glance showed the pinnace forging ahead. A second flash and report, this time from closer inshore – there were two gunboats, then. They would be converging on the raiders as fast as they could pull. The western headland was abeam now, and looking ahead he saw the frigate's flank less than three hundred yards away and rising higher (it seemed) at every stroke of the oars. Lights blinked from the ports and other lights moved along her deck. Hamilton's pinnace was a length ahead of the gig, her oars beating the water furiously.

'Pull – pull – pull!' Antonio yelled. 'Lay yer bloody backs into it!'

'Larboard bow, remember,' McMullen said, trying to keep his voice steady.

'Aye, sir. Best make ready.'

As McMullen stuck the cutlass into his belt and stood up there was an outburst of shots and shouts. He saw that the other four boats, some distance astern of the leading pair, were engaged with two larger craft; either they had been caught by the gunboats or had foolishly waited to intercept them. In any case the boarding-party was now reduced to thirty-two men.

Thirty-two against three hundred. The words thumped absurdly in his head as he hastily thrust his way through to the bows of the gig. *Hermione*'s starboard side stood up like a wall, light flooding along its rim from lanterns hung in the rigging. Antonio was steering away to larboard to get round her stern and Hamilton's pinnace was heading straight for her – Hamilton would be boarding in a matter of seconds. A hubbub of shouting swelled, then a bright irregular line of flashes and the crash of musketry along the rail. No bullets came near the gig – the Spaniards appeared to be firing at the six boats clumped in a warring mass farther away. And now the gig was foaming round under the high stern clear of the rudder, with the quarter-gallery whence he had dropped so long ago close above him. Just in time he ducked to avoid being swept overboard by the stern cable as they passed beneath it, and when he straightened himself the bowman had shipped his oar and was standing beside him ready with his boathook. The high wooden side with its closed gunports slid past a few feet away. Above and beyond it the din of musketry, continuous until now, suddenly slackened and a frenzied outburst of yelling took its place in the midst of which McMullen thought he could distinguish English voices. Hamilton was leading his sixteen men up the side.

'Way 'nough!' snapped Antonio. 'Bows!'

The gig rasped alongside, the bowman hooked on, McMullen sprang for the side and got his fingers over the top of a gunport lid. One hand slipped off and he hung precariously for a few seconds until a mighty hand under his buttocks thrust him upward and Seaman Bragg's roar sounded in his ears: '*Hup* an' over!' He threw a hand across the rail above his head, glancing up as he did so and ready to dodge the expected shot or blow. None came. He swung himself over the rail unopposed and stood on *Hermione*'s fore-deck.

It was odd to find himself thus landed in a clear space when every other part of the frigate's deck was packed with milling, shouting Spaniards. The mob was thickest all along the starboard side from forecastle to quarterdeck, and amidships pistols flashed and steel gleamed in the lantern-light. He had just time to note this before a pistol flamed and banged six feet away and half-a-dozen men rushed at him before he could lug the cutlass from his belt. He ducked under the downward sweep of a sword, hurled himself sideways, whirled round cutlass in hand to see one of his attackers pitched bodily over the side by the gigantic Bragg and the others cut down by the men who had sprung over the rail. They had gained the deck close to the larboard gangway which ran, six feet wide, from forecastle to after-deck, and now a pack of Spaniards ran at them yelling from the forecastle. Bragg and his fellows charged straight at them like a herd of bulls, their sheer impetus sending the Spaniards reeling back until they turned and ran, leaving three of their number dead or wounded on the deck.

McMullen, left behind by this headlong charge, had a second or two to look about him for his friend and captain. Almost at once his eye caught the blue and gold in the mêlée on the starboard gangway and instantly he grasped the situation. Hamilton and his handful of men had tried to fight their way to the quarterdeck, which the captain had named as the rendezvous; but the Spaniards massed on the quarterdeck were pushing aft along the gangway and forcing them back.

'Gig's party all on board, sir,' said Antonio at his elbow.

McMullen yelled with all the force of his lungs. '*Surprise*! Come aft – follow me!'

The men who had chased the Spaniards to the forecastle came running back as he turned and dashed along the larboard gangway with the coxswain and the later arrivals at his heels. Most of the *Hermione*'s men on the quarterdeck were pouring down onto the opposite gangway, as he had seen, but a number of them had seen his own party and came shouting to oppose them. The leader, an officer by his heavily-braided coat, snapped a pistol at him and the bullet hummed past his ear a second before his cutlass hacked down between neck and shoulder. The officer fell against him with a groan and he stumbled forward, so that the boarding-pike that thrust fiercely at him passed over his bent head and ripped his coat. He glimpsed the flash of Antonio's long knife and felt hot blood spurt on his face, heard steel clash overhead and Bragg's roar mingling with a man's scream. Then he was up and on the quarterdeck, conscious of a savage exaltation that, owing nothing to reason, yet sharpened every sense so that decision was instantaneous.

Hamilton and his party were fighting desperately at the for'ard end of the gangway, pressed back by the quarterdeck Hermiones in front and harassed in rear by their fellows on the forecastle. The last Spaniards were driving down from the quarterdeck when McMullen and his sixteen fell on them from behind like a thunderbolt and slashed their way onto the gangway. There was little room for sword-play on the long six-foot platform, cluttered as it was already with the bodies of dead and dying. By the tricksy light of smoky lanterns and the glimmer of the stars the Surprises, with McMullen raging at their head, smote and stabbed and cursed their way along it, those in front striking and twisting through the tightly-packed Spaniards and leaving those they passed unhurt to be dealt with by the men behind. Beyond the whirl of brandished weapons and swaying figures McMullen saw the burly form of Maxwell the gunner grappling with an antagonist, and an instant later he was chest-to-chest with Edward Hamilton, sword in hand and hatless.

'Well done, John – saved us.' The panted words were barely audible above the uproar. 'Must get – quarterdeck – in case the others – '

He was gone, running aft along the gangway. McMullen, hesitating momentarily, was engulfed by his own followers rushing to aid the gunner's party who were surrounded on the forecastle. He broke free, conscious for the first time of blood streaming from a cut on his left thigh and the sting of the pike-thrust that had grooved his back. Flesh wounds, no more. Muskets and pistols were firing from the maindeck and a bullet knocked the cutlass from his hand, numbing his fingers. He stooped to pick it up and was almost knocked over by a big man who clutched at him excitedly.

'The cap'n, sir, yonder!' yelled Bragg. 'Them buggers is at 'im!'

McMullen was running aft before the seaman had finished speaking. Fast though he went, leaping on and over the bodies that littered the gangway, the dimly-lit action on the quarterdeck seemed to take place with infinite slowness – Hamilton beset by three Spaniards, a fourth behind him swinging a musket by the barrel, the musket descending on the unprotected head, Hamilton felled to the deck. McMullen was still twenty paces away when it happened, that blow smashing down on the very place where with infinite care he had inserted a thin plate of silver four years ago. He went mad. Roaring Spanish oaths (*hijos de puta* the least of them) he flung himself forward, cutlass swung back for the avenging stroke. The musket-wielder fell across Hamilton's prostrate body with his head nearly severed from his shoulders. Red flame stabbed at McMullen from a yard away and the pistol-bullet seared across his upper arm a second before his assailant was cut down by Bragg, who with another two seamen had followed him. The remaining two Spaniards ran for the ladder-head pursued by Bragg and his mates. Before they could escape they were checked and borne back again by a howling mob charging up the ladder from the maindeck.

McMullen had not even time to ascertain whether his friend was alive or dead. The three seamen might hold their ground at the head of the ladder for a few seconds but they were facing a hundred Spaniards. He sprang across to hack and thrust at their side, the hot fury of a moment ago giving way to cold despair. The tremendous odds against them must prevail – it was impossible that they should not.

The deafening screeching of the *Hermione*'s men changed of a sudden to yells of dismay. McMullen, stabbing with his point at one man as he kicked at the face of another who sought to knife him from below, saw that the attack had turned into a rout – though without changing its direction. The Spaniards struggled now to hurl themselves past and between the four defenders of the quarterdeck, running for the starboard gangway when they broke through. Then through the drift of powder-smoke the scarlet-and-white of the marines came surging with Turpin whirling his sword at their head. It was their bayonets that had turned the Spanish assault into panic flight. Cursing, thrusting, they herded the Spaniards like sheep up the ladder, hunted them into corners, bayonetted them as they fell. In less than a minute they had cleared the quarterdeck.

'Form! Form!' Turpin screamed at them, his cherubic countenance transformed by a diabolic grimace. '*Dieu-de-dieu!* form here – at the taffrail!'

Dodging between hurrying marines, McMullen ran to where Hamilton had fallen. The captain was on his feet and leaning against the rail, his face a mask of blood.

'Never mind that,' he snapped, cutting short the surgeon's inquiries. 'What are the boats doing? Where's Ritchie? The bower cable should be – '

'Present – *fire!*'

The crash of the marines' volley was followed by a chorus of screams and shouts from the close-packed mass of men on the maindeck.

'Bayonets!' shouted Turpin. 'Forward, *mes garçons* – down again and at them!'

The rousing cheer as the marines swept down to the maindeck seemed to bring a double echo from for'ard, and the uproar of fighting on the forecastle intensified.

'Wilson's boarded, thank God!' said Hamilton. 'Ham too, I fancy. Get me to the after rail, John.'

'I want to look at that head-wound. You're bleeding like a stuck pig.'

'*Tu quoque*. Get me to the rail.'

For a moment theirs were the only figures erect on the quarterdeck. McMullen steered Hamilton between the bodies of motionless dead and writhing wounded to the rail. Boats were down there on the dark water and the thud of blows came to their ears.

'Is that you, Mr Ritchie?'

'Aye, sir.' A grunt and a thud. 'We'll – have her – parted in a jiffy.'

'Cap'n Hamilton, sir!' This came from a man who had arrived panting behind them. 'Foretops'l's loose an' ready, sir.'

Hamilton turned. 'Very well. My compliments to Mr Wilson and why the hell hasn't he cut the bower cable – look sharp about it!'

As the seamen sped back along the gangway there came a dull thump below the rail and the frigate's deck swayed and shifted underfoot with the parting of her stern cable. Down on the maindeck another volley of musketry crashed above the tumult. Simultaneously a knot of struggling men appeared at the head of the quarterdeck ladder and a tall Spaniard broke from it to rush at the two by the rail with upraised sword. McMullen remembered for the first time that he had a pistol. He lugged it from his belt, thumbed back the hammer, and fired at six yards' range. The sword flew harmlessly over his head. The Spaniard – dead or dying – pitched headfirst into McMullen and he was flung to the deck. It was one of *Surprise*'s men who pulled him to his feet. The quarterdeck, he saw, had once again been cleared of the enemy, this time by the second cutter's party led by the boatswain.

'Explain later, Mr Turfrey,' Hamilton was saying sharply. 'Four hands to shake out the mizen tops'l and two to the helm. The rest for'ard to help Mr Wilson.'

'Aye aye, sir.'

Lieutenant Turpin came springing up the ladder as the seamen rushed away for'ard with the boatswain leading. He had lost his hat and powdered wig and his shaven head gleamed in the smoky lantern-light.

'We triump', sir!' he announced breathlessly. 'A grand many of the dogs are closed in the cabin, each one crying to *se rendre*.'

'And the others?'

'The others, sir, fled themselves down the after-hatch. *Par encouragement*, I fire the volley into them. But you are hurt bad, sir, I fear?' Turpin added anxiously.

'It's nothing. Post half your men to guard cabin and hatchway, take the rest to the forecastle.'

Before Hamilton finished speaking the *Hermione* had lurched and quivered and it could be felt that she was moving through the water, albeit very slowly. Except for the ceaseless groans and sobs of wounded men the after-deck was quiet now, though at the for'ard end of the ship cries and sporadic shots told that the fighting on the forecastle was not yet done. McMullen, when Turpin had gone leaping down to the maindeck, felt the stimulus of wild excitement drain from him, to be replaced by a lethargy of exhaustion. For a few seconds he stood slack and dazed, literally unable to move, while his senses slowly accepted things ignored until now: the pain of his wounds; the pools of blood at his feet, black and shining in the lantern-light; a half-naked man lying under the taffrail with a broken boarding-pike sticking in his side. He saw, above the smoky shambles of the deck, the network of rigging moving across a backcloth of brilliant stars, and the stars blotted out by the great black square of the foretopsail as it filled with wind. He heard the loud flap of the mizen topsail and Wilson's voice shouting orders to the men at the wheel; heard Wilson again close at hand in anxious exclamation and Hamilton's voice in reply telling him to hoist what sail he could. Suddenly he was aware that all sound of fighting had ceased – he could hear the steady wash of *Hermione*'s wake and the hiss of the following breeze in her shrouds. His strange languor fell from him and he turned to go to the captain.

Hamilton had been leaning with his back against the rail but now he had slid down to a sitting posture.

'By God, John, I believe we've done it,' he said faintly as McMullen bent over him. 'We've to run the gauntlet of the forts yet, but – '

'Hold steady,' the surgeon cut him short. 'I must have a bandage on this head-wound.'

He pulled bandaging from the pouch at his waist. A hand dropped on his shoulder.

'Mr McMullen? Tillotson here, sir – Mr Maxwell, he's wounded very bad, up for'ard.'

'I'll come as soon as I can. And Tillotson – get a party and find our wounded. Better carry them up here.'

A flash and a heavy report drowned Tillotson's response. The forts had opened fire. *Boom-boom*! A double report – and a hit. The heavy spanker-gaff smashed down across the starboard rail twenty feet away, but McMullen continued his work unheeding, peering and groping in the half-darkness. It was impossible to assess the gravity of the oozing wound on the head until they were back on board *Surprise*; if they ever reached her, he added to himself as a shot crashed into *Hermione*'s quarter.

'Hulled us, by God!' The captain shifted uneasily. 'If they – '

'Hold still, confound you!' McMullen growled, tying-off the head bandage. 'There's enough bleeding without your aggravating it. I'm going to put a tight lashing above this gash in your thigh.'

Hamilton's chuckle was just audible. 'Lacking – the famous – McMullen styptic, eh?'

'And I believe there's a pistol-ball lodged here, above the gash.'

To this Hamilton made no reply. He had fainted.

The rapid irregular firing from the forts continued as McMullen worked on, dimly aware of Wilson's shouts as the boat-crews were taken on board. He finished the little he could do and stood up, wincing at the pain of his stiffening wounds.

Hermione was moving much faster through the water now they had more sail on her. The black outline of the hills above Puerto Cabello was already low and distant astern, and though the gunfire still flashed from the forts and the booming of the guns came loudly on the breeze no shot fell near the frigate. She was out of range.

Two men carrying a wounded man between them were coming slowly aft along the gangway. There was Maxwell, badly wounded, to be looked to; and doubtless two-or-three-score others. McMullen braced his weary body for the work to come, unable as yet to find pleasure in success. They had done it, as Edward Hamilton had said. They had done it – but it remained to count the cost.

4

John McMullen stepped out of the temporary sickroom in Sir Hyde Parker's Jamaican residence and closed the door softly behind him. The draught he had given had taken effect and Edward Hamilton was sleeping at last; when the attendant promised by the Admiral arrived he would be free to visit the Beauchamp plantation again – after an interval of two years and three months, he remembered.

The long entrance hall of the Admiral's mansion was empty. He walked, stiffly because of his wounds, across the cool marble floor to the magnificent fireplace at the end opposite the portal. Sunlight from the tall windows sparkled on the myriad crystal pendants of the hanging chandeliers, big tropical plants in pots stood along the white-panelled walls, chairs upholstered in Aubusson tapestry stood about here and there. It was a world removed from the shambles of *Hermione*'s deck where he had stood nine days ago.

Yesterday, November 1st, *Surprise* had come proudly in past Gallows Point with her prize, to be greeted by saluting guns on the forts and cheering crowds on the quays; a fast sloop, spoken on the previous day, had carried the news of her success to Kingston. McMullen had been too preoccupied to enjoy this welcome, for Captain Hamilton had proved to have suffered severe internal injuries and had been in a high fever for several days.

Now, in this big cool house on the hillside above the port, he could relax almost for the first time and give his mind to his own future, which largely depended on his reception by Miss Lucy Preston. The lapse of two years since they had last met must to some extent spoil his prospects, he thought, but the dual character he had displayed would surely be the chief obstacle to renewal of their friendship. If she had thought him a hero to side with the mutineers, what would she think of him now – reinstated as the opposer of mutiny, a man who had played an active part in the recovery of *Hermione* for the 'tyrants'? He would have to make a clean breast of the whole affair to Lucy, he told himself. Unless she had changed, she could be trusted as he trusted Edward Hamilton. But perhaps he would never get as far as to tell her his story. Perhaps she would refuse to see him. Perhaps –

The sound of wheels on the gravel outside the portal cut short his uneasy thoughts. Sir Hyde Parker came in through the door and crossed the hall towards him with short quick steps, his old-maidish face wreathed in smiles.

'Ah, McMullen – apologies for not being here to receive you,' he said as he came. 'You will allow me, I hope, to felicitate you on your part in the – um – recent operation. So resounding a triumph has not been – ah – reported during the whole of my service as Commander-in-Chief on this station.'

McMullen, finding his hand grasped in the Admiral's, remembered his previous meeting with Sir Hyde and concealed a smile. If he had been living under a cloud it was indeed dispelled. No doubt the fact that Sir Hyde's credit with the Admiralty would be much increased when the news about the *Hermione* reached London had something to do with it.

'You're very kind, sir,' he said. 'But it's for me to apologise. I fear my letter of yesterday must have seemed to you a trifle peremptory. It was essential that Captain Hamilton should receive medical attention ashore, but I was resolved that he shouldn't go to the hospital in Kingston. The only alternative I could think of – '

'My dear McMullen, you were quite right, quite right. A

terrible place, that hospital. I'm glad to have Edward
Hamilton under my roof.' Sir Hyde produced a small gold box
from his larboard waistcoat-pocket and flipped it open. 'You'll
take snuff? No? Then allow me.' He took a pinch and sneezed
heartily. 'He'll be attended by Dr Ken, who – um – attends
both myself and the Governor. Until, that is, the packet sails
on Wednesday, when he'll go aboard her bound for England
with Dr Ken. How is the – ah – patient, by the bye?'

'Asleep, sir. The fever is somewhat abated. But as I
mentioned in my letter he needs someone constantly at the
bedside.'

'Quite, quite. You saw the note I left for you? I have been
with the Governor this morning and His Excellency has sent
for the attendant you require.' The Admiral took a watch from
his starboard waistcoat-pocket and consulted it. 'His
Excellency's carriage was dispatched immediately to fetch the
man – he should be here at any moment.'

'Thank you, sir,' McMullen said with relief; he would
probably be able to pay his momentous visit within the hour.
'The fever's not dangerous, but the severe bruising of loins and
kidneys – '

'Of course, of course. But about this fever.' Sir Hyde
hesitated and frowned. 'Do you consider – but pray forgive me
for a moment. Captain Hamilton's report reached me by
messenger last night and I have it in my desk.'

He bustled out through a door on one side of the fireplace
and returned almost at once with a small sheaf of papers.

'I consult you as Captain Hamilton's medical attendant, Mr
McMullen,' he said, with a doubtful sidelong glance, 'and I
trust you will not mistake me when I say that to – ah – some
who read it this report could well appear – shall I say – totally
incredible. It is dated October 26th. Was Captain Hamilton at
that time – um – in a feverish state?'

'Not in the least, sir.' McMullen's tone was sharp. 'He was in
pain but there was then no trace of fever.'

'I ask so much, McMullen,' said the Admiral confidentially,
'because, as you realise, the packet will take this report to Their
Lordships at the Admiralty. And I read here – ' he consulted
the papers – 'that two hundred and forty-six Spanish prisoners

were put on board a captured schooner and sent back to Puerto Cabello, while the number of Spaniards killed in the fighting is stated as one hundred and nineteen, including their captain.' He looked up. 'That means that three hundred and sixty-five men were engaged against *Surprise*'s boarding-party of less than one hundred.'

McMullen had a momentary mental picture of the scene on *Hermione*'s crowded deck when the prisoners, some of them wounded men he had tried to tend, were being transferred to the Spanish schooner.

'Those figures are entirely accurate, Sir Hyde,' he said coldly.

'I don't doubt it,' nodded the Admiral. 'But you must confess it will raise some eyebrows at the Admiralty – more especially when they read that *Surprise*'s casualties amounted to twelve wounded, including the captain, and not one single man killed.' He sucked in his breath and blew it out. 'As God's my life, McMullen, the thing is little short of a miracle!'

'So I thought, sir, when I found it to be so.'

'That the initial success of boarding should have been gained by thirty-two men,' Sir Hyde continued, 'is as miraculous as the rest. And you, McMullen, were among them, as I read here. Most creditable, most creditable.'

And some of the credit, reflected McMullen with an inward chuckle, would rub off on a senior officer whose implicit orders had been that *Hermione* was not to be cut out by *Surprise*. Those orders, he thought, would be suppressed in the Admiral's report.

'Well, well,' the Admiral was saying as he folded his papers, 'there'll be a whole *Gazette* devoted to this affair, I don't doubt, and we shall hear of *Sir* Edward by the next mail from England. Mr Wilson, of course, will be made post. For yourself, sir, who – as Captain Hamilton writes – turned the tide of battle by your heroical conduct at a crucial moment, the Navy has no such – ah – rewards, I fear.'

'I'm content, sir, I thank you,' said McMullen. 'I believe Captain Hamilton has represented that I should rank as lieutenant for a share in the prize-money,' he added with a smile.

The Admiral nodded absently and pulled out his watch. 'The Governor's carriage should be here by now, with that attendant fellow,' he said. 'The man, by the bye, is a medical orderly appointed by the Governor to a small hospital which his Excellency has lately taken under his wing. This hospital, curiously enough, is administered – ' He stopped as carriage-wheels ground to a halt outside the door. 'This, I fancy, will be our man.'

The door at the other end of the hall opened and two people came in. One of them was a man – the medical attendant, doubtless – but McMullen had no eyes for him. The other was Lucy Preston, Lucy in a grey dress, a little hat perched on her dark curls. Sir Hyde had gone forward to meet her and she was beginning her formal curtsey when her eyes fell on the tall man by the fireplace. Instantly, and leaving the Admiral in the middle of his bow, she ran – ran straight across the marble floor with both hands outstretched. McMullen caught her hands in his and they stood gazing into each other's eyes without a word spoken.

Sir Hyde, raising his eyebrows very high indeed, surveyed this *tableau à deux* with astonishment for a moment. Then he shrugged, beckoned to the medical orderly, and led the way into the sickroom. The door closed behind them.

Historical Note

The mutiny of the *Hermione* and her retaking by the *Surprise* are on record, in some detail, in James's *Naval History*. Captain Hugh Pigot and Captain Edward Hamilton were real persons and their actions were as I have described. John McMullen, ship's surgeon, was also a real person and the description of his behaviour in the cutting-out of *Hermione* is factual; I have, however, taken liberties with his career prior to October 1799.